Catherine Tinley has loved reading and writing since childhood, and has a particular fondness for love, romance and happy endings. She lives in Ireland with her husband, children, dog and kitten, and can be reached at catherinetinley.com, as well as through Facebook and on X, @CatherineTinley.

Also by Catherine Tinley

A Waltz with the Outspoken Governess

The Heiress Switch miniseries

The Maid's Masquerade

The Triplet Orphans miniseries

Miss Rose and the Vexing Viscount
Miss Isobel and the Prince
Miss Anna and the Earl

Lairds of the Isles miniseries

A Laird for the Governess
A Laird in London
A Laird for the Highland Lady

The Ladies of Ledbury House miniseries

The Earl's Runaway Governess
Rags-to-Riches Wife
'A Midnight Mistletoe Kiss'
in *Christmas Cinderellas*
Captivating the Cynical Earl

Discover more at millsandboon.co.uk.

THE UNDERCOVER HEIRESS

Catherine Tinley

MILLS & BOON

All rights reserved including the right of reproduction in whole or in part in any form. This edition is published by arrangement with Harlequin Enterprises ULC.

This is a work of fiction. Names, characters, places, locations and incidents are purely fictional and bear no relationship to any real life individuals, living or dead, or to any actual places, business establishments, locations, events or incidents. Any resemblance is entirely coincidental.

Without limiting the exclusive rights of any author, contributor or the publisher of this publication, any unauthorised use of this publication to train generative artificial intelligence (AI) technologies is expressly prohibited. HarperCollins also exercise their rights under Article 4(3) of the Digital Single Market Directive 2019/790 and expressly reserve this publication from the text and data mining exception.

® and TM are trademarks owned and used by the trademark owner and/or its licensee. Trademarks marked with ® are registered with the United Kingdom Patent Office and/or the Office for Harmonisation in the Internal Market and in other countries.

First published in Great Britain 2026
by Mills & Boon, an imprint of HarperCollins*Publishers* Ltd,
1 London Bridge Street, London, SE1 9GF

www.harpercollins.co.uk

HarperCollins*Publishers*, Macken House, 39/40 Mayor Street Upper, Dublin 1, D01 C9W8, Ireland

The Undercover Heiress © 2026 Catherine Tinley

ISBN: 978-0-263-41873-6

03/26

Printed and Bound in the UK using 100% Renewable Electricity at CPI Group (UK) Ltd, Croydon, CR0 4YY

For my RNA besties—
Saoirse Morrigan, Katie Ginger, Lulu Morris,
and Ali Henderson. I can never thank you enough
for all your support, advice, and love.

Chapter One

The Atlantic Ocean, Summer 1818

The trouble with good ideas, thought Sophia Van Bergen, is that once they had occurred to you, it was very, very difficult to get rid of them.

This particular good idea had its origins in a number of factors—Aunt Agatha's unexpected death, for one. As the ship's chaplain went through the words of the funeral service, Sophia stood immobile, her face impassive, as befitted the eldest daughter of Mr Oscar Van Bergen, a director of the New York Bank, signatory to the Buttonwood Agreement, member of the newly formed New York Stock Exchange, and one of the most influential men in Manhattan.

When Alexander Hamilton—one of the fathers of the United States of America—had founded the bank in a coffee-house at the corner of Wall Street and Water Street back in 1784, Sophia had not yet been born. By the time she had come along, Papa's position and wealth was secure, and the only life she had ever known was one of pampering and ease.

Pampering and ease was all very well, but it was tedious, and safe, and held nothing of adventure. And Sophia longed for adventure. Had *always* longed for adventure. It had been she who had made up games involving pirates and brigands and evil English soldiers for the amusement of her younger sisters. She had written little plays and built fortresses from sheets and blankets and generally sent her nursemaids and governesses to distraction. Occasionally she had been sent to her father's study for chastisement, but once he had heard the detail of her tales he would generally pinch her cheek and tell her he liked the fire in her belly—to Mama's endless frustration.

As she had grown, Sophia's thirst for adventure had changed—from making up wild tales, to taking what Mama described as 'shocking risks'. Well, why should she not climb all the way up the bell tower in Manhattan's North Church near their home on William Street? The views were said to be remarkable, and she had wished to see them. Yes, the stairs had been rather rickety, but she had been perfectly safe with the group of young ladies and gentlemen. And it had been exciting!

'It is unbecoming,' Mama had declared, her lips pressed tightly together, 'for the granddaughter of a marquess to be behaving like a hoyden. It would not be tolerated for an instant among the *ton*.'

Sophia had eyed her blankly. Sometimes it was as

though she and Mama spoke different languages. 'But the marquess is long dead, and we are not in England!'

After Sophia had been caught for the third time kissing a young man—three *different* young men, that is, not the same one three times (which would have been both predictable and tedious), Mama declared she had had enough. Casting her hands up in despair, she announced that the best thing to do to manage Sophia was to marry her off.

'Despite your wild notions and rash behaviour on occasion,' she had declared, her clipped English accent in stark contrast to Papa's New Amsterdam drawl, 'you have been raised properly, and so we should be able to find you a suitable husband. Your dowry will be substantial, naturally, and your pedigree—on the maternal side at least—impeccable.'

Sophia had bristled at the notion of her dowry and pedigree being the main attractions, but Mama had spoken firmly. 'It is your duty to marry—as it was mine. Your father came to London seeking an aristocratic wife, and my family benefited from the marriage settlements. They arranged the whole between them, and your papa and I have made a harmonious marriage, I think.'

This was true in that Papa and Mama never argued, and it was untrue in that they basically lived separate lives—as did most of the couples in their social class. Papa was always working—either in his study, at the bank, or meeting with his colleagues. Mama's domain, on the other hand, was her well-appointed home, her children, and the Manhattan social calendar. Still, Mama and Papa genuinely liked one another, which was a good thing, no doubt.

Sophia had been out in New York society for three years, having made her debut at seventeen, but none of her would-be suitors had impressed Mama and Papa enough for them to agree to a marriage. Mama seemed to dislike all her possible suitors for being 'too American' (which was nonsensical, since they were in America) while Papa had been critical of many of their families, having done business with all of them over the years. At the age of twenty Sophia was beginning to despair of ever escaping her life as a rapidly ageing spinster, when a letter had arrived from England. Aunt Agatha, Mama's older sister, had written to say that she had been considering Mama's dilemma regarding dear Sophia, and had identified that the Earl of Linford was in want of a wife.

An earl! Sophia's heart had skipped at the notion, but really it was the idea of London that had made her consider agreeing to the betrothal. To be so far away from home, away from Mama's scrutiny and the judgements of those who had known her from the cradle… now that would be an adventure indeed! Mama had been delighted, and Papa had no objection, so it had fallen to Sophia to deliberate over the matter.

'Is the Earl a gambler, or ugly or *cruel*?' she had asked. 'For I do not wish to find myself shackled for life to someone I cannot respect. I should like to *like* my husband.'

Mama had seen the sense in this, and so correspondence had flowed over the Atlantic and back—with long waiting times in between, as even the fastest ships took around four weeks to travel across the ocean. The parties had exchanged miniatures, and Sophia had been pleasantly surprised by the Earl's likeness. He was young and fairly handsome, it seemed—although miniatures were not always a great likeness. The artist who had painted her own miniature had got the main details right—brown hair, blue eyes—but honestly, the image might be held to represent any one of a dozen brown-haired maidens in the New York social set.

Aunt Agatha provided written assurances that Lord Linford was a man of character, with no suggestion he would treat his wife with anything other than the greatest respect. Sophia was also assured that he was no rakester or gambler. Although this was the answer she had hoped for, part of her could not help but be disappointed. *He sounds tedious!* She quite liked the notion of marrying a rakehell.

Still, being married and living in faraway London was tempting… And so she had graciously accepted the Earl's proposal via her father, and the two men had then agreed the marriage settlements.

Aunt Agatha, despite being on the wrong side of sixty, had made the arduous journey to New York last month, since storms were rare in June and July. Sophia had vaguely remembered her from a previous visit eight years ago, and had quite enjoyed taking her aunt out and about to see the rapidly growing city of New York. Papa, naturally, could not afford to be away from the bank for weeks on end, and so it had been agreed that Mama and Aunt Agatha would travel to England with Sophia, to see her safely married.

Disaster had then followed. Two of them, in fact. First, an outbreak of yellow fever in the city, just days before they were due to travel, had sent Mama into a panic. Instantly, she had instructed the servants to begin packing, as she declared she must immediately take Sophia's sisters to safety in their country house north of the city, while assuring Sophia that Aunt Agatha would be perfectly capable of looking after her. Sophia, rather taken aback by the speed at which she was being abandoned, soon came round to the notion. Freedom from Mama's strictures was one of her goals, and this meant she would achieve it sooner than expected.

And so she had boarded the three-masted sailing packet with Aunt Agatha and her aunt's personal maid, her heart thumping at the notion that finally, here was a deed worth doing. Glancing up as she stepped off the gangway, she noted the symbol of the Black Ball shipping line—a dark disc painted on the fore topsail, and she shuddered with a mix of excitement and nerves. This was the greatest adventure of her life. It was novel, and daring, and ever-so-slightly frightening. It felt perfect—until, two days out to sea, Aunt Agatha had keeled over and died.

The funeral was over, Aunt Agatha respectfully buried at sea. Sophia had been fascinated to understand that this was a euphemism for a rather stark expulsion of poor Aunt Agatha's body into the ocean. Afterwards the captain had bowed to her, assuring her of her safety on board. Sophia, her face hidden behind a black veil given to her by one of the first-class passengers who had herself recently emerged from mourning, simply nodded, inwardly wondering whether Aunt Agatha had really been such a guardian of her safety. She certainly could not have rebuffed an assailant by force, being physically rather frail. But perhaps some would-be assailants might have been deterred by a fierce look. Aunt Agatha, like Mama, had been a master of the fierce look.

Sophia was not so naive as to think that a young maiden like herself was necessarily safe just because the captain had said so. She and her friends had often been about in the city, shopping in the genteel stores or walking in the park, and they had been careful to keep their wits about them at all times. Yes, she would have to take great care until she reached her destination. Aunt Agatha had told her that the Earl was to send a carriage for her on arrival at Liverpool, and that they were then to travel by road to London—a journey of four days at an easy pace.

'May we assist you with anything, Miss Van Bergen?' The captain's wife, a stoutish matron with grey hair and a closed expression, asked—her expression not particularly warm or encouraging. The couple lived at sea—a strange life, no doubt. But since Sophia's previous life experience had been largely limited to four dozen wealthy families in Lower Manhattan, she could not honestly say what was strange, for her notions of normal were limited by her own narrow experience.

'Oh, no, thank you. I shall retire to my cabin until dinner. My maid is there.'

'Excellent.' As the captain's wife turned away, clearly relieved at not having to deal with histrionics, Sophia shook her head slightly. While she had not known Aunt Agatha particularly well, she was still sad at her aunt's death. Sophia's grandfather, the marquess, had had only the two children—both daughters, fifteen years apart. Mama's mother had been the marquess's second wife, and when she too, had died without giving him an heir, he had apparently declared his intention not to re-enter the marriage mart at his advanced age. The title and most of the holdings had passed to a distant male relative, while the marquess's two daughters had been left with only a modest settlement each. It had been Agatha who had brokered Mama's marriage to the wealthy New York banker, and Mama had never seemed to regret it.

And now here was Sophia, bringing wealth to what surely was another impoverished aristocrat through her marriage. Sophia frowned as she walked to her cabin. Something about it did not sit well with her—even though she knew it to be the way of the world. Two of her friends from school were already married, their husbands having essentially been selected by their parents. While no one would force a marriage if a maiden actively disliked the man, the whole enterprise still seemed rather cold to Sophia. She was not romantic—at least, not in the sense of seeking courtly love. Her notion of romance was adventure, and freedom, not domesticity.

'Cabin' was something of a misnomer, thought Sophia as she stepped inside. It was a first-class suite with a modest sitting room, a bedroom containing two beds, and a tiny dressing room where their maid slept. Sophia and Agatha had needed to share a maid as there would literally have not been the space to house a second girl. The bedroom even had a small round window, from which Sophia could look out at the horizon—a line of blue-grey with the sea below and the sky above. She had never before appreciated the vastness of the ocean—indeed, if she thought about it too much, it gave her the shivers to think how vulnerable they were. *One storm, and...* But no. Aunt Agatha's funeral had clearly lowered her spirits. She would be back to herself shortly, no doubt. The voyage itself was an adventure, and she must show no fear.

The cabin was done out in mahogany, with plush crimson draperies and a thick carpet underfoot. As Sophia entered, Daisy—Aunt Agatha's maid—emerged from the small dressing room to take Sophia's gloves and veil.

'My slippers, please,' she asked, longing to be out of her stylish but uncomfortable half-boots.

'Yes, miss.' As Daisy bent to her task, Sophia eyed the girl assessingly. She and Daisy were about the same age and build, and Daisy had brown hair...

'All done, miss. I shall fetch your slippers.'

Sophia waited, her mind racing. The idea in her head just would not go away, even though the rational part of herself was telling her it was madness.

'Where are you from, Daisy?'

The girl looked startled, her blue eyes wide for an instant. 'I've lived in lots of places, miss. I was born in Shropshire, though.'

'And did you live with my Aunt Agatha in London?'

'No, miss. I was hired for the New York trip only. My employment ends when we get to Liverpool.'

'I see.' She thought for a moment. The girl's accent was refined—at least to her ear. 'And have you more work lined up?'

'I do, miss. I have a posting at a country estate in Derbyshire—Lord Hartington and his sister are hosting a house party and have hired additional staff.'

Derbyshire. Vaguely, she knew that was not particularly near London. 'For how long?'

Daisy shrugged. 'Until the end of the summer. The *ton* will stay away from London until September, for the city is too warm and too odorous in July and August. From mid-September on it is usually busy again.'

Sophia thought about this. They were expected to reach England sometime in mid-July—although the captain could not predict the date with accuracy. *Mid-July until early September.* It did not seem very long—and yet, was quite long enough to satisfy her plans, her thirst for adventure. Perhaps domesticity could wait awhile. 'And is this how you work? Taking different posts, one after another?'

Daisy looked decidedly uncomfortable. 'Yes, miss.'

'But I thought most servants worked for the same family?'

She shook her head. 'Oh, no. Most are like me, moving around wherever the work is. The lucky ones are retained by a particular household, sometimes for life.'

'Then—forgive me—you have no security? No pension for old age?'

'No, miss.' She bowed her head, but not before Sophia had seen the gleam of unshed tears in her eyes.

Lord! What a life! 'I am sorry, Daisy.'

'Yes, miss. May I be excused? I have to mend the tear in your green silk.'

'Of course, of course.' Sophia watched as the girl made her way back into the dressing room, where she slept on a small cot among Sophia's and Aunt Agatha's clothing. *I have upset her.* She felt bad about it.

Sighing, she made her way to the chest of drawers where Aunt Agatha had kept her correspondence and other personal items. Now that her aunt had died, she was in charge of the travel arrangements, and needed to review what was in place. Even that was a thrill, for she had never had such an opportunity before. Taking her aunt's wooden box from its drawer, she placed it on the dressing table and set to work.

Chapter Two

Half an hour later Sophia's review was completed. She had made a list of all of the inns booked and the prices agreed, and had diligently read through the correspondence associated with the bookings (Aunt Agatha had been very specific about the level of cleanliness required). There was also a letter from Aunt Agatha's man of business in London, a Mr Lynch, confirming he would pay all of her bills while she was away. *Lord, I shall have to sort out her affairs!*

Or perhaps Lord Linford's man of business would do so? The notion made her frown, as the idea of being involved in managing the complexities of Aunt Agatha's estate held a strange appeal. What, exactly, did she want from life? To raise children and attend balls and soirées, like Mama? Or to become involved in her husband's business, as some of Papa's friends' wives did? She understood the banking world fairly well, having always been curious. Papa had taught her—indulgently at first, then with a sharper focus, and Sophia always enjoyed their lessons and conversations.

Pondering over this for a moment, she discovered only murkiness in her mind when she tried to imagine her future. She did not know what she wanted. She hardly knew who she was. In truth, she had never been *herself* before. At twenty years of age, she had only ever been Papa's daughter, Mama's daughter, Lady Agatha's niece. She was a sister to her sisters and a friend to her friends. And now she was to be someone's wife. Lord Linford's wife. A man she had never met.

She sighed. She was at a crossroads, and knew not what path to take. The easy choice would be to be compliant, travel to London, say 'I do', and be done with it. But the restlessness within her was growing by the hour.

Was it not fate that had prevented Mama from travelling, that had decreed Aunt Agatha would go to her eternal rest exactly *now*, exactly *here*? For it offered Sophia a glimmer of freedom—the chance to be someone entirely different, if only for a short time. To discover who she was. She, herself.

But she could not ask such a thing of Daisy. The girl was limited by her choices too—though in a very different way to Sophia. Similar age, similar looks, but one was rich and one poor. All they had in common perhaps, was the need to keep going.

Daisy had returned to help her dress for dinner. Sophia's wardrobe—including many new dresses created especially for this trip—was entirely based on her status as a young unmarried woman. It was all pale muslins for day wear and gentle colours for evening gowns—mostly blues and greens, for they suited Sophia's colouring. Nowhere among them was there anything black, grey, purple, or lilac—the colours of mourning. On Daisy's advice Sophia decided on the green silk that Daisy had just mended, teamed with one of her aunt's dark shawls.

'I shall dress your hair simply, miss, if you please,' Daisy offered.

'An excellent suggestion! Thank you, Daisy.' Sophia thought for a moment. 'And I shall wear no jewellery.' Vulgarity, Sophia knew, was the one thing Mama found unforgiveable. *She has trained me well—or at least, so I hope.*

Sitting before the mirror as Daisy pinned her hair up, Sophia decided to bring up the matter of her marriage. Daisy might know things that she did not. 'You know I am to marry Lord Linford?'

Had she imagined it, or was Daisy's expression suddenly closed? Surely there was a tightness about her that had not been there a moment ago?

But perhaps she had imagined it, for the maid's voice was even as she replied, 'Yes, miss.'

'Daisy, you will have worked in many *ton* houses, I am sure.'

'Oh, no, miss! Not very many at all.'

'Have you ever met Lord Linford?'

'Once. Many years ago.' Her tone was clipped.

'And what did you make of him?'

'I can have no opinion of my betters, miss.'

Sophia bit back frustration. 'Of course,' she said soothingly. 'But what have you *heard* of him? What do you know of him?'

'I cannot say, miss.'

Why is she being so evasive?

Sophia laughed lightly. 'If you will say nothing to praise him, I must assume you know something about him that is not good.'

Daisy's demeanour was now entirely rigid, her face set and rather pale, and her lips clamped tightly together. Sudden realisation swept through Sophia, the shock of it sending coldness through her entire body. *She wishes to tell me something, but cannot.* And whatever it was the girl knew about Sophia's future husband, it was not good.

Lord! What manner of man was he? Someone that her aunt thought to be perfectly amiable, but a serving maid did not?

Servants knew everything. They were required to be discreet, but they *knew.* So what was it, then? Was he a cheat? Did he, perhaps, engage in the awful slave trade? *Oh, why did I not think to question my aunt more?*

One thing was for certain. She must not rush into marriage with this man. She needed to evaluate, to consider.

Sometimes in life one gets the opportunity to be

brave, to take a chance. This was such a moment, and the significance of it tingled at the edge of Sophia's awareness. She took a breath. 'Daisy.'

She had made her decision. *It can do no harm to ask.* 'I am going to tell you something. And then I am going to ask you something.'

'Yes, miss?' The girl looked decidedly nervous.

'I am...unsure whether to go ahead with the wedding. I do not know if I even wish to be married. My head is awhirl with worries, and fears, and doubts.' She shook her head. 'This must sound conceited to you, who has genuine concerns to worry about. But it is real to me.'

'Oh, no, miss. I understand—a little, at least.' Daisy's eyes had softened in sympathy. 'It is difficult when one's choices are limited.'

'Thank you. Yes.' She took a breath. 'I have decided I wish to take some time away, when we arrive in England. Time for myself. Time to *think*.' She grimaced. 'But Lord Linwood will expect me to go straight to London, and to marry him within a few short weeks. My mother is not here, and now I shall not even have my aunt's counsel.'

Daisy's eyes were wide. 'You will have no one to advise you, save his family!'

'Precisely. And this is all about my money for him. He has never met me, knows nothing of me save the size of my dowry.'

The maid looked grim. 'Now that I can believe. But how are you to manage it, miss?'

This is it. 'I wondered if I could perhaps…be you. Just for a short time.'

Daisy looked stunned. 'Whatever can you mean?'

'I should like to work as a housemaid in Derbyshire—to fetch and carry, clean and mend. To do honest work with my hands and learn new things and *not* be a dashed heiress!'

'But—but—'

Sophia waited.

'But Lord Linford will still expect you in London!'

'Yes. This may sound nonsensical, but you look a little like me.' She turned back to the mirror, seeing Daisy's shocked face behind her in the reflection.

'We look very different, miss.'

'Yes, but you have brown hair and blue eyes. You are a similar build to me, too. The miniature that Lord Linford received was not very accurate.'

'I…see…'

'Besides, you will be in mourning for my—*your* aunt. It is likely that you will see little of him—or anyone. You will simply rest, and not work, until I return.'

Sophia waited, while Daisy considered the matter. Numerous expressions flitted over the maid's face—uncertainty, anger, then determination.

'Let me check if I understand you, miss. You wish for me to go to London, to make Lord Linford believe that I am Miss Van Bergen?'

'I do.'

'But what will happen when he finds out the truth?'

Sophia shrugged. 'He will be very angry with me, I have no doubt. It should not affect you, for you can always go back to your old life. And if you are worried that I might be a terrible maid and earn you a bad reference from the household in Derbyshire, I can tell you that you are probably correct. But I shall more than make up for it with a glowing reference. And I shall pay you handsomely.' She named a sum that was trifling to her but which would equate to double wages for Daisy.

'But...your marriage...'

'The truth is I have yet to decide whether I wish to go ahead with the marriage.' She frowned. 'I do not wish to undermine my parents and my aunt, who have made the arrangements in good faith. For me to refuse would reflect badly on them.' She thought for a moment. 'Seeing how someone behaves when they are angry is often quite revealing. It may help me decide if I wish to go through with the wedding.'

'Or he may decide he wants nothing to do with you!'

Sophia smiled mischievously. 'That, too! And then I would be free to decide for myself what to do next.'

'I see. And you believe I can do this? Fool them all?'

'Can you?'

Daisy bit her lip. 'Maybe,' she said slowly, then shook her head. 'But this is madness, if you do not mind me saying so, miss!'

'I do not mind at all, for you are entirely correct.

Now, I shall go to dinner, and leave you to reflect on this.'

'Yes, miss.'

This is madness. Daisy's words stayed with Sophia as she made her way to the ship's first-class dining room. Madness it certainly was, and yet the notion was the most wonderful, exciting, *daring* madness that Sophia had ever considered carrying out. *And I am determined to do it—if Daisy agrees.*

Dinner was uneventful—full of people treating her like she was made of china and might break if they so much as mentioned her recent bereavement. Sophia asked the captain if he would carry a letter back to New York informing her mama of Lady Agatha's death. He agreed instantly, informing her that the ship would stay in Liverpool for just three days before setting off again, with a similar break on the New York side. Sophia did a quick calculation in her head. Since they were due to dock around the fourteenth or fifteenth of July, that meant even if Mama left for England immediately, she could not possibly arrive in England until September. In fact, if the packet took broadly the same number of days to cross the Atlantic each time, then the ship carrying her letter would only reach New York in mid-August, and Mama could not arrive in Liverpool until the thirteenth day of September at the earliest. *Plenty of time for my masquerade to run its course.* She would simply have to ensure she was safely back in London by then.

She ate little—partly because she was genuinely disturbed by her aunt's death, and thinking of her. Agatha had lived quietly—an elderly spinster with a married sister in New York whom she rarely saw. Mama had gone to London twice during Sophia's childhood, and Agatha had visited New York occasionally. That had been daring, surely, for Aunt Agatha to travel on a ship across the Atlantic with only a serving maid for company? *Perhaps despite living quietly for the most part, she is the source of my need for adventure.*

Finally she was free to return to her cabin, and as she opened the door she felt a sense of trepidation. Would Daisy agree? It all hinged on Daisy, for the notion of temporarily becoming a serving maid had taken firm root in Sophia's mind. Daisy covering for her in London meant there would be no manhunt for a missing heiress, and even if Daisy's ruse fell, Sophia would have had at least a taste of freedom, and the experience of real work. And if her betrothal fell… Sophia shrugged inwardly. She had never met Lord Linford. His opinion was of little interest.

Daisy was there to take her gloves and fan, and as Sophia made for the settee and kicked off her slippers, she waved at a nearby armchair.

'Please sit, Daisy. I have been gone for nigh on two hours, so I am hoping you have had a chance to think.'

Daisy sat, looking uncomfortable. 'I have, miss.' She took a breath. 'I have questions.'

'Of course you do.' This was encouraging. The girl had not given a flat No.

So Daisy asked her questions, and Sophia answered them. They mostly involved practical matters like what knowledge Daisy would be expected to have, whether there was anyone in London who would have met Miss Van Bergen previously, and how on earth an American heiress was expected to behave. Over the hours that followed, as both girls engaged their brains in a lively way, something between them changed. Daisy became more relaxed, the liveliness of her character showing through, and Sophia found that she liked her. Had they been of the same class, she would have wished to make a friend of her. And somehow, as they talked, they both gradually changed their way of speaking, from 'if' to 'when', from 'would' to 'will'.

'So, are we going to do this, then?' Sophia enquired, sometime around one in the morning.

Daisy grinned. 'I think we are, miss!' She put a hand to her head. 'It is madness, but only a temporary madness. Once our masquerade is done, we can both return to our old lives.'

'I shall probably be entirely ready to return to a life of ease, having known real work for a few weeks!'

'And I shall be glad to have enjoyed a life of ease, even if only for a few weeks.' Her brow furrowed. 'I shall have to teach you how to be a maid before we reach Liverpool.'

Sophia grinned, excitement bubbling within her. 'I shall enjoy being Daisy Jennings, I think!'

'And I hope to enjoy my sojourn as a lady, miss.'

'Oh, please call me Sophia. What we have done has broken all notions of rank, I think.' Sophia stuck out a hand, equal to equal. 'Then we are agreed?'

Daisy took it. 'Agreed.'

Chapter Three

'I would speak to you of your marriage, brother.'

Joshua Banfield, Earl of Hartington, looked up from his newspaper. 'Good morning, Eliza. I trust you slept well?'

Her lips tightened. 'Do not think to evade the subject, Hart! We both know it is time for you to settle down and produce an heir.'

'I merely said good morning, dear sister. Will you be seated?' He indicated the armchair opposite, recalling as he did so that as children they had often been sent here—to what had then been Papa's library, not his, when they had misbehaved.

Eliza sat, her spine rigid, and a martial look in her eye. *Oh, Lord, she has the bit between her teeth!*

'You will soon be thirty, Hart. Thirty!'

He sighed. 'You wound me, Eliza! I am but eight-and-twenty, and do not need to cloud this sunny day with thoughts of my own mortality.' He sent her an innocent glance. 'Does that mean you are nearly forty?'

'I am not! I am five-and-thirty, and a long way from—' Despite herself, she smiled. 'You wretch, Hart!'

'That is more like it,' he murmured.

'But I mean to be serious!'

'So I see.' He eyed her closely. 'Something is bothering you, Eliza. Spit it out!'

She exhaled. 'Louisa met our cousin in Derby recently. She has written to tell me of it.'

'I begin to understand you. How was the delightful George?'

'Drunk as a loon at midday!' She grimaced. 'And Louisa says he means to come for your house party. His mother, too.'

He shrugged. 'He is my heir. I had no choice but to invite him—both of them.'

'You know as well as I do that he is entirely unsuitable! The very thought of him inheriting Walton House gives me palpitations!'

'While I have nothing but respect for your palpitations, dear sister, the law is set. The earldom, and the lands and properties that go with it, are entailed through the male line.'

'Which is precisely why you need to marry and produce an heir!' She sent him a keen look. 'I notice you did not mention monies. Are you still washed up?'

He frowned. 'Not *entirely* washed up, no. I have worked hard these past four years since Papa's death to discharge many of his debts. With good stewardship, our ship may remain steady.' *Or may gradually, slowly sink.*

'But a good dowry from your future wife would help, would it not?'

'There is, at present, no "future wife", Eliza.'

'Which is exactly my point! Louisa says—' She broke off, piquing his interest.

'Pray continue, Eliza. What does our dear sister say?'

'The same as me—that you should marry soon, and ideally you should marry an heiress!'

'And where am I to find such a creature in the wilds of Derbyshire?'

She sniffed. 'There are a couple of possibilities coming to your house party, for I made sure to include them and their parents in the invitations. And if they will not do, then you will have to go to London!'

'Well, I fully intend to go to London in September, as always.' He shuddered. 'But you would have me prance and preen at Almack's, I suppose. No, thank you. I have an abhorrence of the marriage mart and its matchmaking mamas.'

'And yet, you must marry. You know it.' There was no response. 'Well!' She rose, smoothing her skirts. 'I have done my part. Now, I have much to do. The extra servants I hired for the party will begin to arrive today. I do hope the agency has not let me down! The house must be cleaned from top to bottom by Friday!'

He picked up his newspaper. 'I am sure you have it all in hand, Eliza.'

She went to say something more, then seemed to think better of it. Lips pursed in disapproval, she exited, leaving Hart to his reading.

It was dawn, and finally the ship had arrived in England. The Liverpool docks were as busy and as bustling as New York's had been. The accents, however, were decidedly different. Sophia looked left and right, trying to catch her bearings, her heart pounding with excitement—excitement not just because they were finally in England, but because she was dressed in the unfamiliar garb of a maidservant, while Daisy was wearing one of her best day dresses, teamed with a cloak and the black mourning veil.

A liveried carriage sent by Lord Linford awaited Miss Van Bergen, and Sophia followed Daisy directly to it, trying to act the part of a demure servant rather than a confident heiress. They had decided to leave the ship early, Sophia missing breakfast in the sumptuous dining room in favour of eating a couple of rolls in her cabin while Daisy dressed her hair primly in the severe style of a servant. Sophia then returned the favour, dressing Daisy's hair in one of the elaborate up-styles currently favoured by the young ladies of New York, and which she had practised on her sisters.

Daisy, wearing the mourning veil—which had proved to be quite the blessing—had preceded Sophia down the gangway, having carried off a brief farewell from the captain with aplomb. *It is a good thing*, thought Sophia, *that the man was so distracted.* But he had seen what he expected to see—a slim, elegant lady in a mourning veil, followed by a servant. Sophia had not earned a single glance. Servants really were invisible, in a sense.

Over the years Sophia had played many parts in the little plays she had written for her sisters. Always though, she had been centre stage in the performances in their elegant drawing room. This part was entirely different, requiring her to cultivate invisibility, to walk slowly with eyes downcast, to be nothing, and no one, and unseen. While she was used to giving way to married ladies and older ladies—like Mama and Aunt Agatha—she still remained a young lady, daughter of a wealthy banker and granddaughter of an En-glish aristocrat. In her new role as 'Daisy', she was no one of consequence.

She would have to be careful with her accent. While Mama herself was English, and had always insisted on employing English governesses for her girls, Sophia knew that her own accent contained hints of refined New York. Daisy had been coaching her ruthlessly these past weeks, as the ship had made its slow progress over the Atlantic—and not just on how to speak correctly. Sophia now knew the basics of how to wash and mend her own clothes, how to clean furniture and carpets and how to simply dress her own hair. Dressing Daisy's hair had been easy, for she and her sisters often played with new styles.

Daisy had complimented her on it. 'You have quite a talent, Miss Van Bergen!'

Sophia had grinned. 'Perhaps it will come in useful!'

'It actually may, for even as a housemaid I am frequently called upon to attend ladies at house parties.'

'As a personal maid?' Sophia had frowned. 'I don't think I should spend too much time with any individual. I anticipate that it may be difficult to keep this up.'

'Do not.'

'Do not?'

'Yes. You should not say "don't" or "can't". It sounds American.'

'Noted.' Sophia filed the information somewhere in her brain, along with sailboat and eggplant and dollhouse. *So much to remember!*

She had also been teaching Daisy—about her family, her schooling, and her life in New York. Thankfully, the girl was an apt pupil, and could also read and write very well.

'What of languages?' she had asked. 'Young ladies are expected to speak at least one other language. I know Dutch and Spanish well, and my French is reasonable.'

Daisy had nodded. 'I cannot speak Spanish or Dutch, but my own mother was French, so I should be able to manage.'

'Mais ça, c'est magnifique!' Sophia had responded, and the two girls had often spoken to each other in French after that.

'Where to, miss?' the coachman was asking, and Daisy, with a hint of an American accent, directed him to stop first at The Saracen's Head in Dale Street. That was where Sophia would take the Derby stage, where she was then to present herself at the offices of the Earl's man-of-business, who would apparently arrange the final leg of her journey to Walton House. It all sounded extremely daunting—particularly as other people had always arranged such things for Sophia before.

Daisy was sympathetic. As the coach rumbled over the cobblestones of the docks, she said, 'When my own parents died, I had to fend for myself. I had a small amount of money, but knew I needed to find work. The benefit of becoming a servant is that you will always have food and a roof over your head—and relative safety.' She grimaced. 'There are many bad people out there.'

'I do not doubt it.' Sophia thought for a moment. For her, this was simply a ruse—something she would be able to end as soon as she tired of it. For Daisy, this was her life.

'You do realise that when Lord Linford discovers how we have deceived him, he will likely not wish to marry you?'

'I am counting on it!' Sophia grinned. 'But no, try if you can to keep him engaged, for when I do reappear, I should like to decide for myself if I wish to marry him.' Daisy had steadfastly declined to elaborate on her reservations about Lord Linford, beyond assuring

Sophia that neither young woman would be in any danger from him—which gave Sophia some reassurance, for she would not wish to be sending Daisy into peril. Daisy had promised to consider observing the man as much as she could over the coming weeks, in order to possibly provide information for Sophia.

'By that time I may have your assessment of him,' she continued. 'Plus, if our masquerade is only discovered when I choose to return, he shall be unsettled whereas I shall be confident. My papa talks about having an advantage when one is entering a business arrangement.'

'And that is how you see your marriage? As a business arrangement?'

Sophia shrugged. 'How else can I see it, when we have never even met one another?'

'I suppose. It does not seem…right to me.'

'Is it not normal?'

'Not uncommon, yes. Normal?' Slowly, Daisy shook her head. 'My parents loved one another very much. That is my idea of normal.'

'Then you are lucky indeed.' The coach stopped, Sophia bracing herself against the seat at the sudden jolt. 'It is time.'

'You do not have to do this, miss.' Daisy's voice was low.

'Oh, but I do. I most definitely do.' The coachman was unstrapping a small bag from the back—a bag that had belonged to Daisy, and which now contained the few possessions Sophia would need during her sojourn as 'Daisy'.

Opening the door, she climbed down, then turned to ask one final question. 'Tell me, how old were you?'

'Excuse me?'

'When your parents died, and you had to make your own way.'

'Oh. My mother died when I was fourteen, and when Papa died I was seventeen.'

The coachman had climbed up on his perch, and was now lifting the reins.

This is it.

Abruptly, fear rippled through Sophia. This was madness. Why was she even thinking of doing such a thing?

No!

By sheer force of will she remained silent and immobile, watching until the coach had turned the corner and was out of sight. Then, hefting her bag—surely the heaviest object she had ever been required to carry in her entire life—she walked to the front door of the inn and stepped inside.

Chapter Four

'Hart! I must speak with you! Oh, my apologies, I believed you to be at your lei…' Eliza's voice tailed off.

'At my leisure?' Hart indicated the pile of papers on the desk before him. 'My steward has provided me with enough work to fill a week.' He set down his pen. 'But of course I am ready to serve you, dear sister.'

Eliza sniffed. 'Well, how was I supposed to know when it always seems as though you have little to do!' She paused, as if awaiting a response. Hart declined to give her one. 'I wish to go through the guest list with you. It would not do for you to show surprise as people arrive.'

'Oh, no,' he replied mildly. 'But then, I rarely show surprise, I believe.'

She cocked her head to one side, considering this. 'It is true. Nothing seems to surprise you, or anger you, or *please* you, indeed. I find it most unnatural.' She shrugged. 'Still, you should at least know whom you have invited.'

'Please enlighten me then, Eliza.' He leaned back. 'I am entirely at your disposal.'

She began to go through the list, which contained the names of about a dozen people—some of whom he knew fairly well, others barely at all. George Banfield, his first cousin and heir, was likely to be a handful, for he always had been. Reared by an indulgent mother in the full expectation of inheriting the title, George frequently made demands on Hart's purse, as well as behaving in a manner not befitting the Banfield name. Hart hoped he could behave himself during the upcoming house party.

'…and then there are the Chesters. His inheritance was modest at best, or so it is believed, but he has managed to turn his fortunes around. His daughter's dowry is likely to be substantial. She is the most delightful creature! I met her at…'

Hart was no longer interested. His mind was elsewhere, speculating about Mr Chester's change of fortune. With careful management, he himself had managed to just about stabilise the Hartington finances, but he always had an ear open for opportunities to add further security to his holdings. He felt a strong responsibility to all those who depended on him—from family retainers to farmers. If he fell into bankruptcy—something that had been a strong possibility four years ago when he had first inherited the title and all the tangled finances that went with it—then all of them would suffer.

It could happen yet. His mind flicked to some of the people he cared for most in the world—his old nurse, Bess, who had a pension and a cottage on the estate. John, the head groom—who refused to retire despite being near seventy. John loved his work, loved the horses, and the other grooms all deferred to him even as they took on some of the heavier physical tasks so he would not have to.

'Your friend Lord Linford—' Hart's attention was back on his sister, 'has written to say he may not attend, or might join us late. He does not give a particular reason, though I believe I may know it.'

'You do?' Why should Eliza know something about one of his closest friends, when he himself did not?

She lowered her voice theatrically. 'I believe him to be awaiting the arrival of a significant person.'

Hart raised an eyebrow. 'He is? Whom?' Hart's friend Linford, who was a similar age, and with whom he had enjoyed many escapades during their time together at school and at Oxford, had visited Walton House on many occasions.

'An heiress, currently on her way from New York. She is related to my dear friend Lady Agatha Palmer. I had it from her—though it is all hush-hush, and not to be spoken of. You must recall I told you about it.'

Hart could not recall anything of the sort. Unfortunately, he often became lost in abstraction when people were speaking, unless he was keenly interested in the topic. His sister's long speeches, sadly, were rarely interesting.

'What is this heiress to do with Linford?' *New York*. 'And where did he meet her?'

'The couple has not yet met, but Lady Agatha hinted that certain negotiations have been taking place, via correspondence. The girl is of good lineage on the maternal side, and her father is a banker. But they do not wish for it to be widely known, she said.'

'I see.' He thought about it. 'I see.'

And he did see. Like himself, Linford had inherited a mess on his father's death, and like Hart, he was trying to achieve stability. Linford's appetite for risk, however, was higher than Hart's, and he had engaged in some hazardous investments, some of which had failed—or, at least, had threatened to fail. *His circumstances must be worse than I believed.* If the man was selling marriage to an American heiress, the situation must be dire indeed.

Linford's father had been a gambler, whereas Hart's papa had suffered from something far, far worse: the desire to spend money on those he loved. Money he did not have.

All of which served to remind Hart that marrying an heiress was probably a sensible thing for him to do also. Particularly since he was determined not to 'fall in love' with his future wife, whatever that meant. If the dowry was substantial enough, it would move his finances from being tolerable to being safe—and he would spend only what he had to spend to discharge his responsibilities. He stifled a sigh. If only they had known about Papa's extravagance...

Guiltily he recalled his father's excessive gifts to his family—diamonds for his wife and daughters, horses, carriages and expensive trips for his son. Papa had loved them very much, but had failed to show proper prudence, being led by his heart and not his head. Hart would never make the same mistake. There were people he loved, yes, but his affection for his sisters and their children, and for those servants who had helped raise him, had nothing of passion in it—passion that might lead to poor decisions. He must be careful to choose a wife who would incite no passion in him—though at the same time she must be tolerable.

'Who is the other heiress?'

Eliza blinked, mid-sentence. Lord, he had done it again. His mind often did this—went off on its own side road, and frequently people would be surprised when he spoke as the subject matter was often unrelated to the topic now at hand. This time, however, it was close enough that Eliza accepted it.

'Alongside Miss Chester, I have invited Lady Caroline, daughter of the Earl of Pashley. Her parents will both be here.'

'Lord Pashley.' Hart remembered the man—florid, with strong opinions and a fondness for port. *Do I really wish for such a father-in-law?* He chastised himself inwardly. Pashley was essentially reasonable and good-hearted. Why should he judge the man? And besides, the Pashleys were fixed in Kent. If he did marry the daughter—which was far from certain—he need not see much of them.

'...substantial dowry, as has Miss Chester.'

'Very well.' He nodded. 'I am making no promises, Eliza, but I shall give the matter my consideration.'

'Over there.'

The clerk barely lifted his head. One of the things that Sophia had noticed already was the way servants were treated. *It is as though I am nothing—a class of human that deserves no respect.* Still, at least she had not been accosted inappropriately. Or at least, not yet. She was fairly certain that in New York, she'd already have had to fend off at least one leering man.

After nine hours in a rumbling coach she had finally arrived in Derby, and a passer-by had directed her to the office of Lord Hartington's man of business. She had shown him the letter of introduction from the employment agency, but had barely got through half of her prepared speech about being employed by the Earl's sister when the clerk had interrupted, handing back the letter and indicating with a wave of his hand that she was to go to the other side of the room.

Fighting exhaustion, she took a seat amid a group of other servants—both maids and manservants, setting her bag on the floor with a great deal of relief. This time she had only had to carry it for the ten minutes it had taken to get from the coach to this building, but her arms ached and her palms stung from the leather handle digging into them. She would have to physically toughen up in the coming weeks, for sure.

'Hello.' The girl on the seat beside her offered a timid greeting. 'I'm Mary Thorpe.'

'Hello, Mary. I'm Daisy. Daisy Jennings.'

'You are for Walton Park, too?'

'I am.'

Mary was pretty, with soft brown eyes and brown hair tied up in a simple twist—just like Sophia's own.

'I've just finished working a house party in Cheshire. Always good seasonal work in the country houses at this time of year.'

Lord, is she going to ask me which other houses I've worked in? Sophia's mind was blank—in this moment, she could hardly remember anything Daisy had told her, and did not wish to draw attention to herself at this point by mentioning Daisy's transatlantic posting. So she murmured a mild agreement, but thankfully all eyes now turned to the door, where an elderly man wearing the black coat of a groom had entered. He was tall, with a shock of grey hair, a weathered face, and merry blue eyes. Sophia liked him on sight.

'Servants for Walton Park, come with me.'

They all rose, pressing to follow him outside. By the time Sophia had hefted the damned bag outside she was last, and there was no space left in the large travelling coach.

'You will have to ride upfront with me,' said the groom, taking her bag and throwing it on top of the others. 'I am John.'

'Daisy.'

She walked to the front, where John had already climbed up to the driver's perch. There was a space beside him, but how Daisy was supposed to reach it, she had no idea, having only ever ridden *inside* carriages.

'Well, come on then, Daisy!' He sounded exasperated. 'Use the footboard!'

Daisy could see the small metal step at about the height of her knee, but was unsure where to hold on, or how she would get further up the massive carriage. Stretching, she grasped the metal bar below the seat, hauling herself up inelegantly. From there, she discovered a small step recessed into the carriage, and so managed to lever herself further upwards, collapsing into the seat beside John like a sack of meal.

He chuckled. 'Well done, lass.'

Humour danced in Sophia's eyes, and she sent him a merry glance. 'Thank you, John.'

They were on their way soon afterwards. My, this was so much more exciting than sitting inside! Exhilaration rushed through her as they left the town behind, and John urged the horses to greater speed. Despite herself, she could not prevent a small whoop of glee escaping her.

'Not sat up top before, eh?'

'No, sir!' Catching a hint of New York in her pronunciation, she added, in proper English. 'This is my first time.'

'And?'

'I love it!'

And she did. From so high up, she could see the English countryside in all its glory. Rolling green fields, hedgerows in their summer finery, high hills in the distance. *I am in England!* They chatted idly as they journeyed, Daisy confessing she had never been to Derbyshire before. John—who was clearly proud of his home county—named the villages as they went through. The names were novel, and endlessly fascinating. Duffield. Belper. Crich. The road was rising now, steep in parts, and Daisy held on to her seat as the coach rolled and rocked along.

'Here we are,' John muttered gruffly, as he dexterously turned the carriage into a wide driveway to the right of the road, and Sophia sat up straighter, eager to see the place that would be her home for the next few weeks.

'Oh, how beautiful!'

The architecture was new to her—she being rather more used to the three-storey brick-and-render mansions of Manhattan and the sprawling timber country houses of the wealthy. This was built in warm stone, the evening sun warming it from the left. It seemed to her that, if such a thing were possible, the house *smiled*.

Shaking her head slightly at her own nonsensical thoughts, Sophia appraised the building more objectively. It was a substantial mansion, with three main floors, a line of smaller windows at the top, and skylights signalling fifth-floor attics. Sophia counted seven windows across the middle floor, above the portico. Strange to think none of the main bedrooms would be hers. When she and her family visited with their friends, the girls were usually housed in comfortable bedchambers on the main floors. This time... Sophia glanced again at the skylights, which surely must be where the servants were housed. *I shall see the sky in the mornings, perhaps.*

The house was surrounded by well-tended gardens giving way to woodland, while the hills rising behind it gave an air of protection—altogether an idyllic setting. It all spoke of care, of beauty, and of Englishness. Every moment here was an adventure.

'Woah!' John pulled the horses up at the corner of the house. *Of course!* Servants would not be entering by the front door. Jumping down lightly, he turned back, offering his hand.

'Don't want any accidents, Daisy. I saw how you climbed aboard!'

She took his hand and jumped down, thankfully with an appearance of grace. Before letting go of his hand, she curtsied, as though at a ball. Laughing, he matched her with a bow. 'Now, get on with you, lass, or Mrs Stone will likely box my ears.'

She snorted, having got his measure during the journey from Derby. 'I should like to see anyone try such a thing!' It was strangely liberating, being free to befriend servants as equals. *I am one of them now.*

John handed down her bag and she followed the others down a side path and round to what was clearly the kitchen entrance. She had arrived.

Chapter Five

How curious! Hart, standing idly by the window, was half watching a new batch of servants arrive. John had clearly volunteered to fetch them from Derby—a return journey of nearly three hours. At his age he should be resting, not driving solo over such a distance! But John would never hear of anything that might suggest he was getting older.

As he watched, John assisted a serving maid down from the driver's perch—there must have been no room for her inside the coach. The girl, laughing, swept into a curtsy as elegant as any that graced the ballrooms of the *ton*. Hart took a closer look. She was remarkably pretty, with clear skin and blue eyes currently brimming with humour.

All traces of character, he knew, would be suppressed as soon as she donned her uniform, but Hart was glad to have this brief reminder of the humanity of all his servants. And it was good to see John smile. The pretty maid had clearly lifted his spirits.

Yes, and mine, too. It had been a while since Hart had enjoyed a flirtation. Despite youthful infatuations with entirely unsuitable maidens, his heart remained untouched, and he had not so much as attended a ball in over a year, being altogether too focused on working with his steward and his man of business to ensure the estate was in good shape and his investments sound. He stifled a sigh. Somehow, he would have to find the desire to spend time with the debutantes his sister had invited—yes, and propose to one of them, if he liked her well enough. And, naturally, if she liked him in return. Either way, his peace was to be disturbed, and he was unsure if it would ever return.

'Mary Thorpe!' The housekeeper, an efficient-looking woman in her middle years, was calling out names from a list.

'Yes, Mrs Stone.' Mary stepped forwards, standing still as the housekeeper looked her up and down.

'Sally, Mary will sleep in your room.'

One of the two senior maids flanking the housekeeper nodded, not a hint of a smile cracking her granite-like visage. Sophia was conscious of a sick feeling in her stomach. *Lord, I have not felt like this since school!*

'Daisy Jennings!'

Copying Mary, Daisy stepped forward. 'Yes, Mrs Stone.'

The housekeeper eyed her keenly, making Sophia feel as though she could see directly into her heart. But her secrets were not so apparent, it seemed, as after a moment, the woman nodded. 'Sally, another for you.'

Her hands trembling, Sophia walked to stand behind Sally, by Mary's side. She did not dare to exchange a glance with the girl, for fear of drawing attention. They stood like that while Mrs Stone completed the list, assigning all the new staff to their allocated sleeping spaces.

'My staff will provide you with your uniform. It is your duty to make sure it is spotless at all times. Report here at six o'clock tomorrow morning, where you will be assigned your duties. You are dismissed.'

And that was that. No 'good-night'. No supper, even. The coach had stopped for dinner at an inn in Halton, but that seemed a lifetime ago.

Climbing the stairs all the way to the attics, with her bag seeming heavier than ever, her tummy rumbling with hunger, and aching tiredness in every part of her, Sophia briefly yearned for her other life. Even now, Daisy would be sleeping in a comfortable inn, with good food and servants to attend her.

'Here we are!' Sally declared crisply, opening the door. She lit two tallow candles, and in the dim light Sophia could make out three narrow beds. 'This one is mine, as is that closet. You may both use the cupboard in the corner.'

Wordlessly, Sophia and Mary moved to the other beds, Sophia dropping her bag onto hers with a huge sense of relief. Sally left then, to fetch their uniforms, and Mary and Sophia sat on their beds, both exhaling in relief.

'Lord, that Mrs Stone is frightening!' Mary's brown eyes were wide.

'She is. I was terrified when she was looking me up and down!'

'And Sally seems…'

Sophia grimaced. 'She is not the most welcoming of people, I think.'

'I am glad you are here!'

'I feel exactly the same, Mary!' They shared a wan smile, before rising to unpack their meagre possessions. Their clothes went into the corner cupboard, Sophia leaving her treasures hidden in her bag, which she stuffed under her bed. It would not do for anyone to see the bag of silver sovereign coins she had there, as she did not wish to have to explain why a girl with such riches was working hard for a servant's paltry wage. The coins she had carefully wrapped in individual rags before leaving the ship, to prevent any clinking that might draw attention to her wealth, but the rags had probably added to the overall weight of her bag. She had kept a few shillings and pennies out, and these she placed under her pillow in a little drawstring purse.

Thank goodness Papa had sent her away with so much money, for even when she split it between herself and Daisy, there had been plenty to go around. Daisy had needed money for the inns on the journey—including food and accommodation for the coachman, and

Sophia had advised her to seek out Aunt Agatha's man of business if she needed more. Aunt Agatha's money she had not touched, but charged Daisy to take care of it until she came to London.

Her jewellery she had also left with Daisy. Fleetingly, she wondered if Daisy could be trusted. She knew very little about the girl, it had to be said. She might decide to take Sophia's things and run away. If Daisy sold the jewellery there would be enough money for her to live on for many years. Sophia shrugged inwardly. She did trust her, somehow. Besides, it mattered little, for the price was worth paying, for it represented her own chance to enjoy a taste of freedom.

Indeed, leaving the jewellery with Daisy was *necessary*, for the girl would require it in order to maintain the fiction that she was indeed a New York heiress. And Sophia definitely did not need it in her role as servant.

Yet already, she missed it. She was used to wearing jewellery every day—usually a simple cross on a chain for day wear, and then pearls or discreet diamonds at night.

It will do me good, she told herself, *to be without such fripperies. This is likely to be the only adventure I shall ever have, and I intend to make the most of it.*

Chapter Six

Walton House, situated between Belper and Cromford in the idyllic setting of Derbyshire, had neither the Elizabethan solidity of Hardwick Hall nor the glamour of Chatsworth. It was a fair mansion, solidly built by the third Earl over fifty years ago, with a façade of grey limestone trimmed with warm sandstone. Hart rode up the drive after his usual early morning hack, trying to see it through the eyes of his expected guests. Would Lady Caroline be impressed? And what of Miss Chester, whose home was apparently a lavish manor set amid the lush swards of Essex?

He frowned, suddenly uncomfortable with his own line of thinking. Walton House might not be the largest home in England, but he was proud of it, of his ancestors, and of the people who worked so hard to maintain the place. He pulled up, dismounting beside two of the gardeners who were already hard at work before the day became too warm. He lingered for quite a few minutes talking with both men, whom he had known since boyhood. A groom came and took his horse, so once he had finished his conversation he made his way round the side of the house to the kitchen door.

'Ah, my lord, now you know they don't like it when you come this way.' It was John, seated at the massive kitchen table with a cup of tea in his hand.

'John! Good day to you.' Hart slid onto the bench opposite, with a comment about the fine weather.

'Aye, it's like to stay fine for a few days yet, so your guests may walk about the garden and the woods at their leisure.' He rolled his eyes. 'There's a mad frenzy of cleaning going on upstairs, as I'm sure you realise. I plan to stay out of the way of it, for once my Nancy is in this humour she will brook no delay or opposition.'

Nancy was John's daughter, Mrs Stone. 'She is a fine housekeeper, John. You should be proud.'

'Well I am. Just don't tell Nancy!' He winked, and Hart laughed, feeling the tension ebb out of him. His father would have strongly criticised Hart for befriending the servants, but Hart had always followed his own path. Papa had saved all his emotion for his family; Hart preferred to bestow his affections on a wider range of people—his sisters, certainly, and their husbands and daughters, but also those servants he had known since birth. *Affection* was safe; it required neither grand gestures nor grand spending. Papa's great love for Mama had been all-consuming, and had transferred itself to the children of the union. Unlike other gentlemen he had never strayed, not once—laudable, no doubt, until one looked at the state of the Hartington finances.

'She is currently "training" the new housemaids, may the good Lord have mercy on them!' John jerked his head towards the servants' hall next door. 'The poor girls are terrified, no doubt!'

'I saw you arriving with some of the temporary servants last night. You really should not be driving so far!'

'Pah! I had the company of a pretty young maid all the way back. At my age, one takes whatever opportunities one can find for such a pleasant pastime.'

'I saw her curtsy. Nicely done!'

'Aye, she's a handsome lass, that is for certain. Quick-witted, too. And...' He paused, his brow creased. 'There is something unusual about her. I cannot quite say what, but...yes, definitely something about Daisy.'

So her name is Daisy. The name did not suit the elegance of the curtsy he had seen. Still it was pretty, and rustic, and perfectly suitable for a serving maid.

'What are you suggesting? Do you think she means to steal the silverware?' He accompanied his provocative words with a smile, so John would know he was not serious. Still, Mrs Stone, along with Knox, his butler, would be wary of the temporary servants. If ever silverware might be stolen, the coming weeks might provide a clear opportunity for a nefarious temporary servant. 'I think I shall call in on them,' he said, rising.

John chuckled. 'Not too many things that might disturb my Nancy, but your arrival in the servants' hall might just be one of them!'

With a final grin in John's direction, Hart made for the door to the servants' hall. Here, Mrs Stone and Mr Knox reigned supreme. Here the servants ate, and received their daily orders, and even slept at times—or, at least, the junior footmen did, for he had seen them, stretched out on pallets by the smouldering fire in winter. Oh, they all had beds—he had made certain of it—but they often chose to sleep here for warmth during the winter storms while Hart shivered in his cold four-poster, the wind rattling at the windows. *Those windows need to be replaced before next winter.*

Composing his features, he opened the door. All eyes turned to him, Mrs Stone immediately rising from her chair to drop into a curtsy.

'My lord!'

There was a collective gasp as the four serving maids currently seated on a bench realised who had entered. Two were wearing the plain uniform of scullery maids, the other two the rather more expensive garb of upper housemaids. As one, they rose, curtsying with various degrees of elegance. These then, were some of the new temporary hires. His eye, naturally, had gone directly to the one called Daisy, who was just as pretty as he remembered, though her soft brown eyes currently held a slightly terrified expression. *What has Mrs Stone said to them of me?*

'You may be seated.' He turned to his housekeeper. 'I trust all is in order, Mrs Stone?'

'Yes, my lord. The two new housemaids will shortly be assigned to help the others. The rest of the scullery maids have already begun their tasks, and these last two will be assisting with preparing the best china, once I have finished speaking to them. All will be ready before your guests arrive, my lord.'

'I have every faith in you, Mrs Stone.' He turned to the serving maids. 'I do hope you will enjoy your time here. I appreciate all your efforts.'

With a nod, he left again, entirely aware of the consternation he was leaving in his wake.

Well! So that was Lord Hartington! From what Mrs Stone had been saying, Sophia had envisaged some sort of ogre. They were never to speak to my lord. They were never to meet his eye, unless he directly addressed them. If he or any of his guests passed their way, they were to instantly rise, to stand with their backs to the nearest wall, hands by their sides and looking straight ahead.

A thousand times, Sophia had seen servants do exactly that, when she had passed them. Never before though, had she thought of what it must be like from the perspective of the servant. As Mrs Stone resumed her (detailed and specific) teachings, Sophia's mind drifted back to the Earl. He was handsome, with dark blue eyes, dark hair, and a fine, strong form. *Lord, if*

Linford is anything like as handsome, I shall be very well pleased. If a girl had to marry, the man should at least be handsome. Hopefully the miniaturist had conveyed accurately Lord Linford's good looks.

Lord Hartington's manners were also excellent, she thought, trying to imagine Papa making the effort to meet new servants, much less temporary servants. Papa was a good man, but had no time for what he would no doubt describe as trivialities.

There had been something *more* with Lord Hartington. A liveliness of thought—she could not describe it exactly, but there had danced in the Earl's eyes a hint of a good mind. Sophia herself had often been praised by her tutors for her voracious desire for learning, her quickness in picking up new ideas and concepts. Only rarely had she come across someone who seemed to have a similar appetite for life, for learning.

No, she was decidedly impressed by the Earl. A pity she could not have met him as Sophia…

'… And if you follow those very simple rules, you will do very well here.' Mrs Stone seemed to be nearly finished. 'But remember, I will have my eye on you at all times.'

She looked at them, as if expecting a response. 'Yes, Mrs Stone,' Sophia said, Mary echoing her.

'Right. Follow me!'

She led all four of them up the narrow servants' staircase to the ground floor, assigning them to various tasks. The scullery maids were to empty chamber pots regularly, wash and scrub the kitchens and the front step, as well as carry coal upstairs if fires became needed in the coming weeks. Sophia thought this unlikely, since the weather remained pleasant, but then, what did she know of typical August weather in England?

'Daisy, this morning you will help Sally to brush and clean the stairs, including the balustrades.' Her hand swept towards the grand staircase, where Sally was already cleaning.

'Yes, Mrs Stone.' Her heart sank, for she had not warmed to Sally. Still, at least she would be able to copy what Sally was doing, for she placed no reliance in her own ability to figure it out from scratch.

Sally pointed to the bucket of soapy water by her side. 'Use the wet brush first, then wipe with this.' She handed Sophia a cloth. 'I shall start the balustrades.'

Nodding, Sophia took Sally's place, sinking to her knees on a stair about a third of the way from the top. The stairs above had been cleaned, the carpet running down the centre was a little damp, the tufts disturbed. Dipping her hand into the bucket, Sophia extracted a stout scrubbing brush and set to work.

By the time she had done the next third of the stairs, her back was aching and her hands stinging from whatever was in the bucket. Still, she persisted. Well, she had no choice. *This is my life now.* She had *wanted* to work, and to feel what it was like to be a servant.

A noise from above caught her attention. A lady approached, in an elegant morning dress of jaconet muslin in a striking shade of dark green, indicating she was married. This, then, must be the Earl's sister, Mrs Dawson. According to the limited information provided by the housekeeper, she was to be hostess for her brother's summer party, and it was she who had instructed the housekeeper to hire additional staff. Rising, Sophia moved to the far side of the staircase then, belatedly remembering the bucket, she dashed for it, just getting it out of the way in time. The house was to be cleaned invisibly, with no inconvenience to the family. Sophia could just imagine the horror of Mrs Dawson tripping over a carelessly abandoned bucket!

'Sister?'

Instinctively, Sophia looked upwards—meeting the eyes of the Earl! Instantly there was a roaring in her ears and her heart was pounding, as though she had been running. Tearing her eyes away, she adopted the required pose, staring into the middle distance as Mrs Dawson paused to allow the Earl to catch up with her. He had discarded the riding jacket and was now clad in thigh-hugging buckskins and an olive green superfine jacket. *My, he is handsome!* If she had met him at a ball or assembly in New York, she would gladly have danced with him. Yes, and kissed him too, perhaps.

Stop! She was in enough trouble as it was, for she had looked him in the eye—a cardinal sin, according to Mrs Stone. While she did not expect to be let go over it, she would need to be careful. It would not do to be *noticed*, when one was meant to be simply a uniform—invisible and unimportant. Still, she could not help listening as the Earl and his sister continued down the stairs, chatting about the weather.

The day was indeed pleasantly warm—though with nothing like the heat of New York. Sophia's exertions however, meant that she was a little uncomfortable. Still, there was nothing else for it. Taking the bucket back to the centre of the stairs, she reached inside for her scrubbing brush and knelt once again.

'How was your day?'

Mary and Sophia were finally able to take to their beds, having worked steadily until eleven in the evening. Sally had yet to join them, having stayed behind with others of Mr Knox and Mrs Stone's senior staff in the servants' hall for a late night meeting.

'Exhausting! You?'

'The same.' Mary moved her shoulders, as if to loosen them. 'I am used to hard work, but a deep clean before guests arrive is the bane of a maid's life!'

'I believe I have discovered muscles that I never knew I had!' said Sophia, slipping her feet under the covers. 'I shall sleep like a dead thing tonight.' It was true. Never in her life could she recall ever feeling so tired. Yet she also felt strangely satisfied.

'Me too. And another day of cleaning tomorrow.'

'Is tomorrow Friday? I have quite lost track of the days.'

'Yes, Friday the seventeenth. The guests will come on Saturday.'

'Hmm.' Tomorrow, the ship would leave Liverpool bound for New York, with her letter to Mama on board. This reminder that her time for adventure would be short had come at a good moment, strengthening her resolve. *I wanted this!* Now she had to see it through.

Mary lay down, but neither of them blew out their tallow candles. 'Did you see the family at all?'

'Yes, I saw the Earl and his sister when I was cleaning the stairs.'

'Mrs Dawson is a formidable matron, I am told.'

Sophia reflected on her brief glimpse of the woman—stout, stiff, and stately. Yes, formidable was probably an appropriate epithet.

'Are there more of them? I mean, is it just the Earl and his sister in the family?'

'One of the footmen told me there is another sister, also married. She has two daughters. And Mrs Dawson and her husband also have two daughters.'

'All girls.'

Mary grimaced. 'Indeed. The estate is entailed, along with the title.'

'So who will inherit, if the Earl dies childless? The rules for aristocrats have always confused me, especially entails.' In truth, things were generally done in a much more straightforward way in America, where the eldest child was often bypassed if a younger sibling showed more promise or endeavour, and where daughters like herself were increasingly involved in learning banking, business, and commerce.

Mary was happy to explain. 'Heirs of the body come first—that is, males directly descended from the previous earl, so if one of the sisters produces a son, he will be the heir. If there are no *direct* heirs they will look to the collateral branches of the family. Apparently there is a male cousin. He is coming to the house party.' Mary screwed up her face, as if trying to remember. 'Name of Banford or Banfield. Something like that, anyway. I cannot recall exactly what Reuben said.'

Sophia grinned. 'Reuben, eh? The footman, I presume. And just how *well* do you know Reuben?'

Even in the dim candlelight, Sophia could see Mary flush.

'I met him yesterday, as you well know!'

'I am only teasing. Is Reuben handsome, though?'

The girl sighed. 'He is. I am sure he has many admirers from among the serving maids.'

'Yet he took the time to speak to *you*.'

'That means nothing. He seems generally pleasant and amiable.'

They quietened then, as Sally had arrived. 'You should not waste your candles, girls,' she declared crisply. 'Mrs Stone will not be impressed with any profligacy.'

Obediently, they blew them out just as soon as Sally had lit her own. As sleep overcame her, Sophia was aware again of that strange satisfaction coming from her own aching bones and muscles. And something else…an odd sensation swirling at the pit of her stomach. She did not know exactly what it was, but she knew the cause. It was the Earl, and the way he had looked at her.

Chapter Seven

After another day of deep cleaning, Mrs Stone had declared the house to be 'reasonably presentable'—and just in time, for it was Saturday, and Lord Hartington's guests were due to arrive. Sophia and Mary, along with the hordes of other servants, were up at six again, carrying out the normal daily clean, as well as making final preparations to the guest bedrooms. Mrs Stone personally inspected each one, and Sophia was surprised by how nervous she felt as she stood to attention in the blue room, as Mrs Stone checked the sheets, ran a finger along the top of a shelf, and bent to closely eye the fireplace brasses.

She tutted. 'There is a mark here.'

'I shall see to it straight away, Mrs Stone.' *Lord!* Cleaning the fire irons had proved to be challenging, for Sophia could not ask for directions, which would show that she had never done it before. She had seen Mary begin with oil, and so had oiled and scrubbed the metalwork, but had been unable to remove that stubborn spot.

The housekeeper looked at her more closely. 'You are Daisy Jennings, is that correct?'

'Y-yes.' The lie did not come easily. Bracing herself for more questions, it took all of Sophia's strength to appear composed.

Mrs Stone eyed her for a moment longer, then nodded. 'You are well-spoken, and have a neat demeanour....' She thought for a moment. 'When you are finished here, come to the kitchen. I wish to try you with a tray.'

'Yes, Mrs Stone.'

Well! Sophia could not recall being so pleased with herself since that time she had performed exceptionally well at a test of history while at school.

The entire experience of being a housemaid, Sophia thought, as she knelt to her brass again, was not dissimilar to school. Sharing a bedroom with other girls. Eating plain food with no choice as to what was served. Being continuously under instruction.

Taking the emery paper that had been included in her cleaning kit she tentatively tried scouring the mark—which to her relief eventually began to give way. Having been wary of scouring the brass with such an abrasive material she was relieved to see no damage to the fireiron itself.

Returning to her school memories, she considered the matter further. Alongside the similarities there were differences, too. Physical work rather than studies. And anonymity. All her life she had been Miss Van Bergen, with all of the expectations and judgements that brought—even in school. Here, she was just another anonymous housemaid, free to hide amid the crowd, to watch and not be watched—apart from by Mrs Stone, and she could hopefully manage that.

Indeed, Mrs Stone was honouring her by even considering her for upstairs work. Serving food to the family and guests was a privilege reserved for only the most skilled and demure of housemaids. It would also give Sophia access to the drawing rooms and morning rooms, where she could enjoy observing the members of the *ton* in discourse. It might even help prepare her for a future among their ranks.

Still, she must not build up her hopes. She was a housemaid, and as such her main responsibilities were cleaning and needlework. She would not normally be allowed into rooms containing her 'betters'—as the staff called them. A shame, since the Earl's good looks had caught her eye, along with something more—some quality of wit, or liveliness of mind which she found intriguing. It would be decidedly entertaining to be able to observe such a man from a position of anonymity.

Hart was conscious of a feeling that burdens were about to be placed on him. On awakening all had been well for a moment, then his heart had sunk, as he realised it was finally the day his house guests would arrive.

He was not normally averse to social interaction. Indeed he grew frustrated when left on his own for too long. But this house party felt somehow different.

His mind went immediately to George Banfield, his heir. The man was a good ten years older than Hart, and for the first decade of his life he had been the direct heir to the earldom, Hart's father at that time having produced only daughters. The arrival of a baby boy when the countess had been at the end of her childbearing years had surprised everyone—not least the couple themselves, who had apparently given up all hope of such an outcome.

Banfield's mother, Hart's aunt, had expressed her dissatisfaction with this turn of events on many occasions, and George had been raised with a slack hand. The man was a notorious spendthrift, and frequently came to Hart when his debts became too pressing. His spending habit was the only way in which Hart saw a family trait, for Banfield held none of Papa's warmth, humour, or good-naturedness.

Still, duty decreed that Hart welcome his heir, and fund him when needed. *Duty*, Hart reflected sourly, as he rose from his bed, *is a hard taskmaster.*

As he washed and dressed—his valet assisting him into his riding jacket—he reflected further. His friend Linford was not coming—or at least, could not come to start with. *Because he is to marry.*

If Linford was to settle down, then perhaps Hart should, too. The sick feeling that followed the thought was immediate and striking. This then was his true burden—the knowledge that he must do his duty, marry, and produce an heir.

Abruptly, the constraints of his title tightened about him like chains. Why had he not the freedom to choose his bride freely, and at a time of his own preference? Why was he forced to manage a set of finances that wavered from safe to unsafe and back again without ever reaching the heady heights of thriving, while at the same time funding the lifestyle of a weak buffoon like George who could not live within his means if his life depended on it? No, he must choose a bride from among the few whose dowries were substantial, and hope that she liked him well enough to accept his offer.

George may marry whomever he wished—whomever would have him—while Hart, as earl, could not. That was his fate.

Knowing the risks of being an emotional creature like his father, Hart had cultivated a studied mildness—a containment that contrasted sharply with Papa's effusive jollity and warmth. Where Papa had been emotional, and effusive, and fascinated by every action of his family, Hart was normally mild, and disengaged, and slow to rouse.

But not today.

Striding directly to the stables, and ignoring the servants scattering left and right before him, he mounted his stallion for the usual morning ride, hoping it would assuage some of the restlessness within him.

Sophia jumped up and stood to the side as the Earl approached, his expression fierce. Lord, what had occurred to overset him so early in the morning? Turning her head, she watched his back as he made his way along the main ground floor hallway. *Perhaps he is not such a nice person after all.* There was a lesson in it—seeing what the servants see. Lord Hartington might be the sort of person who was perfectly amiable to friends and family, yet showed his true self in unguarded moments such as these.

As she went about her cleaning tasks, Sophia reflected on this. To a certain extent, everyone had a face for public events. She well recalled occasions when she and her sisters had been arguing over some trivial matter, only to instantly cease when a visitor was announced. Servants were always witnesses to such moments, yet were trained to not react by so much as a flicker of expression.

Mrs Stone had spent more than half an hour with her in the kitchen, teaching her how to correctly lift, carry, and set down a tray, and by the end had declared herself satisfied.

'My lord's guests will arrive later, and will likely assemble in the morning room and drawing room in the coming days and weeks. They will also require refreshments in their chamber from time to time. My own Walton House maids will serve them first, but I shall need some of you temporary girls to assist on occasion. I shall try you this morning, when we have only the Family, to see how you go on.'

'Yes, Mrs Stone.' Sophia had been surprised to feel a sense of pride flash through her. She might be green and untried, but her mind had been lively enough to learn Mrs Stone's precise requirements in a fairly short period.

'Now go and help the girls finish with the hall floor, then report back here for your next task.'

Which was how Sophia had happened to be in the hallway when my lord had strode through, giving her some insight into how he behaved when something vexed him. As she knelt again to her task, she suppressed a chuckle. Being an invisible servant was proving to be just as interesting as she had hoped!

'Tea, brother?'

'Very well.'

As Eliza rose to ring the bell, Hart pored over the guest list. He had previously given it only a perfunctory glance, but now that arrival day was upon him, he found himself much more interested in the names of those who would be his constant companions these coming weeks. It contained the usual names—many of the great and the popular of the *ton*, all seeking diversion outside of London to escape the August heat in the city.

'You have done well, Eliza,' he murmured after a few moments. 'I am surprised that some of these would come so far north as Derbyshire.'

She gave a short laugh. 'All too true! We have standing yet, despite Papa doing his best to ruin us with his spending.' She sighed. 'Mama always tried to keep him in check, but after she died…'

They exchanged a look of shared understanding, Hart recalling clearly the day when their steward had first given him a full account of Papa's habits, three days after Papa's death. Following the pain of loss, the shock created by these revelations had rocked Hart deeply, and his world had changed forever. In the background, the footman opened the door to admit a housemaid with a tea tray.

'I suspect grief was part of it,' Hart mused. 'They were very fond of one another.' Papa had always been prone to excessive spending, but after Mama's death he had lavished even more gifts upon his children as if worldly goods could ease the pain of bereavement. By that time Hart had begun to be involved in matters of business, and had been horrified by Papa's spending. Having informed his sisters of his concerns about the state of the family's finances, they had all three rejected as many of Papa's presents as they could, but the harm had already been done. It was only when Papa had finally succumbed to a fever three years after Mama's demise, that Hart was able to take full stock of financial matters—matters that had been his responsibility ever since.

'Indeed. Love matches are uncommon, but then our parents were uncommon.'

'True, true.' He sighed. 'So tell me about these two young ladies you expect me to court.'

The maid set the tray down on the side table and began rearranging the china in the usual manner, unstacking the cups and saucers and placing each cup on its own saucer, right way up.

'I am glad you are being so sensible, brother.' Eliza's tone was matter-of-fact. 'Both Lady Caroline and Miss Chester are in their first season, with good dowries and impeccable lineage. Lady Caroline is the higher ranking, being the daughter of an earl, but Miss Chester's family are probably wealthier.'

Hart was now only half listening. The housemaid who had brought the tea was none other than the delectable Daisy. Surreptitiously he perused her fine figure—nicely outlined by her uniform—then moved on to enjoy her perfect features. Her eyes were downcast as she focused on her task, her eyelashes fanning out on her flawless skin. The urge to reach out and run a finger gently along her cheekbone was strong, but a lifetime of decorum allowed him to resist.

As if feeling her gaze on him, she glanced up—and he found himself caught in the snare of her beautiful blue eyes. For a timeless moment he was lost—then, flushing slightly, she broke the gaze and bent to her work again, a moment later bringing the china to Eliza, followed by the teapot and milk jug.

'... Miss Chester is probably the prettier of the two.' Eliza was still speaking, seemingly oblivious to the interaction between her brother and the housemaid. 'Though you may beg to differ. I declare gentlemen's notions of beauty are oft times different to that of the ladies. Have you ever noted it?'

Thankfully, Hart was awake enough to make a sensible response. Shuffling slightly in his chair to ease his sudden discomfort, he shook his head.

'Surely notions of beauty are universal? Would gentlemen and ladies not agree?'

'I think not, for I am quite bemused at times to discover a maiden with looks no better than ordinary receiving marked attentions, while a notable beauty sits with only one or two admirers.'

'Ah, but you must allow for the effect of *character* on beauty, my dear sister.' The housemaid was walking towards the door, and he recalled the merriment with which she had curtsied to John. 'A maiden who is pretty but insipid soon becomes tedious, while a lady who is no more than "ordinary", as you describe it, may have countenance enough to attract attention. The perfect combination therefore must be looks *and* character, surely?'

'Lord, you have exacting standards, brother. I can

only hope that either Lady Caroline or Miss Chester can meet them!'

The door closed. She was gone. Hart sighed. 'I hope so too, Eliza. I hope so, too.'

Chapter Eight

Sophia felt very strange.

As she made her way back to the kitchens, her heart was racing, her mind confused. What on earth had just happened between her and the Earl? When their eyes had met, she had been overcome with the strongest sensation she had ever felt in her life. It was a little like the attraction she had felt towards a couple of the young men in her set at home, but the scale of impact was a thousand times more. How she had managed to finish setting the china without trembling she did not know, for she was now shaking from head to toe.

Reaching the safety of the dimly lit servants' staircase, she leaned against the wall for a few moments, trying to slow her breathing and allow her mind to return to its place. Why was she so affected?

He was handsome, for certain, but she had seen handsome men before. Had even flirted with a few. But this was different. A solution came to her. Perhaps it was because as a housemaid, she was forbidden from flirting with him.

The notion pleased her, so she embraced it. *Yes!* Her instincts, honed by a lifetime of being Miss Van Bergen, had wanted her to join in their conversation, to send him an arch glance as she opined on the matters he and his sister were discussing. But she could not do so, for at this moment she was not Miss Van Bergen. She was Daisy Jennings, housemaid.

With a pang, she recalled the rest of their conversation, to which she had eagerly listened. So he was to choose a bride during the house party? He, like Sophia, could not escape being forced to marry. Something about it felt very wrong. Who on earth had decided that a housemaid or footman could marry whomever they wished, while an earl or an heiress must marry for money, or position?

'Well? Any difficulties?'

'No, Mrs Stone.' *Apart from the fact I am fast developing a little tendre for Lord Hartington.*

The housekeeper nodded. 'Go back in twenty minutes and collect everything. In the meantime you may do some sewing.'

She indicated the needlework basket, filled to the brim with bed linen, aprons and clothing, all in need of repair. With a sense of determination, Sophia selected a pile of handkerchiefs with frayed edges and set to work. She had been trained to set a neat stitch, and knew this was one task where she had little to learn. Here housemaids and debutantes were all the same, with nothing between them.

Twenty minutes passed quickly, and Sophia set her needle aside, wiping her hands on her apron. In just a few moments she would see him again. Predictably, her heart began racing as she approached the drawing room.

What would Lord Hartington and his sister be discussing now? The ball, perhaps? The servants all knew that an extravagant ball was planned for early September, just before the house party came to an end, with guests invited from among the local gentry to boost the numbers.

Abruptly, Sophia's mind provided a vision of herself emerging from the shadows to dance with the Earl. In her mind's eye she was wearing one of her most stunning ballgowns—a gown of white net over a blue satin slip—currently in a trunk on its way to London. She could be the Lady Incognita, just like the girl in the fairy story of the glass slipper.

Chuckling, Sophia dismissed the nonsensical notion. She was here to work as a housemaid, nothing more. Her ruse would only succeed if she disappeared from Walton House unnoticed, to re-emerge in London as Miss Van Bergen. She must never be uncovered as her true self—for the shame of it, she had no doubt, could never be overcome.

During the long journey across the ocean Daisy had expressed a willingness to take the blame for their masquerade, since she had no reason to require society's approval afterwards. If the worst were to happen, the *ton* may decline to employ the girl after her true identity was revealed. In that situation, Miss Sophia might recommend her to someone in New York, if that was what Daisy desired. Daisy could even change her name and start afresh if she chose.

But for now Sophia must continue to play her own part—be a quiet, demure serving maid, then leave with the other temporary servants after the house party, sliding back into anonymity.

The footman outside the drawing room door opened it for her and Sophia stepped quietly inside. Lord Hartington and his sister were laughing about something, and for the first time, Sophia felt a pang of what felt suspiciously like loneliness. She and her sisters fought and argued at times, but they loved one other dearly, and she missed them. Yes, and her parents, too. The Earl was lucky to have his sister nearby.

As she tidied the tray she kept her eyes on her task, knowing that being unobtrusive was the main requirement—including avoiding any clatter that might accidentally draw attention to her.

She need not have worried, for the rumble of a carriage outside drew the attention of Mrs Dawson, who rose to look.

'Oh! It is our dear Louisa and her girls! I declare it will be a delight to see my nieces again!'

'A delight indeed.' Something in the Earl's tone suggested he was anything but delighted, and Sophia only just managed not to look at him.

'How old are they now?'

Mrs Dawson tutted. 'Why is it that men can never remember such things? Francesca is eleven, and Amabel is nine—old enough to attend an informal house party like this. My sister does well to fledge them here. I shall hope to do the same, when my own girls are old enough.'

Lord, I am altogether too interested. Carefully lifting the tray, Sophia took a few steps towards the double doors, then quickly stood aside as the footman opened them, announcing,

'Mrs Smyth, Miss Smyth, Miss Amabel Smyth.'

Taking two more backwards steps, Sophia felt the reassuring hardness of the wall behind her. Keeping her eye gaze straight ahead, she nevertheless listened with interest as the family greeted one another, sensing genuine fondness between them all. Another carriage had arrived outside, but the family seemed not to have noticed. The girls, Sophia observed, seemed to treat their uncle and aunt with easy familiarity, and once again Sophia felt the lack of her own sisters. The youngest two Van Bergen girls were only a little older than Mrs Smyth's daughters, and were being introduced to New York society events in a similarly gentle manner.

'Tea! We shall have more tea!' Mrs Dawson declared, with a glance in Sophia's direction. With a nod to show she understood, Sophia made for the door, where she paused. The footman was outside, and could not know that she needed to leave, and her hands were full with the tea tray.

Lord! Carefully balancing the tray between her left arm and her torso, she reached for one of the door handles with her right hand. Slowly, carefully, she turned the handle and pulled the door ajar, then quickly grabbed the tray with both hands—just as the china began to slide downwards. The door—which, naturally, had decided to be entirely contrary, had decided to close itself, so she stuck a foot into the rapidly decreasing space.

Whew!

Her relief was short-lived, for at that precise moment the footman pushed open both doors with significant force, the left door clattering into her. The tray tipped upwards and she jammed the edge of it into her ribs, at the same time bringing her elbows in to create a kind of cage within which to hold the precious china. Warm tea spilled all over her front, but she barely noticed, so intent was she on protecting the china. A single silver spoon flew off to the right, hitting the floor with an almighty clatter.

'Oh!' Consternation was writ all over the footman's face. Recovering himself, he bent to retrieve the spoon, setting it on the—thankfully now stable—tray.

There were guests behind him, so for the second time Sophia gave way, retreating this time to the wall behind the door.

'Mrs Edgar Banfield, Mr Banfield, Mr Forsyth!' the footman announced, while Sophia stood stone-still, trying to ignore the fact her clothes were soaked with tea and her stomach tight with nerves. The housekeeper would surely banish her from the drawing-room when she heard of the incident, which was a shame, for Sophia had discovered herself to be mightily intrigued by the family and their guests. From her current vantage point she had a perfect view of the family as they greeted the latest arrivals.

'My dear, dear cousins!' declared the man in the mulberry jacket. 'It is such a delight to see you!'

His cousins did not seem quite so delighted to see Mr Banfield, Sophia noted. Their responses were perfectly polite, but lacked the effusiveness being demonstrated by Mr Banfield—and his mother, who declared she was always pleased to come to Walton House, as she quite thought of it as her second home.

Mrs Dawson almost recoiled at this point, Sophia noticed, but Mrs Edgar Banfield, seemingly oblivious, rattled on about their journey, and how she had been determined to arrive early, '… For I know you will welcome my assistance with hosting, my dear Eliza!'

Her dear Eliza looked decidedly nonplussed, and Sophia had to stifle a highly inappropriate chuckle. It felt as though a play was being performed in front of her.

'Cousin,' Mr Banfield brought the Earl's attention back to himself, 'I have brought my friend along. I knew you would not mind. This is Cedric Forsyth.'

His face impassive, the Earl nodded to Mr Forsyth. 'We are always ready for guests here at Walton House.'

That was it. No warmth. No assurances that Mr Forsyth was most welcome. *Ouch!* The Earl was adept, it seemed, in the subtleties of verbal fencing.

The footman had kept the doors open, and now stepped around the door to send Sophia a significant look. *All is clear for me to leave.* Carefully she tiptoed to the door and out, sending a grateful look to the footman before heading for the servants' stairs.

Hart watched her go, conscious that he had quite enjoyed her reactions to unfolding events. Unlike most servants, Daisy seemed to be unable to completely smooth out her responses, and he found himself keeping a subtle eye on her. Earlier, she had suppressed a smile when he had allowed a hint of irony to enter his tone as he had professed his delight at the impending arrival of his young nieces, and she had clearly sensed his distaste for George's having brought an uninvited guest. Unlike George himself, who was so thick-skinned as to be oblivious.

Hopefully Mrs Stone would continue to allow Daisy to serve upstairs, for watching her had provided much-needed diversion from the reality that the onslaught of guests had now begun. He glanced at his nieces again. Despite a liveliness of mind they were well-behaved, and he really had few concerns that they would make the house party more difficult. No, that honour was already being claimed by his Aunt Edgar and her son.

And the audacity of George, to bring an extra guest when the house was full! He had no idea where Mr Forsyth was to be housed, and regretted giving another headache to Mrs Stone, just when her work would no doubt be at its height. Lord, this was not an auspicious start to his house party.

Chapter Nine

'What on earth happened?' Mrs Stone was looking in horror at Sophia's wet uniform. Her eyes narrowed. 'Did you drop the tray? Any breakages?'

Sophia remained outwardly calm. 'Oh, no. The footman pushed the door open *just* as I was there, but I managed to keep all the china on the tray.'

'Hrmph. You may get changed, quickly. Go to the laundry room and they will find you a clean uniform.'

Sophia set the tray down, relieved that Mrs Stone had not banished her. She paused.

'Yes? There is something else?'

Sophia grimaced. Much as she wished to avoid being the bearer of bad tidings, she knew that Mrs Stone would wish to know as soon as possible about the extra guest.

'Mr Banfield has brought a friend to stay.'

'What?' The housekeeper put a hand to her head. 'But there is not a single bedroom left! Who is his friend?'

'I believe he introduced him as Mr Cedric Forsyth.'

Mrs Stone rolled her eyes. 'Yet another of his profligate hangers-on, I have no doubt. And I do not have enough older housemaids!' She straightened. 'Very well. I shall think about what solution may be possible. You may go.'

'Yes, Mrs Stone.'

The solution, it seemed, was that Mr Banfield and Mr Forsyth would be forced to share a bedchamber—a most satisfactory outcome, in Sophia's opinion. By the time Mrs Stone was summoned to the drawing room to hear the news of Mr Forsyth's unexpected arrival, she had already rearranged her chamber allocation, and asked three of the footmen to remove the large bed from the green chamber, replacing it with two narrow beds. Sophia and Sally then made up the beds, Sally complaining at length about the inconvenience, extra work, and sheer selfishness of both gentlemen. For once, Sophia was entirely in agreement with her, and said so.

'I shall warn you,' Sally offered, straightening the bedcover, 'that Mr Banfield has been known to behave in ways that he should not.'

Sophia looked at her blankly. *Ways that he should not* could mean anything.

'With the serving maids,' Sally clarified. 'Which is why Mrs Stone will try to ensure younger maids like yourself and Mary have little contact with him.' She sniffed. 'I have no doubt his friend is equally fond of debauchery.'

Lord! Sophia's eyes grew round. Were men really so depraved that they would try to take advantage of a housemaid, knowing she might be disgraced if news of any molestation emerged? *I am green indeed.* Despite increasingly assisting Mama to run their household, she could not recall having to consider the possibility that guests might molest the female servants. But then, she supposed, Mama would never invite such men to stay… Unfortunately, the Earl could not turn away his cousin and heir, and Mr Banfield had invited Mr Forsyth, so there was not much that anyone could do about it.

Recalling the way some men had behaved towards her in New York—while out with her friends or at a ball—a healthy cynicism rose within her. Such men existed, and they cared nothing for the woman they pestered. The only novel aspect to the current situation was the knowledge that a house guest would attempt to importune a good-living servant. Sophia resolved never to be alone with either of them, and sent a silent prayer of thanks for the fact that good men also existed.

The rest of the day passed in a flurry of activity, as the remaining guests arrived, some bringing their own servants. Those without valets or abigails would have to be served by the Walton House staff—a fact Mrs Stone had taken into account in deciding how many additional female servants to hire.

'Mary, Daisy,' she called crisply, as they were rising from the servants' supper table to finally seek their beds. 'Come to my room.'

'Yes, Mrs Stone.' Daisy did not dare to even glance at Mary as they followed the housekeeper to her private room. As befitting her station, Mrs Stone had her own quarters—shared with her husband, who was the head gardener. He was there, puffing on a pipe and reading a newspaper.

'Good evening, Mr Stone,' the girls offered politely, feeling decidedly uncomfortable that they had disturbed his peace.

'Evening,' he replied laconically, unfolding himself from his armchair and making for the door. 'Happen I'll take me last walk for the evening.'

His wife sent him a grateful look, then turned her attention towards the girls.

'Despite the unfortunate incident with the tea tray earlier—' she sent Sophia a piercing look '—Sally tells me that you two are the best of the temporary maids. You are diligent, and prettily behaved, and you obey orders without any nonsensical quibbling.'

Sophia was almost afraid to breathe. Mrs Stone rarely praised anyone. Was this the preamble to some criticism? But no, for she continued, 'We have two young ladies staying at Walton House, and neither has brought an abigail. That is a challenge for me, for Sally will be looking after Mrs Chester and Lady Pashley, and my own housemaids will be busy with the Earl's sisters and supporting the governess of the two children.' She looked from one to the other.

'Tell me, have either of you previously washed and repaired delicate fabrics—beaded silks and satins, lace-trimmed gowns? Have you ever dressed hair, or assisted young ladies to dress? I have seen you manage petticoats and bed linens well, but I am unsure as to whether to let you loose on more delicate fabrics. Mary?'

While Mary gave her reply Sophia was thinking furiously. She and her sisters had routinely helped one another dress and done one another's hair, but naturally, had never cleaned their own gowns. The hurried lessons given to her by the real Daisy on board ship might not be adequate. Briefly, Sophia imagined accidentally destroying an expensive gown made by a fashionable modiste in London, and shuddered.

'Well, Daisy? What have you to say?'

'I have assisted young ladies to dress—many times, Mrs Stone, and I believe I am reasonably skilled at dressing hair. But I confess I am nervous of caring for delicate fabrics.'

'Hrmph! So you are content to do the glamorous work of assisting the ladies to dress, but will not put yourself out to clean their gowns. I see.'

'Oh, no, Mrs Stone. You misunderstand me! I am entirely willing to clean the gowns. I just might need some instruction so that I do not damage them.'

Mrs Stone's eyes narrowed, and she stood silent for a moment. Sophia could sense Mary beside her, still but tense—just as she herself was. Such an opportunity did not present itself very often. Kitchen maids dreamed of being allowed to work upstairs as housemaids, while housemaids dreamed of becoming ladies' maids. Even ladies' maids aspired in turn to be retained as a lady's abigail—her dedicated personal maid. Such a role—if one did it well—often led to a job for life, the ultimate goal of any servant.

'And Mary? You have told me you can clean fabrics, but what of dressing hair?'

'I am the opposite to Daisy, I think. I have cared for many delicate gowns, and have occasionally helped ladies to dress, but I have little skill with the curling irons.'

'Very well. I shall try you both. Help one another with the skills you are yet to acquire. But you must mix to support both Lady Caroline and Miss Chester, and if I hear any reports of encroaching behaviour, you shall be in the kitchen washing pots for the rest of the summer! Do you understand me?'

'Yes, Mrs Stone.'

'You may go.'

Outside in the dimly-lit corridor, they shared a quick hug, unable to contain their excitement. 'Imagine!' said Mary, with a sigh. 'We shall get to see and touch all their beautiful clothes. Lord, I hope I do not do anything wrong!'

'Why must we mix in with both? Surely it would make more sense to assign one of us to each?'

'I imagine she does not wish for the young ladies to become attached to a particular maid. This way, we perform tasks, but we do not *belong* to them.'

'That makes complete sense, Mary. Why are you so wise?'

Mary giggled. 'I am not a bit wise, but I am skilled at giving the impression of it occasionally!'

'Not at all. You are wise, Mary, and I am grateful to have you by my side in Walton House.'

'And I you. We are friends now, are we not?'

'Yes,' said Sophia slowly. 'I believe we are.'

A rush of warmth spread within her. Here, possibly for the first time in her life, was a friend who liked her for herself, without the complications of the Van Bergen name. Inwardly, a moment of guilt stabbed at her, that she could not be fully honest with Mary. If the girl knew who she truly was, she would recoil in horror. Never could she be so friendly or unguarded with a Miss Van Bergen.

Which was, she reminded herself, exactly why she had decided to become Daisy for a time. Daisy had freedoms that Miss Van Bergen could only dream of. Freedom to travel alone, to befriend a girl like Mary, to learn new skills—such as cleaning gowns.

'You will help me with the silk gowns, though? I shall be terrified to damage them!'

'Of course! And you shall teach me how to dress hair.'

'We have a bargain, I believe!'

They grinned at one another, making for the staircase that would lead to the attics. As they walked, Sophia reflected further on the opportunities she had gained while pretending to be a maid. Mary was entirely open and unpretentious, able to simply be herself. She had no worries about her dowry or her family's standing or her father's income. Despite the hardships and uncertainties of life as a servant, there was freedom in it, too.

Chapter Ten

Having finished her morning cleaning and attended a brief church service with most of the other servants in the small chapel in the grounds, Sophia was in the servants' hall mending a torn sheet when a bell jangled on the board. Glancing up, she saw that it was labelled as the yellow bedroom. *Miss Chester is awake!*

'Daisy, see to Miss Chester, please. You may bring some hot water when you go.'

'Yes, Mrs Stone.' Folding the sheet and tidying it away, Sophia rose and made for the scullery. 'Miss Chester has rung her bell,' she told the scullery maids. Taking one of the large earthenware jugs she filled it with hot water from the stove, then carried it carefully to Miss Chester's bedroom.

'Good morning, miss.' She set the jug on the dresser, then crossed to open the curtains. How many hundreds of times had she been on the receiving end of similar ministrations?

She looked around. The towel she had left out the

day before was lying on the floor, and there was cool water in the washing bowl. Carefully pouring the used water into yesterday's jug, she rinsed the bowl with hot water, then filled it properly.

'I shall fetch a clean towel.'

Miss Chester, who had climbed back into bed after ringing the bell, stretched and yawned, but did not reply. Well, and why would she? In Sophia's exclusive school, they had been taught that thanking servants was a sign of ill breeding, yet Papa did it all the time, and he was one of the most respected gentlemen in New York.

When Sophia returned with a clean soft towel as well as curling irons and hairpins, the scullery maid was leaving with the chamber pot and Miss Chester was up, standing near the window in a fine linen nightgown, and with her hair unbound. She was about Sophia's own age—or possibly a little younger—and pretty, with dark hair, wide blue eyes, and a plump figure. Wordlessly, Sophia set the items on the dresser, then stood by the wall, waiting.

Eventually, Miss Chester turned, and for the next half hour Sophia assisted her with washing and dressing. Just as she was doing up the last wrist-button on Miss Chester's fine muslin morning gown there was a scratching at the door, and a middle-aged lady in puce entered.

'Oh, my dear, you are awake!'

'Good morning, Mama.'

'How did you sleep, my dear?'

'Very well.' She indicated her gown. 'I have worn this gown, as you wished. But do you not think it is too plain to attract the Earl's attention?'

'Too plain? No. That embroidery cost me a fortune, Serena!'

The girl was clearly unhappy with this response. 'Yes, but I am covered to the neck!' She tugged at her neck ruffle. 'How is he to appreciate my *assets* if he cannot see them?'

Mrs Chester sniffed. 'You will have plenty of opportunity to show him your bosom—yes, and you should allow him to touch, if he wishes. He may then feel obligated to marry you. But you know as well as I do that high-necked gowns are to be worn in the mornings.'

Her daughter sighed. 'I suppose so.' She sank into the chair before the dresser. 'You may dress my hair.'

Sophia jumped to attention. The comment had been given in an offhand manner, and without so much as a glance in her direction. Yet this was her duty, she knew.

'Very well, miss. What style do you prefer?'

'Just make me look as pretty as possible.'

Sophia eyed her assessingly. Miss Serena Chester had regular features, a short, plump figure, and a petulant expression. Of the three the only one the young lady could do anything about was her attitude, but Sophia had no power to influence that.

'As pretty as you *are*, my dear,' counselled her mama, who had clearly noticed Serena's unfortunate phrasing.

'Haha! Yes! I am already pretty, and you are required

to…to *enhance* that prettiness, so that the Earl will fall in love with me!'

Walking to the side table, Sophia collected her box of hair pins and set to work. It was challenging, for Miss Chester's hair was bushy, and springy, and resistant. But she persevered, and when she stepped back she was reasonably pleased with her efforts. The irons were rapidly cooling, but even Miss Chester's side curls looked reasonable.

'Not bad,' the girl declared, turning this way and that to look at herself in the dresser mirror. 'What say you, Mama?'

'I say she has done an excellent job. I know how difficult your hair can be, Serena.' She eyed Sophia keenly. 'What is your name, girl?'

'My name is Daisy, Mrs Chester,' said Sophia, dipping into a small curtsy.

'Daisy,' she echoed, as if committing the name to memory. 'Let us go, Serena, for no doubt the other guests will already be assembling for breakfast.'

And that was that. They sailed out, without another word to Sophia. Chuckling to herself, she tidied up and made her way downstairs.

'Well? Where have you been?' Mrs Stone was bustling about the servants' hall, a list in her hand.

'Dressing Miss Chester's hair.' She paused, then greatly daring, added dryly, 'For which I believe I deserve a medal.'

Mrs Stone stilled. 'Was the young lady…difficult?'

'Not particularly, although I suspect she can be. But her *hair...*' She rolled her eyes. 'Her hair is difficult.'

'Mrs Stone!' It was one of the footmen. Reuben, if Sophia was not mistaken. Taking a closer look for her friend's sake, she saw that he had a handsome, open face.

'We need more eggs—boiled and poached, if you please. And the bacon is running low.'

'Lord save us, they will eat us out of house and home if they carry on like that! Follow me. You too, Daisy.'

In the kitchens, Cook was unflappable. 'Aye, I put more on when I heard how quickly they were getting through what I already sent up. Many of them ate very little yesterday evening, after travelling all day. Here you go, Reuben.' She handed him a tray jammed with poached eggs and bacon, and he took it.

'The boiled eggs should be just about done,' she declared, spooning them carefully out of the saucepan and into a china dish. 'Grab that tray there, Daisy.'

Impressed that at least someone apart from her attic mates knew her name, Daisy complied, and a moment later was on her way up to the dining room. Nodding to the footman guarding the doors, she steered her way inside, aware of a babble of conversation. Making straight for the sideboard, she set down the dish of boiled eggs for the footmen to serve, then began stacking empty dishes onto her tray. More than half her attention, however, was given to the Earl and his guests, as they breakfasted together for the first time.

'I must say, my lord, that your home is *delightful!*' Miss Chester was losing no time in attempting to ingratiate herself with their host, it seemed.

'I thank you. We are fond of the place.' The Earl's tone was neutral, curt even. It contrasted sharply with Miss Chester's gushing tones.

'The gardens are also pleasant, Miss Chester.' That was the voice of Mrs Dawson, the Earl's sister. 'After breakfast we might perhaps have a walk about, since the day is so mild and dry. There will be plenty of time before church.' The family and guests would have their service at noon, Sophia knew.

'What an excellent notion!' A male voice, young. Mr Banfield, perhaps? Or his friend? 'I should be delighted to accompany you, Miss Chester.'

As some of the others joined in, Sophia reflected that the upcoming walk was likely to look quite comical. Ten or fifteen people traipsing through a garden at a snail's pace, telling each other how lovely the flowers were, how mild the weather, how delightful their surroundings… She suppressed a small smile. Until very recently, such a life had been hers. Empty compliments, meaningless excursions, insincere company.

Today, instead of strolling around a garden twirling a parasol, she would be cleaning and mending. She would be industrious, purposeful, *useful*.

Her tray was full. Time to go. As she turned, she saw that the Earl was looking at her, so, very properly, she dropped her gaze and left the room.

Chapter Eleven

She is doing it again! Something about their conversation had amused Miss Daisy. He could see her profile from where he sat. Oh, she was busy with dishes, but he knew for certain that she was listening, and that she had...*opinions* about their conversation.

It had never occurred to him before that housemaids had opinions. Not because he did not see servants as people—he counted John as a friend, and the Stones were something similar. No, it was just that there were so many of them, and they were trained to deliberately make themselves seem invisible. Miss Daisy, he thought wryly, must have missed her schooling that day.

As she left the room he watched her, noting how her new uniform tightly hugged her bottom...it was the same dark grey linen as worn by all the other housemaids, but after yesterday's soaking with tea Daisy had clearly been issued with a new dress that was a little smaller. He approved.

'...join us, my lord?'

Lady Caroline was speaking to him, so he agreed with what he hoped was the right tone. It would not do to let his guests know that, rather than following the conversation, his mind had been entirely taken up with speculation about Miss Daisy, and his body entirely taken up with the sight of her bottom, outlined in a tight uniform.

'And this is why I am much more suited to the role of housekeeper!' Mrs Stone was saying, when Sophia returned to the kitchen.

'Aye, horses for courses!' Cook replied, stirring a pot on the stove before opening the bread oven to check on progress. 'I know how much to cook for a typical crowd, that is for certain. Now, I shall need a day or two to understand their preferences, but the footmen and maids will keep me right. Daisy!'

Sophia sent a thankful smile to the scullery maid who took the tray of dishes from her. 'Yes?'

'Did you happen to notice what the ladies were eating? Gentlemen are easy pleased, for all I must do is offer them plenty of meat. Ladies can be trickier.'

Sophia thought for a moment, bringing to mind her brief vision of the ladies' plates. 'Mrs Chester and her daughter were eating heartily, I believe. The other ladies had opted for rolls, and fruit. A couple had eggs or porridge.'

'Just as I thought. Good to know about the Chester

ladies, though. I shall count them as men for the purposes of working out how much meat to provide.'

Mary had now appeared, her brow furrowed.

'How did you get along with Lady Caroline?' Mrs Stone's demeanour made it seem as though this was a casual enquiry, but Sophia knew better. The housekeeper was on top of every little detail.

Mary was still frowning. 'Dressing her was no real challenge, but I think...that is to say, I believe I disappointed her.'

'How so?'

'She is used to wearing beeswax perfume, and has forgotten to bring it from home. She was most distressed about it, and demanded I make her some.'

Demanded. That did not sound good.

'Make *perfume*?' Mrs Stone's eyes were round. 'What on earth does she think you are? A French perfumier?'

'Apparently they have a maid at home who has such a skill.'

'Ridiculous!' The housekeeper's tone signalled her outrage. 'The two young ladies are already proving to be just as much trouble as Mr Ban—'

She stopped, seeming to remember just in time that it would not be seemly to criticise the Earl's heir—who one day might be her employer, if Lord Hartington failed to marry and produce a male child. That the two young ladies were vying for the role of countess seemed to bother her less, and Sophia briefly wondered why.

'I can make beeswax perfume.'

All eyes turned to Sophia.

'You can? Well, and why did you not say so?'

'What do you need, Daisy?' Cook had moved directly to the practicalities.

'Hmmm…let me think. Dried herbs and flowers—and maybe a few fresh. Oil and beeswax. Then it's just a matter of simmering, straining, and pressing it, and leaving it to set.'

'A useful skill,' Mrs Stone murmured, 'and one for which a London perfumier would charge a fortune, I have no doubt!'

'The skill is in mixing the herbs to find aromas that are pleasing. I do not claim to have the nose of an expert, but when I have done this before, my—er, the ladies I made it for seemed content.'

She had almost said 'my sisters', but had caught herself just in time. Daisy had no sisters, Sophia did. And Daisy had not the money to be wasting on fripperies such as perfume making. Sophia on the other hand had spent an entire summer two years ago experimenting with making perfumes. She still occasionally made them as Christmastide gifts.

Mrs Stone sighed. 'Very well. My lord would expect us to meet his guests' needs where we can. Mary, go to the dining room to clear more dishes. Daisy, you will continue to help there, but after the breakfast is cleared I may need you to spend time making perfume to satisfy the whims of a young lady.' She frowned. 'Where is Lady Caroline now?'

'She has returned to her bedchamber briefly,' Mary offered. 'They all intend to walk in the gardens shortly.'

'Very well. Help here for a few moments Daisy, while I check as to the vehemence with which Lady Caroline requests this.'

She departed in a bustle of jangling keys and irritation, returning a few moments later.

'Well!' She rolled her eyes. 'Lord save me from demanding young ladies! Lady Caroline and her mother both insist that we create a perfume for the young lady. They seem to have no understanding of the amount of work we must do, nor how stretched we are.' She turned to Sophia. 'Daisy, do your best. We must hope it satisfies her.'

'Yes, Mrs Stone.' Sophia turned to Cook. 'Might I use your distillation equipment? And what dried herbs and flowers do we have?'

Cook shrugged. 'Use away. Everything is in the stillroom, including quite a number of different herbs—but I got no dried flowers, I'm afraid.'

'Right. With your permission, Mrs Stone, I shall pick a few flowers from the gardens...and maybe the woodland.'

Mrs Stone waved this away, clearly not interested in the details. 'Whatever you need. But clear the dishes first. Lady Caroline's demands can wait.'

* * *

Breakfast was done, the guests gone, but Hart had lingered, a cup of tea in his hand. Twice Daisy had come to clear away dishes, and twice his heart had thundered when he saw her. The door opened, and in she came again, an empty tray in her hands.

Instantly his heart began a thunderous tattoo, his eyes sweeping over her face and form as though sipping a particularly fine wine. She got prettier it seemed, each time he saw her.

What on earth is happening to me? Oh, in a sense he knew exactly what was happening. He wanted her, as he had wanted women before. But on previous occasions, the women had been appropriate. *Suitable.* A merry widow. A courtesan. A saucy tavern maid. Not a respectable unwed housemaid.

The ladies he had dallied with in the past had not been so young, nor had they been in his employ. Only the worst of men importuned servants, who were reliant on them for employment, for a roof over their heads— for basic food and shelter. Never would he dream of doing anything so wrong, yet surely it could not hurt to indulge his unexpected attraction, just a little? So long as he did not act on it.

So when the footman left with a heavily laden tray, leaving just Hart and Daisy, he decided to speak to her. There was no harm in that.

'Er… Daisy, is it not?'

She whipped round, colour rising in her cheeks, and curtsied. 'Yes, my lord. How may I serve you, my lord?'

Such a question! Instantly he had a vision of asking her for a kiss. Of his lips on hers, his hands on her…

Stop!

'Are you liking your time here?'

She frowned, as though she had not understood the question. 'I am here to work, my lord.'

I am a fool! She is not here for pleasure. 'But the work itself? You find it…acceptable? Interesting?'

Interesting? What am I even saying? Seeing decided confusion on her face, he almost groaned aloud.

'It is perfectly acceptable, my lord.'

'Good, good.' Now what? She was waiting, perfectly still. 'You may continue.'

Just as she turned back to her task the door opened.

'My lord.' It was one of the footmen. 'Your guests are ready for their walk around the gardens.'

'Yes, of course.' He rose, relief rushing through him. What on earth was happening? He was a grown man—an earl, for God's sake—yet he could not speak to one of his own servants without becoming tongue-tied and foolish! Stomping though the hallway, he saw a large group of people awaiting his presence, and bit back a sigh.

And it was only day one of the party.

Chapter Twelve

Well, that had been decidedly odd. Never had Sophia, nor to her knowledge, any of her family, questioned a servant about whether their work was *acceptable* or *interesting*. Either Lord Hartington was a particularly caring employer, or…?

Exiting via the kitchen door, Sophia made for the shed belonging to the head gardener. Her heart was racing, as a new possibility occurred to her. The way he had looked at her…the way she had felt when their eyes met… If she did not know better, she might think he had a liking for her. For *her*, specifically. As Miss Van Bergen, she had encountered that look before—from young men who wanted to kiss her.

More importantly, his gaze had seemed to be…seeking, somehow. As though he wished for connection with her. A meeting of minds as they kissed…

For Sophia, who had only ever kissed good-looking wealthy young men who were, sadly, her intellectual inferiors, the notion was astounding. Just imagine, she thought, what it would be like to experience such a kiss. A kiss that involved a meeting of minds as well as lips...

Was her employer the sort of man who seduced serving maids—women who were vulnerable to the power he held over them as servants?

Every instinct she had rejected the notion. *No!* He was not that kind of man, she was certain of it. Then why...?

She tapped on the door, setting speculation aside for now.

'Come in!'

'Good morning, Mr Stone. I am Daisy.' It was the first time they had had a proper conversation. 'Ooh, what manner of plant is that?' He seemed to be transferring a small, knobbly-looking plant from a small pot to a larger one.

'Pineapple,' he said, 'although I am still uncertain as to whether they will take.'

'You are growing pineapples!' Sophia was astounded. 'But why?'

'As to that, you must ask the master,' he replied, 'for it was his notion.' He shook his head. 'They are the most devilish things I've ever had to grow. Constant re-potting, plus they fail if they are removed from the hot wall for too long. Must be near as bad as that damn cedar my grandpa had to look after!'

Her eyes widened. 'You have an actual cedar tree?'

'Oh, yes. Edge of the woodland.' He gestured to his

right. 'We have a cluster of redwoods too, brought from America fifty years ago. Capability Brown planted the cedar himself, from seeds obtained from Highclere Castle, for they have fine cedars there—all the way from Lebanon. There were five saplings originally, but this was the only one that survived.' Setting down the pots he walked towards her, his expression one of puzzlement. 'Now, Daisy. What brings a housemaid to the gardens?'

She gave a crooked smile. 'Lady Caroline.'

He raised an eyebrow. 'One of the guests, I assume? Then let me attempt to guess your task. She has had a sudden craving for a particular herb, or flower, and nothing will do but that she must have it?'

She chuckled. 'Sadly, you are almost correct. She has come without her perfume, and has…requested that we make her some.'

'Requested? Or demanded?'

'As to that, you may ask your wife.'

'Oh, I shall, you may be certain of it. And have you the skill to make perfume, Daisy?'

She shrugged. 'The proof will be in whether Lady Caroline is satisfied with my efforts. I have done it before, but never with this level of expectation and responsibility on me.'

'Then I shall do my best to help,' he replied simply. 'What do you need?'

'Thank you. Cook has some dried herbs in her stillroom—a great starting point. But I need your advice as to which scented flowers—garden or woodland—are currently in bloom.'

'Ah. Something with a strong scent. Roses?'

She wrinkled her nose. 'Attar of roses reminds me of death. Honestly, I do not know why some people like it so much. A fresh rose on the stem, yes. But something changes when we try to preserve scented rose petals. I do not know why.'

He considered this, much struck. 'I believe you are right! Well, I have been gardening for fifty years, and have learned something new this day.'

'Perhaps I do have something of a nose for this work, after all!'

He began to speak, then—of feverfew and meadowsweet, evening primrose and tansy, of what they looked like and where they might be found amid the trees in the nearby woodland.

'Try the gardens, as well. The sweet alyssum is in bloom, and so is the lemon verbena.' Helpfully, he described these two—to Sophia's relief, for she was not at all familiar with some of these plants.

'And what of the cedar? Might I be permitted a small piece—a branch, perhaps? Cedarwood oil is greatly prized in perfume making.' This she knew, for her father had spent a pretty penny on a small vial of oil for her, during her perfumery summer.

He frowned. 'That would be a matter for the master, I believe.'

'Of course. Thank you for your advice.'

'Here—take this.' Reaching to a high shelf, he handed her a trug made from rows of neatly plaited willow.

'Thank you,' she said again. People were so *kind*.

'Ah, 'tis nothing, Daisy. Good luck with the perfume!'

Her heart lifted, Daisy stepped outside. Blinking in the bright sunshine, she made her way first to the flower gardens surrounding the front and sides of the house. Walking directly past the rose garden, she made for some of the beds near the corner, bending to sniff at some pale alyssum carpeting the edges of the path. *Oh, yes.* The sweet scent was delightful, so she plucked some of the clusters of white blossom, placing them carefully in her trug. Now to find the lemon verbena which, if its name was accurate, should give her the dash of citrus that would reach the senses first. Hurrying along, her gaze focused on flowers to the left and right, she almost failed to notice that the guests were almost upon her, led by the Earl himself!

Miss Chester had his right arm, and a young blonde lady whom she assumed to be Lady Caroline had his left. He looked extremely dashing, his blue coat echoing the colour of his eyes, and displaying his broad shoulders and narrow waist to advantage. His buckskin breeches clung to his thighs, and his outfit was completed by gleaming top boots—no doubt polished that very morning by the Earl's valet—a lofty, self-important man who did not deign to speak to female servants unless forced to.

'My lord, your gardens are truly delightful,' gushed Lady Caroline, as Sophia stood to the side to let them pass.

'Indeed they are,' agreed Miss Chester, her tone so sycophantic it was a wonder the Earl was not immediately motivated to retch.

Sophia had seen such behaviours before, among the men and women of her set. People were fawned over by those who wanted something from them—in this case, the ladies were both trying to capture the Earl's attention in the hope she would be his bride. *I wish them good luck!* Sophia thought with a shudder. *All of them!*

Thankfully her own situation was settled. She would not have to try to persuade Lord Linford to marry her, for he had already agreed to do so.

Unless…

She frowned. As she and the real Daisy had discussed, Lord Linford might well take exception to her little masquerade and refuse to go ahead with the betrothal. But why should she worry about such an eventuality? She was Miss Van Bergen, heiress, and daughter to one of New York's leading bankers. She could marry at any time of her choosing. Or not at all, if she so chose, like Aunt Agatha.

Turning her head, she cast an eye over the threesome as they walked away. Lady Caroline, tall, fair, and willowy. Lord Hartington, strong and fine. Miss Chester, diminutive and fashionably well-rounded. Neither lady was taking the right approach with Lord Hartington.

She caught her breath. What a strange thought! She had known the man for less than two days. Who was she to think she knew him? Knew how his mind worked?

Yet somehow she did. He liked intelligence and humour. She had seen these qualities in his own expressions, in his interactions with others. Rather than flirting in such a mortifying manner, the young ladies would do better to tease him, or debate with him. Or learn something from him. He had looked tired just now. Tolerant, but tired.

He is filled with ennui. Their conversation is wearing him out. She did not know how she knew this. But the instinct was strong within her.

They had stopped, in response to a shout from behind. Out of the corner of her eye she saw the two gentlemen who had hailed them hurry to catch up.

'Cousin!' declared Mr Banfield. 'Are we not to show the ladies the fountain?' He bowed. 'Lady Caroline, Miss Chester, permit me to tell you that there is the most delightful fountain over there, and Mr Forsyth and I should be delighted to show it to you!'

Now what? Would the young ladies stay with the Earl, the man they had targeted? But no. Both giggled and simpered at Mr Banfield's exaggerated courtesy.

'I should *love* to see the fountain,' declared Lady Caroline coquettishly, 'if it is as pretty as you say, Mr

Banfield. I wonder that Lord Hartington did not think to show us!'

'Indeed,' agreed Miss Chester, seemingly determined not to be left out. 'I cannot account for it! My lord, how could you have forgotten such a detail?'

This was clearly the Earl's cue to say he was distracted by their beauty, or some such other flattery. Instead, he replied in a flat tone, 'The fountain will still be there when we have finished with the rose garden. But by all means, go with my cousin and his friend. I shall go and find Lady Pashley and Mrs Chester, as they seem to have dropped behind.'

And with that, he turned on his heel and went back the way they had come, Sophia, standing stock still, felt the rush of air as he passed—so close she could have touched him. Although he did not look towards her she had the oddest feeling he was aware of her presence, as she silently watched the little drama playing out before her.

'Well!' Lady Caroline sounded less than impressed. 'He departed rather rapidly, did he not?'

'Ah, Lady Caroline.' There was a kissing sound as Mr Banfield had clearly lifted her hand to his lips. Sophia suppressed a shudder. 'My cousin Lord Hartington has something of a reputation for brusqueness, I am sorry to say. But fear not! Forsyth and I are here to pay you both the attentions you deserve!'

Somewhat mollified, the young ladies thanked Banfield and Forsyth for their consideration, and Sophia heard them walking off to her right. Stealing a glance, she saw that Lady Caroline was on Mr Banfield's arm, while Mr Forsyth had Miss Chester by his side.

Stifling a grin, Sophia resumed her task, reflecting that the Earl had risen in her estimation by not adhering to the expected script, and that his cousin's standing in her eyes had decreased further—particularly since he had lost no time in criticising Lord Hartington to the ladies after he had left them. *A reputation for brusqueness*, eh? If they had any wit at all, the ladies would realise that the Earl's display of distaste for play-acting had given them a valuable insight into his preferences. Whichever of them could learn from the incident just now would, she guessed, have the upper hand in winning his approval—if, indeed, that was what they were seeking.

Listening to the giggling coming from the general direction of the fountain, she doubted very much whether either of them had any wit whatsoever. If her own sisters behaved as Lady Caroline and Miss Chester had just done, she would be sending them daggerish looks and telling them off afterwards. *Silliness is not a virtue.*

Soon afterwards she found the lemon verbena and harvested a number of the flowers and stems. The scent was delightful, and reassuringly potent. Lifting her head, she looked to the woodland at the edge of the gardens. Did En-gland have dangerous wild animals? She hovered for a moment, trying to recall if she had ever learned of any. Foxes, badgers...were there still wolves in England? Lord, why did she not know this?

Tentatively, she made her way towards the edge of the woodland. It was delightful, alive with birdsong, wildflowers, and beautiful trees with various shades of bark and leaves. Daringly, she made her way in through the trees, her fears soon giving way to contentment as she harvested various wildflowers that might prove useful in her perfume making.

Among the oaks, ash, elms, and beech trees, she suddenly spotted some interlopers. Foreigners, like herself. Four giant redwoods stood in this English copse as though they belonged there. Stepping forwards, she placed a hand on one and closed her eyes. There, with her bare skin touching the rough reddish bark, she felt a sense of connection with her homeland, so far away across the Atlantic ocean. While redwoods were uncommon in New York, she had seen them in the country estates of her parents' friends, many times. They were American, just as she was.

'Do the trees speak to you?'

Startled, she opened her eyes to find the Earl surveying her, a humorous expression in his eyes.

Chapter Thirteen

Heart pounding, she dipped into a curtsy. 'I must appear foolish, my lord.' She patted the tree. 'This is a magnificent specimen, do you not think?'

'I do, and I am impressed that you have sought it out.' His gaze travelled upwards. 'The tallest tree I have ever seen, yet apparently they grow even taller in California.'

Daringly, she continued the conversation, even though she knew she should not. 'Have you been to America, my lord?'

He grimaced. 'No, though I should like to. The place has always fascinated me. How does one build such a massive country from nothing? Government, laws, culture—all of it. And while there are people here in England from all parts of the world, my understanding is that America is even more of a Babel. I should love to explore the place.'

'It is a special place indeed, my lord.' Sophia heard the catch in her own voice, and swallowed hard.

He eyed her keenly. 'You have been there?'

She nodded. 'I came here directly from Liverpool. I have lately been in New York.' She chose her words carefully, trying to minimise as much as she could the need for lies.

His eyes widened. 'How wonderful! I knew there was more to you than… But you must tell me all about it!'

'Yes, my lord. But…' She eyed him dubiously, 'Will your guests not be seeking you?'

'They will seek me for every minute of every day, which is exactly why I took the opportunity to divert to the woods for a few moments.' He frowned, eyeing her trug. 'But what brings you here? My sister cannot have requested feverfew and tansies for her floral displays?'

'No, but another guest has requested that we create a perfume for her, and so—' She shrugged.

He shook his head. 'Lord save me from demanding ladies!'

'Gentlemen too, may be demanding!' she retorted without thinking. 'Though the manner of it may appear different.'

He seemed unbothered by her speaking to him so directly. Humour lit his eye. '*Some* gentlemen, perhaps.'

'And *some* ladies. Not all of them.'

He threw his head back and laughed. 'Touché. So, what does one need to make perfume? Ah, I see you have some sweet-scented flowers there.'

She looked down at her trug. 'I have nearly all I need, apart from one ingredient.' Lifting her head she sent him a challenging look. 'Though you may not like it, my lord.'

His eyebrow lifted. 'I cannot even begin to guess. Enlighten me, Daisy.'

'Cedarwood,' she said simply. 'Is it true you have a tree here? I was looking for it, but then became distracted by this colossus and his comrades.'

His eyes lit up. 'The Walton House cedar? One of my favourite trees. It is this way.'

She fell into step beside him, and together they made their way through the woods. Conscious of something special in the moment, Sophia tried to take it all in. Birds singing happily amid the soft susurration of rustling leaves. Sunlight. The earthy smells of rich loam, summer trees, and flowers. And Lord Hartington, walking beside her.

'Which guest was it?'

'Hmm?' Lost in thought, it took her a moment. 'Oh, Lady Caroline. She was apparently most distressed at having left her perfume at home.'

He shook his head slowly, as if struggling to comprehend. 'But *why*?'

She sent him a mischievous look. 'Do you not know that if she were properly perfumed, you would fall instantly in love with her?' She clapped a hand to her mouth. *Too late*. The words were already out.

He chuckled. 'Indeed? She has a strange idea of me, then.' He thought for a moment. 'And what of Miss Chester? Does she also believe in the powers of scent?'

'Oh, no. I understand Miss Chester believes that her main assets are her—' She broke off, suddenly conscious that she was chattering with him just as though she were Miss Sophia Van Bergen, his social equal. 'I have been indiscreet. I apologise, my lord. Servants should never behave in such a forward manner.'

'You are right, of course,' he replied with an air of nonchalance. 'And yet I find myself taken up with curiosity. I wish to know about Miss Chester's…er…*assets*. And about New York. Will you tell me of New York?'

Lord, that would be foolish beyond measure! If she spoke of home, she would be much more likely to accidentally reveal her secret. Uneasy, she sent him a troubled glance.

'Hmmm… I see you are uncomfortable. As servant and master, we cannot continue to converse freely, as we have been doing these past few minutes. I understand that.' He paused for a moment, as if pondering this, yet Sophia had the distinct impression his pause was for effect only, and that he knew exactly what he was going to say next.

'Very well. As Earl of Hartington, I propose to use my powers in an unusual way.'

His words were issued in a light-hearted manner, yet there was something else there, too. Something richer, darker. Something delicious.

'I therefore proclaim—as is my right—that within the confines of these woods you are not a housemaid, but an acquaintance. You are Daisy, and I am Hart, who is *not* your master.'

She thought for a moment, liking the notion. 'Is Hart an earl still?'

His eyes narrowed as he considered her query. 'An excellent question. Being the Earl is a burden I carry night and day. A pleasant burden, but a burden nevertheless. I believe I should be glad to shed it for a few moments.' He stopped and stuck out a hand. 'Hart. Pleased to make your acquaintance.'

She took it, sealing their bargain—and recalling a similar handshake she had recently had with Daisy. A bargain which erased the lines of class.

'Daisy.' Why did her voice shake? And why was the feeling of his hand touching hers sending strange sensations running through her?

'Daisy.'

Their eyes held, and something…something *enormous* passed between them. It grew, and strengthened, while all the while Sophia's heart thundered in her chest.

Then, just as though it were the most natural thing in the world, he bent his head and kissed her, and she kissed him right back.

Chapter Fourteen

Hart had kissed a fair number of women in his life. He had even been briefly enamoured of a couple of them. The feeling had worn off within days, however.

This was different. Daisy was different. As his lips moved on hers he was conscious of more than the usual bodily response.

Oh, he desired her. He had known that from the first. But he had desired women before. His arms tightened about her, drawing her to him as he deepened the kiss. She responded with passion, igniting his own.

Lost, he immersed himself in her—her mouth, her breasts pressed against him, the feeling of her back beneath his hands. Around them, the woods cocooned them in a safe circle of birdsong and sunlight.

Then the kiss ended and they simply stood there, her face resting against his chest and his chin on top of her head. Both were breathing raggedly.

'Well!' she said, drawing away and reaching up to check her housemaid's cap before picking up her trug—

its contents still in place despite the fact it had been let fall to the ground during their embrace. Her hand shook a little, he noticed. 'That was unexpected!' She frowned. 'Am I now to be let go from your service?'

'Let go? No, of course not!' His eyes roved over her. *My, she is beautiful!* 'You kissed only Hart, which is perfectly admissible.'

'But—are servants not prohibited from dallying?'

He chuckled. 'If that is the case, then how did my head gardener manage to persuade my coachman's daughter to marry him?'

Her jaw dropped. 'Mrs Stone is John's daughter?'

'She is. I believe there have been other pairings among my staff over the years, too.'

'But you are not staff.' She eyed him dubiously.

'Oh, but I am. My role is a little different, but you know me only as Hart, remember?'

'Like in the story of the glass slipper!'

'Ah, *The Tales of Mother Goose*! I remember it well, from my childhood.'

'As do I.'

They shared a smile, then he asked, 'But what aspect of the tale are you referring to now?'

'Oh, only that she is a maid who dallies with a prince. And that he does not know her true self.'

'Did you know there is another version of the tale, where she meets him first in the woods and he pretends to be a servant?'

'No, truly?' She smiled. 'I like that.'

'As do I, Cinderella.' He offered her his arm and she took it, and together they resumed walking. He did not directly mention the kiss, for truthfully, he was too shaken by it himself to know what to make of it. Hopefully he had at least reassured her that she would not lose her position here because of it. As well as delight, guilt was there within him, for having kissed a servant. But perhaps their agreement negated that?

They had reached the cedar tree. 'How beautiful!' she gasped.

'It is impressive, is it not?'

She stepped away from him towards the tree, setting down the trug before placing both hands on the tree bark and softly exploring. Given recent events, the sight of her hands moving in such a manner was too much for him, and he quickly glanced away.

'So what do you need for the perfume?' he asked. 'I should warn you that the tree must not be harmed.'

'Oh, no! For who would harm such a wonderful specimen? I need only some shavings or sawdust from which to extract the oil. Perhaps by sacrificing a tiny branch, if that is acceptable.'

'Very well. Ask Stone to do that for you.'

'Thank you, my lord.'

He shook his head. 'Hart.'

'Hart.'

There was something compelling about hearing his name on her lips, about watching as she breathed it out, her delectable mouth opening a little... *Lord!*

He grimaced. 'I must return to my guests—and I have asked not even one question about New York!'

'That is true.'

'I shall contrive to return to the woods another time. Do you have any time off?'

'Not during the day. We work from six in the morning until you and your guests have eaten their supper, my l—' She visibly stopped herself from addressing him formally. 'When not cleaning or serving, we are expected to do needlework in the servants' hall.'

'I see.' He was conscious of a feeling of disappointment. 'You work hard. All the servants work hard.'

She shrugged. 'Yes. We have a day off each week, though.'

He brightened. 'You do? When is your next day off?'

'Thursday, I believe. It will be my first day off since arriving here.'

'And Sunday?'

She shook her head. 'No one has Sunday off, though the work is a little easier, and we all leave our duties to go to church early in the morning. The scullery maids here take turns at missing church so that they can keep an eye on the food for Cook.'

He returned to the more pressing matter—the need to see her again, alone.

'And do you have plans for Thursday?'

She sent him a quick glance, which at this moment he was unable to decipher. 'I thought I might write some letters, perhaps walk to the nearest village. It partly depends on the weather.'

A neutral comment. *Does she wish to meet me?* 'Ah, our English weather!' he replied lightly, then took a breath. 'If it is dry, would you consider meeting your friend Hart in the woods, early in the morning perhaps? I normally ride out early, before the others rise.'

'Are we friends then? Not acquaintances?'

My, she has a quick mind! 'I think,' he responded dryly, 'that we can no longer claim to be mere acquaintances.'

She flushed, and his heart swelled at her prettiness. 'No. I suppose not.' She thought for a moment, and he read uncertainty in her eyes. Then she smiled. 'This is an adventure, I suppose. But you must not seduce me, my lord.' Her tone was serious, her expression adorable.

'I shall try my best not to do so!'

'Then I shall come on Thursday, so that we may speak of New York.'

He bowed, taking her hand. 'Farewell, sweet Cinderella. Until Thursday.'

'Until Thursday,' she echoed. As he kissed her hand their eyes met, and held, and once again he was conscious of something powerful between them. Something unanticipated, and significant, and rare.

As he turned away, he was also conscious that his mood had lifted. Gone was the frustration he had felt earlier, bringing a group of rather dull people slowly through his gardens. He felt...fortified, as though she had given him some of her vitality. Smiling, he walked back to the house with a sense of renewal coursing through him. Perhaps, after all, the house party might be tolerable.

Chapter Fifteen

Sophia returned to the house, stopping only to ask the head gardener for some wood shavings from the cedar tree—ensuring he was aware that my lord had agreed to it. She then made directly for the still-room, hoping it would be empty, as her mind, body and heart were in severe disorder. Her thoughts were racing, trying to make sense of recent events.

Was he seeking to make a friend of her? Or was he a practised seducer, with a habit of inveigling young serving maids? Instinct told her that he was no rake—but then, the most skilled of rakes were surely accomplished in the art of seeming to be in earnest with their wooing...

He was certainly skilled in kissing. Her body felt as though it hummed, like the last reverberations of a harp when plucked. Her pulse was tumultuous, her heart pounding in her chest, and there was a strange but delightful feeling in the pit of her stomach and her nether regions. *What is this magic he holds?*

Oh, she knew of desire—had read of it, and heard some friends speak of it. She had thought she had felt it when she had kissed those young men at New York parties. But truly, she had known nothing. Until today. Well, her need for adventure had taken an unexpected turn—but one that was entirely welcome. She had kissed a man, with no need to escape her mother's eye. There had been only him, and her, and the beauties of an English woodland.

Taking the flowers from her trug, she laid them out on a thin muslin cloth, which she placed inside the bottom drawer of the stove. With luck, they would be well dried out in a few hours. Exhaling, she focused on the simple task, allowing her pulse to slow and her body to return to something approaching normality. Pulling the stool out from under the table, she stood on it to take down some of the bunches of herbs suspended from the ceiling, setting them on the table. Tarragon, rosemary, parsley... She sniffed each one, thinking about which she might use for her perfume.

Perusing the shelves, she took down the beeswax as well as a jar marked *walnut oil*, opening the lid and sniffing cautiously. Good. There was only a mild nutty scent, so it would serve as the perfect base for her perfume. Pouring it into a pan, she added her selected herbs and set it on the stove to simmer. She then looked in cupboards and drawers until she found a grater, and grated the beeswax into a large bowl. Checking on the simmering herbs, she was glad to see they were progressing nicely.

The simple actions were familiar, and brought her back to her summer two years ago when she had made perfume repeatedly, gifting it to everyone who would accept. In her mind's eye she could see the scullery at home, the servants she had known for years—some of them had worked for the Van Bergens since before she was born. Now she understood a little of their work, their devotion, their commitment. She also knew why housekeepers insisted that days off must be respected. They had earned it.

Her thoughts drifted back repeatedly to her Cinderella moment back there in the woods, and now she made a new discovery. She did not simply desire Hart: she *liked* him. Liked his wry humour, his sense of responsibility, the way he refused to play along with silliness. Had he been part of her set in New York she would have singled him out and tried to make a friend of him. Would have perhaps wished for him to court her…

Her heart quickened, and she acknowledged what she had been avoiding so far; that her heart was in danger from him. Desire and liking were a potent combination.

Yet, her masquerade meant that he was the one man who could never know the truth. For her scheme to work she needed to remain anonymous—an unnoticed maid in a nondescript uniform. That way she could take her place in society as Miss Van Bergen in a few weeks with no one the wiser apart from Lord Linford.

'Daisy?' It was one of the scullery maids. 'Mr Stone has left this for you.' She placed a small basket onto the table.

'Ah, that is wonderful. Thank you.' As she bent her head towards the wood shavings, the rich, spicy scent of cedar reached her nostrils. 'Perfect.' The scent felt calming, somehow.

Checking the copper distillation vat, Sophia poured a good amount of water inside before lighting the low fire underneath it. Gradually, as the water heated, she added the wood chips, then fixed the dome-shaped lid once the water began to gently boil. Setting a large pan under the pipe coming from the lid, she waited for the steam to gather in the pipe then drip as water into her pan. She was unsure exactly how it worked, but something about the process of turning the wood-water into steam then water again would release the oil from the wood and bring it into her pan.

The process would take a few hours, and would have to be repeated twice, so she returned to stir her simmering herbs and check that her flowers were beginning to dry out in the stove drawer.

Cook appeared then, checking on her, and showing a great deal of interest in the process. Sophia, pleased, explained all to her, and Cook resolved to try and remember it all, since she was always interested in learning new skills. She left in good humour, promising to send some darning to the still-room to help Sophia pass the time. Idle hands were not permitted during the working day.

Darning was perfect for Sophia today. A tremendous, unexpected thing had happened to her earlier, and she welcomed the chance to spend the day alone. So she sat for hours, quietly doing needlework, stirring her herbs and keeping an eye on the distillation vat.

Gradually, her mind quietened. It was only a kiss, after all. She had kissed and been kissed before. She need not read too much into it. And as for their assignation for next Thursday, chances were that it had been a passing fancy on his part and he would think no more about it. Probably, he would not even come.

Hart was fixated on next Thursday. No matter how hard he tried, he simply could not get Daisy out of his mind. That kiss the day before yesterday had stirred him in ways he had not known possible—and he was not lacking in experience with women. While he was deeply uncomfortable at the fact she was a maid in his employ, which meant he was in a position of authority and made a balance of power between them impossible, her behaviour had been so unaffected, so lively, that he could only hope she had not felt importuned. Time after time he had relived their kiss in his head, and time after time he recalled only enthusiasm on her part.

Why now? Why her? Perhaps he was reading too much into it all. Perhaps it was simply due to the pressure he had brought on himself by agreeing to this party—and the inclusion of two eligible young ladies on the guest list. His mind wished to escape from the duties pressing on him, and Daisy was a perfect escape. She was beautiful, and lively, and even their conversation had been stimulating.

Sadly, neither Lady Caroline nor Miss Chester had much in the way of discourse, though both had mastered the dubious art of flirtation. In this they were encouraged by their mothers, and even by Hart's own sisters, of whom he had thought better.

Most of the gentlemen seemed to tolerate the giggles, arch looks, and indirect requests for compliments with a fair degree of tolerance, although Lord Pashley, Lady Caroline's father, had occasionally sent his daughter a quelling look—a habit which made that gentleman rise in Hart's estimation.

The girls, undeterred, had a receptive audience in Banfield and Forsyth, who seemed remarkably content to pay extravagant compliments and behave with flirtatious intent towards the ladies. Hart found it childish, and predictable, and, frankly, tedious.

He had seen Daisy occasionally during the day—always at a distance as she passed before him in a hallway or disappeared into one of the ladies' bedchambers. Disappointingly, he had not so much as locked eyes with her since their encounter in the woods. Despite this, he knew that her perfume making was going well—not because anyone had told him so, but when he had encountered her these past two days, she had smelled strongly of flowers, herbs, and what he supposed to be cedar oil. It was heavenly. Clearly, she was still engaged in creating scents for Lady Caroline. The problem was, he thought with an inner grin as he returned from his early morning ride, he would forever associate the scent with Daisy, no one else. So if Lady Caroline hoped to ensnare him with bewitching scents, her hopes were already dashed.

It was Tuesday morning, very early, and none of the guests would yet be about. This was the time when all of the housemaids were engaged in cleaning duties, but still he looked around hopefully as he entered the house through the kitchen door, which was closest to the stables.

She is not here. Disappointment sliced through him.

'Good morning, Lord Hartington.' Mrs Stone, though disapproving, was fairly used to his presence in the servants' hall and kitchens, him having found solace there throughout his childhood. Being a small boy with two older sisters who delighted in telling him how he must behave had been something of a trial, and he had much preferred the warmth, informality, and relatively tranquil atmosphere of below stairs. While Mrs Stone could not bring herself to endorse his habit, she tolerated it nevertheless.

'Good morning, Mrs Stone. How do you today? And is all well?'

She replied in the positive on both counts, taking the opportunity to discuss with him some aspects of preparations for the upcoming ball, which Eliza was organising. The ballroom had not been used in many a year, and part of him was looking forward to the spectacle and glamour of it. Just a pity there was no lady he particularly wished to dance with. Which led his mind to go elsewhere...

'I understand there was an unusual request from one of the young ladies? For *perfume*?'

Mrs Stone drew herself up, clearly affronted. 'Indeed, my lord, and it has been dashed inconvenient! Mr Stone has had to provide chips of cedar wood, and one of your housemaids has spent a day and a half making the perfume!'

'I am displeased to hear that, Mrs Stone. I know how hard everyone works already.' He frowned, as if considering the matter. 'How on earth does one go about making perfume?'

'Hrmph. Luckily, Daisy—one of the temporary maids—knows a little about it, and is hopeful that today the final product will be ready. Thankfully, she was able to return to most of her duties yesterday, just returning to check now and again. And here she is!'

He turned, to see that Daisy had just entered. She curtseyed, flushing. 'Lord Hartington!'

'Good morning, Daisy. I understand the perfume you were asked to make is nearly ready.'

'Yes, my lord.' She looked at Mrs Stone. 'I have finished my cleaning, Mrs Stone, so I thought I might check to see if the beeswax has set properly overnight.'

Mrs Stone waved a hand. 'Yes, go and check, and if it is ready you may bring it to Lady Caroline yourself. She should at least know who has done this for her. Afterwards come back here for needlework.'

'Yes, Mrs Stone.'

'Do you mind if I come along?' He looked directly at Daisy. 'I confess I find myself beset by curiosity.'

'Yes, my lord.' She sounded less than enthusiastic, which Mrs Stone must also have detected, for she added, with rather more enthusiasm,

'Of course, my lord. Daisy, show the master your work!'

'Yes, Mrs Stone.'

He fell in beside her, asking, 'Where are we going? Where did you create this masterpiece?'

She sent him a side glance, everything about her signalling discomfort. 'The still-room, my lord.'

'Naturally! I should have realised.' They stepped into the hallway, away from Mrs Stone's keen eye, but still Daisy seemed uneasy.

'I can tell you have been making perfume, because the aroma is strong around you.'

She flushed further. 'So everyone keeps telling me. I apologise, my lord. I do not wish to...to offend your senses.'

He stopped, waiting until she looked at him. 'You are not doing so and could never do so! Do you understand me?'

'Yes, my lord.' She dropped her gaze and turned away, pausing until he began walking again.

It took only a few more steps to reach the still-room, and the aromas emanating from it were powerful indeed.

'Apologies, my lord. I have left the door ajar so that the smell might begin to dissipate.'

He waved this away. 'Did you use any cedar wood in the end?'

'Oh, yes. Mr Stone sent me a whole basket of wood shavings on Sunday.' She frowned. 'I am sure he harvested them without risking harm to the tree, though.'

'I do not doubt it. He is very proud of our rare specimens.'

'Apart from the pineapples!' She clapped a hand over her mouth—an action he had seen her do before and which he welcomed, for it indicated she was expressing her true opinions. 'I apologise, my lord. I should not have said that.'

He laughed. 'I am entirely familiar with his antipathy towards the noble fruit. Mainly because pineapples are the very devil to grow successfully. Has he shown you his tan pit and hot wall?'

'No.' There was a spark of interest in her eyes. 'Is that because it is too cold here for them to grow easily?'

'Exactly. They are from warmer climes—South America, I believe. So we have to keep them warm at all times. They also have to be re-potted frequently, and he grumbles every time he has to do it.'

'This I know. He was re-potting when I called with him two days ago.'

'On your way to the woods.'

'Yes.' Her voice was barely a whisper.

There was a silence. 'You look decidedly uncomfortable, Daisy.'

'Yes, my lord.'

'Will you tell me why?'

She glanced at him, briefly, then lowered her gaze again. 'You must know I cannot speak freely, my lord.' Her words were directed to the floor.

Damnation! There she was, right in front of him, looking just as beautiful and enticing as she had in the woods, when he had kissed her. But now there was nothing of her character in her eyes. She was all housemaid—nervous, compliant, and contained. Daisy was entirely hidden from him.

Chapter Sixteen

'Very well,' he said, sighing. 'I see I shall have to make another decree.' She looked at him, clearly puzzled. 'From this moment, in this still-room, we are not master and servant. We are Daisy and Hart, as in the woods.'

He stuck out a hand, waiting.

'I agree,' she said, touching his hand briefly, then stepping back in a decided manner. 'But a handshake is enough to seal it, I believe.'

Relieved to see that the true Daisy had made herself known, he responded to the merriment in her eyes with a smile of his own. 'What? Did you not like how we sealed our bargain two days ago?'

'Hush!' she told him. 'At any moment someone might go into the hallway and hear our conversation. Remember, the door is open!'

'You are telling me to hush?' Lord, how fine it was to see her true character again! No one told him to hush. *Ever.*

'Yes I am, for at this moment you are simply my friend Hart, not the Earl or my employer. Now, hush! Let us speak of the art of perfumery—or I shall cancel our agreement.'

'My! You drive a hard bargain, Miss Daisy.' He grinned. 'Such spirit, hiding behind the demure visage of a housemaid.'

'All of your servants have character, you know. But we are required to smooth away any hint of an opinion, or even a reaction, when among the family and their guests.'

'But you have opinions on them all?'

'Of course we do! We are people too, you know.'

He grimaced. 'It is easier to pretend you do not judge us.'

'*Judge* is a harsh word. But we see things. We *notice*.'

'And what is your opinion of my guests?' He wanted to ask for her opinion of him, but at the last second he veered away, for fear he would discover things he should not.

'I refuse to fall into the trap you have set so neatly, for anything I say will be remembered outside the stillroom. And that will not do.'

Voices outside told them someone was in the hallway.

'So this is the vat for distillation.' Her tone suggested they had been discussing perfume making all along. *How quick-witted she is!*

'The wood shavings,' she continued, 'went inside in water, and as the water boiled the steam went through this pipe. The steam then formed into droplets as it passed through the cooler pipe, and I collected them in a pan. By morning the cedar oil had risen to the top of the pan and I was able to skim it off and funnel it into this jar. I repeated the process a number of times.'

'Fascinating.' Removing the lid of the jar, he sniffed the oil within. 'That is a delightful scent.'

'I hope,' she said, 'that it has been sustained in the perfume. As well as the cedar oil, I used the essence of a range of herbs and flowers, which I stirred into different mixes. I then chose my favourites and set them in beeswax overnight.' She indicated three tiny cups, each filled with solid beeswax.

'So the lady dabs some of this on her skin?' he asked, and she confirmed it.

'Beeswax lasts longer than water-based perfumes. I do still have some cedar water and flower water—' She indicated two jars marked in neat handwriting. 'I shall bring a vial of flower water to Lady Caroline in case she should prefer it.'

As she spoke she began assembling the items on a small tray. Three beeswax options, plus the vial of flower-water.

'Lady Caroline is privileged indeed, to have such a service. I hope she appreciates it.'

She sent him a wry look. 'I shall shortly find out.'

Picking up the tray, she paused. 'May I go, my lord?'

'You are still in the room, my friend,' he reminded

her, then laughed as she took three steps to place herself firmly outside the door. 'Yes, you may go. But, Daisy…'

'Yes, my lord?'

Leaning forwards so that his lips brushed her ear, he murmured. 'I am looking forward to Thursday.'

She flushed, turning away. But not before he had seen what he wanted in her eyes. Desire. Desire so strong that it shook him to the core. *She feels it too!*

The feeling that rushed through him was like nothing he had ever experienced before. She was a strong, capable woman, who could hold no expectations from him. If she wanted him, it was for himself. With her, he was not Lord Hartington, he was Hart.

She wanted Hart.

Chapter Seventeen

'Lady Caroline?' Sophia stepped into the bedchamber. 'I have made some perfumes for you to try.'

Lady Caroline was seated before the mirror, plucking her eyebrows with silver tweezers. Without even looking at Sophia, she said, 'You must fetch my mother, for if there is a choice to be made I shall need her assistance.'

Sophia curtsied, setting the tray on a side table. 'Yes, my lady.' Making her way to Lady Pashley's chamber, she scratched at the door, until she heard the command to enter.

Lady Pashley seemed less than pleased to be so summoned by her daughter, but when Lady Caroline apprised her of the situation, she brightened. Sophia stood by the wall, awaiting their verdict.

Lady Pashley was all busyness. 'I firmly believe that men can be strongly influenced by the right perfume,' she declared. 'Now, let me try them all.' Taking each cup, she lifted it to her nose, trying each in turn, then again. 'This one, I think.'

'That is the one I prefer, too!' Lady Caroline looked delighted. She glanced towards Sophia. 'You may take the others away.'

'Yes, my lady.' Sophia began returning the rejected items to the tray.

'But you must ensure that no other lady uses the others!' she added.

Sophia nodded, though how she was supposed to do so, she did not know. If Miss Chester requested perfume, could she be denied?

'Oh, Mama! This will surely help me gain the Earl's attention!'

'I do not doubt it, my child. Why Miss Chester was also invited, I shall never know. Still, at least there are only the two of you, and you know exactly who your rival is.'

'Indeed. And she is so *dowdy*, too. Did you see that dress she wore to dinner last night?'

'With her bosoms displayed to the world? I was worried she would cover them in soup!'

They laughed then, enjoying their unkindness. *Am I also unkind?* Sophia wondered, as she made her way to the door. For she, too, could laugh at the absurdity of Miss Chester's attire, or at Lady Caroline's self-regard. The trick, perhaps, was to do so (for such absurdity must be noticed) while also maintaining a sense of affinity. Or, understanding, at least.

Both Lady Caroline and Miss Chester had been raised—as she herself had been—to be something like a princess in others' eyes. To be noticed, spoken to, complimented. They had graduated from girls who must be quiet in company, to ladies who must be at the centre of attention. She knew it, for that had been her life until very recently.

And she had taken it as her due. Everywhere she went, people fawned over Miss Van Bergen. Now that she was simply Daisy, people like Lady Caroline and her mother did not even *look* at her unless they must. And yet Miss Van Bergen, heiress, and Daisy, housemaid, were the same person. The same mind, body, thoughts, opinions, needs.

Making for the servant stairs, she reflected that there had certainly been no notion of either of the two ladies thanking her for her work in making perfumes for them to consider. They simply could not conceive of such a thing, and were entirely disinterested in how it had come about. For all they knew, it had been done through witchcraft.

Was I like that? And does it matter if they ignore a housemaid? Sophia could not expect people to thank every servant for every service. Yet, something inside her was changing, learning not just from her fellow servants, but from her new perspective as one of them.

She chuckled as a new thought came to her. While Lady Caroline and her mother saw only one rival for the Earl's attention, Sophia knew differently. The Earl would do what he must—and he clearly intended to choose either Lady Caroline or Miss Chester for his bride—but Hart, she rather suspected, preferred the company of a serving maid to either of them.

Thursday at last. Hart had not slept well, his night punctuated by erotic dreams and by a constant need within him to check if it was dawn yet. He rose, dressing himself in his riding gear, as he had the habit of riding out alone early each morning when he could.

Last night he had told the stable boy not to saddle his stallion for the morning ride, and he had noted the relief in the boy's eyes that he could sleep a little later. The house servants seeing him pass through would think nothing of it, for they were used to his habits.

They were already busy at their work, cleaning all the public rooms before the guests should rise. Since the beginning of his fixation with Daisy, he *noticed* more. Here was a footman, polishing silver. Here a maid washing a floor. The house required a significant amount of work every day just to maintain a good standard.

He suppressed a sigh. All of it had to be paid for. The servants. The cleaning materials. Food and drink… And while his coffers were nowhere near empty, he knew his duty. He must marry an heiress, or in his lifetime the estate could see bankruptcy.

Which was why he should be focusing on his courtship of Lady Caroline and Miss Chester, in the hope that marrying one of them might end his financial woes. Instead he was sneaking outside—hiding from his family, friends, and servants—in order to tryst with a serving maid.

Guilt struck him, for never before had he trysted with an innocent. *But I shall be restrained. I shall enjoy her company, and maybe a kiss...nothing more.* He pushed the feeling of guilt away. Such worries could wait. Right now, he was on his way to the woods to meet with his friend Daisy.

Will she be there? A moment's doubt shadowed his heart, but then he saw her by the giant redwoods, and his pulse quickened.

'I was not sure you would come,' she said as he approached.

'I wondered the same, yet here I am.' He kissed her cheek, enjoying the flush in her rosy skin and the darkening in her eyes.

'I...er...'

She was adorable in her confusion, breaking his gaze to gesture about her. 'This place must be beautiful in the fall.'

He raised an eyebrow. 'I think you mean autumn. How long were you in America for, exactly?'

Her flush deepened. 'Long enough, it seems, to sometimes speak as they do.'

'Tell me more. Who were you in service to?'

She paused, thinking for a moment. 'I think I should not give you her name. That would not be right. But I can tell you that she was an older lady from London—the grand-daughter of a marquess, no less!'

He laughed. 'From your tone, I wonder if she ensured everyone knew it!'

She nodded, humour dancing in her eyes. 'She strongly disapproved of America, yet had arranged a marriage for her younger sister there. This was her third or fourth time crossing the Atlantic.' A wistful look came into her eyes. 'A most redoubtable lady.'

'You became fond of her.'

'I did.'

'And did you see much of the country?' Taking her hand, he led her deeper into the woods. The chances of anyone being here at this hour were slight, but the further away from the house they were, the better.

She shook her head. 'In America, I have never been outside New York state.' There was a definite American twang to her words at times, he noted. It was decidedly endearing.

'And the city?'

'We lived there,' she said simply.

'With your employer's sister?'

'Yes. In the heart of Manhattan Island.' Her gaze grew distant. 'I can picture it all so clearly...the bank on Wall Street, the markets, the mansions...it is a special place.'

They walked on, him questioning her about her time in New York, and her answering in great detail.

'But this is fascinating!' he declared, stopping under

a venerable oak and facing her. Taking her other hand, he raised both to his lips, kissing them in turn. He looked at her. 'Thank you.'

She nodded, seemingly unable to speak. Her gaze dropped to his mouth—her desire clear as day. But he had to be certain.

'Do you want me to kiss you?' His voice was low, his eyes fixed on hers.

'Y-yes,' she croaked, yet rather than waiting for him she took matters into her own hands, standing on tiptoe to press her lips to his.

This. This was what he had craved. This was what he had hoped for, anticipated. Sliding his arms around her, he deepened the kiss, desire rushing through him as he tasted her delectable mouth, his tongue dancing with hers. He stepped forwards, walking her with him until the oak tree was at her back.

Yes! Now he need not worry that either of them would stumble, for the oak was their frame, their buttress of support. Tentatively, he slid one hand to her waist as he kissed her, moving it up and down her side. With the other, he cupped her face, loving the sensation of her smooth skin beneath his palm. Opening his eyes, he looked at her. *Daisy.* Had he ever known a more beautiful woman? He did not believe so.

Now his hand became more daring, sweeping over the side of her breast. She gasped against his mouth, so he did it again.

'Just stop me,' he murmured against her mouth, 'if I do something you do not want.'

For answer she slid her arms around him, pressing closer yet, and he groaned.

I need to touch her breasts. The thought was only half-formed, yet he had already acted, sweeping his hand fully over her left breast, enjoying the little moan in her throat as he lingered over the nipple.

'Hart,' she murmured. 'What—oh!' His other hand had found her other breast, and as he stroked and squeezed them both she threw her head back, lost in the feeling.

My God! Never had Hart known such exquisite discomfort. Daringly, he dropped his right hand to sweep over her nether region, and she stiffened in shock. *Too much.*

Lesson learned, he returned his attention to her breasts, then kissed her again.

How long they were there, he had no idea. They shared many kisses—a dozen, a score...who was counting? He spoke to her about caressing her bosom, and she confessed shyly that no man had ever done so before. Once more he offered to stop, to apologise if she did not want it, but she protested beautifully, taking his hands and placing them on her bosom, then throwing her head back when he obliged with the touches she clearly craved.

'This feels unjust,' she said at one point, and he raised

his head from where his tongue had been giving attention to her bosom through her uniform.

'How so?'

'You are doing everything for me, but I have done nothing to...to please you.'

'This pleases me,' he said simply. 'Giving you pleasure pleases me.'

'Then I wish to give you pleasure also. What may I do, Hart?'

Such a question! 'For men, most of the pleasure is here—' he pointed '—but I think it is too soon for you to do very much there.'

'May I...?' Her hands went netherwards, and he closed his eyes as her inexperienced fingers explored him through his buckskins.

'Stop. Stop!' he said after a few moments of exquisite pleasure, taking her hands away.

'Oh! I am sorry! Did I do something wrong?' She looked distressed, so he kissed her.

'Not at all,' he replied, stepping back and tucking her hand into his arm. 'Let us walk, and I shall explain to you—if you wish to hear it, that is.'

'Oh, I most certainly wish to hear it!' she declared.

'You get another kiss for that!' he told her, and they stood together for another long moment, under the dappled shade of the ancient oak.

They wandered then through the woods for what seemed like an age, discussing desires, and the different workings of male and female bodies.

'And is it true that—?' She asked many questions, based on matings she had seen—mostly dogs and horses—and he supplied her with answers that she seemed to find sometimes odd, sometimes astonishing, but always, she said, fascinating.

Eventually, it was time to part. Checking his pocket watch, he saw that he would have to make his way to the dining room for breakfast. 'Next Thursday?'

'Definitely!'

They kissed again and he left her there, since she wished to stay awhile longer, enjoying the morning sunshine.

As he walked away, he turned back for one last look. She had found a tree stump to sit on, and her perfect profile was clearly outlined amid the other beauties of nature. As if sensing his regard, she turned her head, and so he sent her one final kiss, mimicked on his fingers then sent theatrically on its way to her.

As he walked towards Walton House he was vaguely aware that he had never in his life known such happiness as he felt in this moment.

Chapter Eighteen

Joy was flowing through Sophia. The past hour and more had been magnificent. Her entire being was taken up by him. *Hart.* Had there ever been a man so handsome, so quick-witted, so kind? And as for his kisses… Closing her eyes, she allowed the memories to wash over her. His tongue in her mouth. His hands on her. Shockingly, her hands on him.

Miss Van Bergen knew all too well the limitations on her behaviour. She was to remain pure until marriage. Kisses may be permitted, occasionally—although even they were frowned upon—but anything further was most definitely not.

Yet today, she was not Miss Van Bergen. She was Daisy. And Daisy had freedoms that Miss Van Bergen did not. And so, with the perfect combination of Daisy's freedom to act, and Miss Van Bergen's confidence that ruin would not automatically follow, she had done a bold thing—and loved every second of it!

In fact, she could not wait to do it again. Yes, and

more, if Hart were willing. He had muttered at one stage about not wishing to ruin her. Yes, but what if she *wished* to be seduced, and knew she would manage the consequences, whatever they were?

In an attempt to be logical, she listed these in her mind. Should someone discover them trysting, then Daisy's reputation may well be ruined. But the real Daisy was far away, and could take on a new identity if she moved to America. And the serving maid in Walton House could simply leave. Miss Van Bergen, meantime, could reappear somewhere between here and London. Sophia had money enough in her bag that she could purchase clothing, hire a maid, and stay in the finest inns all the way there. She paused, awaiting a pang of envy for those things, but it did not come. No, she was quite content here, enjoying Hart's attentions as Daisy.

Sophia's understanding of how babies were made had also greatly increased this morning—although she still had questions about some aspects of the process. Whilst she did not wish to find herself with child, even that could be managed, she supposed. She could hire a cottage and a couple of servants and live there in secret for months, then give the baby into the care of a deserving family once it was born, writing letters to her mama to assure her of her safety without giving any hints as to her location. A small voice within her was suggesting it might not be an easy thing to do, but she ignored it.

So those were the risks. And what of the benefits? Instantly, certainty raced through her, along with a tumultuous pulse rate and the rekindling of desire. More kisses. More touching. Untold other pleasures, as yet unknown.

She had taken on the role of Daisy in a search for adventure, and she had found it. This though, was beyond anything great. Never could she have anticipated the elation she was currently feeling.

A dose of realism washed over her. This might be the only time in her life when she had the freedom to choose. Women of her class were governed by their parents, their chaperones...and then by their husbands, unless they remained single, like Aunt Agatha.

Once she went to London, Lord Linford might no longer wish to marry her—a not unreasonable outcome, she supposed. Or he might wish to go ahead. Cynically, she rather supposed it would depend on how desperately he needed her dowry. Like Hart, he might have an expensive estate to manage.

She frowned, allowing herself to properly acknowledge that Hart might indeed marry one of the two house guests who had clearly been invited because of that very possibility. *Perhaps, if he knew I too am an heiress, he might consider...?*

But no. Her deceit of Lord Linford was distant, impersonal. Her deceit of Hart was now as personal as it was possible to be. It would not be forgivable, she knew, if he discovered her dishonesty.

Another problem struck her. Now that they knew one another so well, she could not hope to hide among the aristocratic set—the *ton*, as Aunt Agatha had used to describe it. Hart would likely be hurt and angry if he discovered her true identity, and anything might occur as a consequence. *No, it is best if he never finds out.*

Sadly, she realised she might have no other option but to return to New York soon after leaving Walton House, to once again be Miss Van Bergen and either resign herself to spinsterhood, or choose a husband from among the sons of her parents' friends—men she and her parents had already rejected.

But at least, she thought fiercely, *I will have lived!*

Hart made his way through the house, his entire being radiating happiness. Vaguely, he was aware that he needed to be discreet, and so deliberately made his mouth stop curling up at the corners, distracting himself by noticing each and every servant he passed. As he approached the small door leading to the attics it opened, and he wondered which of the serving maids had found time to go upstairs during their busiest time of day. To his surprise, it was Mr Forsyth, who greeted him effusively.

'I hope you do not object to my exploring the house, my lord. I have a fascination for architecture, you see. Your roof trusses, sadly, are of a standard type. However, I suspect your stable block to be an Elizabethan house—it has mullioned windows to the rear.'

'Indeed!' Hart was ready to be tolerant with everyone just now—even Mr Forsyth. 'Family legend holds that it was the original family dwelling, until my great-grandfather built this place. Have you breakfasted?'

'Not yet. I intended to do so next.'

'I shall join you shortly, once I change to something more suitable for morning wear.'

On reaching his room he called for his valet, then, dressed more suitably, made his way to the dining room. Thankfully both his sisters were already present, along with Louisa's girls and a number of his guests. He sent Francesca and Amabel a warm smile while issuing a general greeting to them all, then took a seat at the side of the table, to reflect the informality of the meal.

He signalled to a footman who served him his usual plate of bacon, beef, and eggs, yet today he found he was not particularly hungry. Sipping his tea, he made conversation with Mrs Chester, who was seated beside him, nodding along with what he thought was great fortitude to her tale of a wasp in her bedchamber.

'I do hope it was a lone intruder. We had a wasps' nest in the stables three years ago.'

Mrs Chester's eyes bulged with horror. 'Lord, that would be like a living nightmare for me. I detest the creatures!'

'Whom is it that you detest, Mrs Chester?'

Lady Pashley's ears had clearly picked up on Mrs Chester's vehemence. 'Wasps,' she replied shortly. 'I detest wasps.' She grimaced. 'I suspect I was stung too many times as a child.'

No one had much to say to this, and the silence that

followed was broken by Lady Caroline expressing a desire for an excursion to some shops.

'We are a long way from London, Lady Caroline,' he told her. 'However, we could go to Derby town for a few hours if it pleases you.'

She clapped her hands. 'It pleases me very much, my lord.'

'Then it is settled.'

No one wished to miss the excursion, and so, two hours later, a veritable cavalcade of people departed Walton House—the ladies and some of the gentlemen in carriages, the younger men on horseback, Hart included. Hart was glad to not be stuck in a carriage, for he could converse easily with the gentlemen if he wished, or remain silent, lost in his own imaginings, or simply *feeling* the joy within him.

Once in Derby the ladies descended upon the shops— with Hart's cousin George and his friend offering to carry packages for them. Truthfully, Hart was relieved, for he was much more inclined to accompany the men on a walk through the town to the Nottingham Road, where they were given an impromptu tour of the porcelain factory where much of the Royal Derby china was manufactured. Mr Bloor the owner was most delighted to receive them—and with good reason, for two of Hart's guests ordered a full set of china then and there.

When the party met up again with the ladies, they discovered that they, too, had been buying Royal Derby china, as select pieces were sold in most of the local shops. Each piece was marked underneath with the same stamp—a crown and the letter *D*, outlined in red.

They all seemed delighted with their outing, and as the carriages wound their way back up the hills towards Walton House, Hart felt a sense of satisfaction. While the house party had taken an unexpected turn, he still needed to do his duty by his guests, and today had been a success.

Still, it was good to be home. And not just for the usual reasons. *Daisy is in there, somewhere.* Foolishly, he scanned the windows, but of course no one was visible. Yet his heart was thundering at the memories from this morning, and his need to see her again.

Lord, I am like a schoolboy experiencing his first tendre! Not only was he overcome by thoughts of Daisy, but his conscience was reminding him she would be deemed highly unsuitable for anything other than a short-lived affair. He disliked the notion, so took his thoughts in another direction. How beautiful she was, and how it had felt to be kissing her, touching her...

'Thank you for today, cousin. It was most enjoyable.' Hart suppressed a sigh. Of course it would be George Banfield who interfered with his happy musings. Still, at least the man seemed in an affable mood.

'I am glad to hear it. What thought you of the porcelain factory?'

'Fascinating, cousin, fascinating. Err...'

'Yes?'

Now what has he to say to me?

'I find myself rather cleaned out at present. I'm at damned low water, if I must be honest. So I wondered if you might see fit to lend me a sovereign or two so I may reach quarter-day without embarrassing the family name.'

'And why,' Hart asked mildly, 'would I do such a thing, since I am still waiting for you to repay me the money I lent you last quarter?'

'Ah, but you do not understand,' Banfield protested. 'My dear mama has her own money, but my allowance is insufficient to support a man of my standing.'

'Then I suggest you apply to my aunt.'

He sighed mournfully. 'She says she will not—or at least, not until we return to London after the summer.'

'Then I do not see the problem. You will be here in the coming weeks, with no cost to your own pocket. You will be living at my expense.'

Banfield shook his head sadly. 'You can have no idea what it is to be rolled up, since you are swimming in wealth.' He gestured towards Walton House. 'Do you have any idea how difficult it is to be your heir, but with no access to your privileges?'

Hart shrugged, unwilling to share the reality that finances were so tight he was even considering sacrificing himself in marriage to some silly girl just to keep the estate steady and safe. 'My question stands, George. Why on earth will you need money in the coming weeks?'

They were nearly at the house, and some of the ladies had already begun exiting from their carriages up ahead. Banfield dropped his voice. 'Today, when the others were purchasing china, I should have liked to do the same.'

Hart was astounded. 'But why? Have you a *need* for new china?'

'Well, no, but I stood there in front of them all, knowing that I could not purchase anything of significance, if I wished to.'

Hart raised his eyes to heaven. 'Lord, what nonsense! So you wished to purchase china that you did not need, just so that the other gentlemen could see you do it?'

'Well,' Banfield replied huffily, 'you can choose to put it like that, but I must say I am disappointed that any cousin of mine is so picksome and strait-laced. You are not like your father at all! Yes, and you can afford to be cocksure, for you do not know what it is to be purse-pinched!' And with that he rode off, clearly in high dudgeon.

Hart was astonished. That Cousin George set great store by his ability to be *seen* to spend money should not surprise him: the man had a distorted set of priorities. He also had clearly developed a spending habit, like Papa—though George was motivated not by love and devotion to others, but by his own puffed-up pride.

But Hart was no green boy, and he could not be so irresponsible as to allow himself to be bled dry. *You are not like your father.* A compliment, unintentionally given. Hart had loved his father, but in this aspect at least, was delighted to be different. To be fair, his cousin could have no idea of the costs of managing the estate. *Perhaps*, he thought, *I should educate him, share with him the burdens I carry. He is, after all, my heir.*

This in turn led to more thoughts—unwelcome thoughts. While he had no desire to shower his house guests with gifts, he could vaguely imagine wanting to do so with Daisy—a notion that was deeply disturbing. Was he, at heart, more like Papa than he knew? Was he in danger of losing his self-control and his carefully wrought containment, to a girl who would only be in his life for a matter of weeks? He needed to be careful there.

And while he had been enjoying his time with Daisy this morning, he would have been better focusing on Lady Caroline and Miss Chester. His responsibilities remained, and ideally he needed to have secured the hand of one or other lady by the time the house party ended.

But now he was home, and dismounting, and bracing himself to once again be the genial host. All else would have to wait.

Chapter Nineteen

Sophia returned to the house after another hour had passed, feeling as though she had settled enough from the heavens to do so. Hart—that is, *Lord Hartington* and his guests had all apparently gone to Derby, and so Mrs Stone had taken the opportunity to initiate a deep clean. Grateful for her day off amid the frenzy of extra work, Sophia made her way upstairs to her room, where she rested, and read part of a book loaned to her by Mary, and wrote a short letter to the real Daisy.

In the letter, she said she hoped that all was well with her, assuring her that she had arrived safely in Derbyshire to take up her new post. She paused, considering, then added that she was making friends and enjoying the work. Which was true. The work—despite being exhausting—gave her a tremendous sense of satisfaction, and she and Mary had become fast friends. The fact that her other friend here was none other than Lord Hartington himself, she kept to herself with fierce joy.

Adding a final sentence, she stated she hoped to see 'Miss Van Bergen' again in early September, and would be grateful to hear back from 'Miss Van Bergen' should she feel able to respond. Hopefully Daisy could provide some assurance that the London part of their ruse had not yet been uncovered. *There!* she thought, as she signed it with her false name. *No one could know to what I am referring.* The letter she passed to the undergroom, with a penny for postage. She was unsure if Daisy would write back, but hoped she, too, was enjoying playing a new role for a time.

After a late dinner in the servants' quarters she went to bed, determined to have a longer sleep than usual. Her dreams though were disturbed, and she woke numerous times during the night. Each time, there was but one person in her thoughts. *Hart.*

With renewed determination, Hart resolved to keep his focus on his guests—in particular the two young ladies. He made an effort to seek each of them out in turn, walking and talking with them, and drawing them out a little. Away from the crowd, neither of them was as silly as he had initially judged them to be, but he always had to stifle a sigh when they reverted to arch looks and playacting in company. He was entirely jaded with Lady Caroline's airs and Miss Chester's chest—the latter being thrust into his line of vision on every possible occasion.

How he preferred Daisy's straightforwardness, the

way her delectable body was hidden beneath a maidservant's gown, how her brow would crease when worrying over something, and how her eyes would dance with merriment during their mutual raillery and teasing. In truth, he preferred everything about her—her kisses that could inflame him within seconds, her lively mind, and her kind heart…

As the days went by, he amused himself as best he could with riding and billiards, finding snatches of interesting conversation here and there with some of the guests. He also found himself particularly enjoying the company of his young nieces, whose lack of artifice and desire to learn appealed to him.

His deeper self though still craved Daisy, and counted the days to Thursday. Each time he encountered a housemaid he had to know if it was her, and so he had learned to know all of them by name. Sally had been here for years of course, along with three others. Daisy and Mary were the temporary housemaids, and would need to seek further employment after their work in Walton House ended. He was even getting to know his footmen better—something he probably should have done years ago.

As the time ticked slowly by, thoughts of Daisy began once more to consume him. By Wednesday evening he could barely focus on anything except willing the hours to pass. Eliza had placed Lady Caroline beside him at dinner, and the occasional scent of her perfume evoked a desperate need within him for Daisy…a need that was unlike anything he had ever experienced.

How? Why? And why now? Was his need for her based on Daisy herself, or was he somehow taken by her because he disliked being compelled to get leg-shackled to a young lady he felt exactly nothing for? But then, what he had learned from Papa was that it might be better to feel nothing for one's spouse. Oh, it was all too difficult!

After a long, long night, finally it was morning, and he made his way through the gardens to the woods. Straight as an arrow he made for the redwoods, only to feel a stab of disappointment.

She is not here.

Had she changed her mind? Had he gone too far last week? He knew her for an innocent. To do even what they had last Thursday might have severely shaken her. *Lord, have I made a mull of it?* Was he a bad person, placing pressure on someone in his employ?

A twig cracked behind him. He whirled around, breaking into a smile as he saw her familiar figure approach. Taking three strides forward he swept her up, swinging her round and planting a kiss on her cheek before setting her down in front of him.

'I was afraid you would not come.' He had said it aloud, with no concern for his own image or demeanour. Lord, it was liberating not having to be an earl with her!

'I could not stay away even if I wished to,' she said

simply, and his heart swelled. Then his lips were on hers and her tongue was in his mouth and all was right with the world.

'Hart,' she murmured at one point, 'Hart.' Surely there was nothing better than to hear one's own name on the lips of the woman you loved?

He froze, feeling as though he had taken an arrow to the heart. *Love? Really?* Shaken, he leaned back to look at her.

'What is it, Hart? What is the matter?'

Do not say it. The situation was complicated enough. To even fleetingly believe that he loved her was a leap of such magnitude that he thought he would need a month just to understand if it was real, and not just a passing fancy in his head.

Be sensible. He barely knew her. It was probably simply a *tendre* exaggerated by its furtive forbiddenness. Not love. Of course not. How ridiculous! This is how Papa might have behaved, losing himself in a manner unbefitting his age and status.

'Nothing is the matter, my lovely Daisy. Not so long as we are together like this.' Bending his head to kiss her again, he decided now was a good time to discover if she wished to repeat their more daring actions from last week, and so he slid his hands down to her bottom, pressing her against his hardness.

She gasped. 'Oh! That feels divine!'

Reciprocating, she explored his back and his bottom, pulling him to her—closer, closer yet.

They kissed, and kissed, and daringly he touched her again through her clothes.

'Lift your skirt,' he muttered, his voice cracking with passion. At this she opened her eyes and he held his breath.

'You do it.'

Exhilaration rushed through him and he complied, stroking her thighs and occasionally brushing his fingers higher, until she was writhing with need. He laid her down then, on the sweet grass amid the redwoods, and touched her with all the expertise he had, bringing her to ecstasy not once but three times.

After the convulsions had eased, he went to touch her again, but she clamped her hand over his, opening her eyes.

'No. You next. Teach me how to touch you.'

And so he did—not that she needed to do very much, so ready was he.

Afterwards they lay together, her head on his chest and his hand gently stoking her hair. He could see the sky through the tree canopy, could hear the sounds of rustling leaves and the singing of birds. And he could feel her breathing. Allowing his eyes to close, he focused on just that for a moment. Her body moving slightly with each breath she took, lying safe against him. How privileged he was, that she should trust him this way. That to her, he was simply Hart.

Daisy.

* * *

Daisy was in alt. The feelings coursing through her were so potent that she felt as though she could barely breathe. Never had she felt so close to another person. When they had touched each other... She would never, ever forget how wonderful it had been. And now, lying here within the circle of his arms, his hand gentle in her hair and his heartbeat in her ear, she felt safe, protected, cared for.

Eventually though, they had to go. Standing, they rearranged their clothing, sending one another grins of delight. They walked through the woods then, hand in hand, and she asked him about his family and childhood.

He had known the love of his parents, that seemed clear. And, although his older sisters had been prone to managing him, it was obvious that he held great affection for them.

'But everyone had expectations of you, did they not?'

He grimaced. 'I never could escape the knowledge that I was my father's heir. The expectations placed on me were not unreasonable, I suppose, but to learn well, behave well, and be ever sensible was a trial at times.'

Growing up as the daughter of the Van Bergens, she knew *exactly* what he meant, though of course she could not say so. Her escape had been twofold: inside the pages of a book, or outside at their country home, running wild in the Van Bergen gardens. A flash of insight came to her.

'This was your freedom, was it not? These woods?'

His eyes widened briefly. 'Naturally you would see that. Yes, here was where I could be myself, playing games of knights and dragons amid the trees.' He sent her a glance filled with affection. 'But you must tell me of yourself. I wish to know everything about you.'

For an instant, three choices stood before Sophia. Use Daisy's story—in other words, lie to him. Tell him the full truth—in other words, admit how she had been deceiving him. Or third, try to tell the truth within the fictitious role she had crafted.

I cannot lie to him. Not anymore. Not now they were this close. Yet to tell him the full truth would risk his anger. His rejection of her. And she wanted to keep this dream alive for as long as she could. So cautiously, she proceeded to tell him of her true self, her likes and dislikes—even mentioning her true parents and her sisters, while omitting any details of their wealth or position.

'My favourite pastime,' she declared, 'was making up little plays for my sisters and me to act in.' She shrugged. 'Now I am grown, I see that we perform roles all the time. I, the housemaid. You, the Earl.'

'Except here, where we are simply two people.'

'Yes.' Stopping, she stood on tiptoe to kiss him—the slightest brush of her lips against his. 'When this is all over, please remember that this is the real me. Nothing and no one else. Just this girl, standing before you.'

A shadow darkened his eyes, and he swooped in to take her mouth in a ferocious kiss. 'Do not,' he muttered, a moment later, 'speak of the future.' They kissed again, until both were breathless, then he released her to check his pocket watch.

'I must go. Until next Thursday!'

She echoed his final words, then watched as he walked away. When he turned back to send one final kiss he was too far away to possibly see that tears were streaming down her face.

Half an hour later she returned to the house, noticing that Sally was cleaning the windows in the drawing room. Had she seen the Earl emerge? Would she put two and two together? *All is well*, she reassured herself. Sally would surely think it simply a coincidence.

Chapter Twenty

The weeks seemed to fly by, and Sophia settled fully into her life at Walton House. As a housemaid she worked hard, cleaning, mending, and seeing to Lady Caroline and Miss Chester. The work was demanding, and she fell into bed each night exhausted, but she was a quick learner, and had now mastered most of her tasks. Meeting the demands of the young ladies was in truth the most challenging part of the role—although, interestingly, both ladies were becoming increasingly unguarded in her presence. Both expressed continuous frustration at the Earl's failure to pay them particular attention, and Sophia could only be relieved that he had clearly not kissed either of them.

His kisses belong to me! He could do what he must after she was gone, as she herself would. For now, he belonged to her, and she to him.

In the meantime she lived for Thursdays, and for her occasional glimpses of him as she went about her duties. Their trysting continued to be delightful, and had now progressed to the use of their mouths to give pleasure, not just their hands. The first time he had pleasured her so, she had been rigid with shock, but had quickly realised this was a new and unexpected delight. Being Sophia, she had promptly asked to reciprocate, and had now learned to satisfy him with both her mouth and her hands.

They had talked of doing more, but had decided not to risk getting her with child. While they both knew it was the right decision, they occasionally spoke wistfully of the things they could not do—like sleeping together in the same bed. *Oh, how wonderful it would be to wake up and find him there beside me!*

Last Thursday, Hart had also spoken sadly about how she could never publicly be his girl, and Sophia had only just managed to bite her tongue. The last days of August were upon them, and there were only ten days left of her employment at Walton House. Ten days. Two Thursdays. Then nothing ever again.

Soon she would make for London, and take up her place again as Miss Van Bergen. Even now, Mama would be somewhere in the middle of the Atlantic, getting nearer and nearer to England with every day that passed.

The real Daisy had replied to her letter a few weeks ago, signing herself Sophia Van Bergen, and assuring 'Daisy' that all was well. Worryingly, she had indicated she was currently staying at Linford House in Kent, which Sophia knew to be Lord Linford's country estate. Lord, she hoped Daisy could maintain the fiction at such close quarters!

Dismissing worries she could do nothing about, Sophia returned to her own conundrum. She was strongly considering telling Hart the truth before she left. Was there any possibility they might have a future together? An earl could never marry a maid, but he might marry an heiress. While she could offer no title, she was granddaughter to a marquess, and her dowry was at least as healthy as Lady Caroline's or Miss Chester's. Of that, she had little doubt, given Papa's wealth.

But a man deceived would surely never marry the woman who had deceived him, and she could not bear the thought that he might react with scorn.

Sophia worried over this constantly. Until she had begun this charade, plain speaking had always been her preference, and it was frustrating not to be able to speak freely with him. Yet she simply had no notion what to do for the best.

The grand ball was to be held next Wednesday night, September the second, with the guests all due to leave afterwards, on the Thursday and Friday, and the temporary staff completing a final deep clean and leaving on the Sunday, September sixth. The date was like a death knell in Sophia's mind.

In preparation, Mrs Stone had the staff in a flurry of extra cleaning. The ballroom had been opened up for apparently the first time in years, and every part of it—including the elaborate glass chandeliers—had to be cleaned. With the others, Sophia scrubbed and cleaned for hours, pausing only when called upon to wait upon young ladies or bring tea to the drawing room.

There was a palpable air of excitement in the house, which Sophia could not help but be infected by. Hart though, seemed to be concerned in case something should go wrong, as his sister had invited all the local gentry and every single one had accepted the invitation. This would be the largest gathering in Walton House in a generation and for Hart's sake, Sophia prayed all would go well.

No, she could not bother him by revealing secrets right now, as he was clearly preoccupied by the ball. But afterwards—she had one final Thursday, and she would try to find the courage to be honest with him.

Making her way to the servants' hall with Sally to fetch more tablecloths as instructed, she happened to hear a discussion between Mrs Stone and her father regarding the stabling of the guests' horses. John had come to the servants' hall for mid-morning tea as he often did, and he had brought with him the stable boy, who had had a tooth pulled and was feeling sorry for himself.

'So we must pray for a dry night, then.'

'Indeed we must, lass, for there is no space in the stables for any of their cattle.'

'And you will be busy, Ben.' The housekeeper smiled at the boy. 'The guests will likely not leave until around two in the morning, and then you will be up early to saddle my lord's horse for his morning ride—assuming he will still ride out after such a late night.'

'Oh, no,' the lad said, 'for my lord never rides on a Thursday no more.'

Sally lifted her head from her folding. Something about the boy's words had clearly interested her... As the conversation moved on, Sophia refused to meet her colleague's gaze, wondering if her own cheeks were flushed. Had Sally recalled the incident from early in the summer, when Sophia had emerged from the woods after the Earl? But no, for the senior maid said nothing, and Sophia continued gathering tablecloths with a strong sense of relief. With the ball upon them, no one had time for speculation. Or so she hoped.

Hart's face ached from smiling, and the dancing was not yet underway. Tonight would be long, and he would have to smile, and please, and be the Earl of Hartington for hours. His house guests were by this point a known quantity, but inviting every member of the gentry for miles around meant tonight would be the largest gathering in Walton House for decades.

He and Eliza had stood in the entrance hall welcoming every single one of their neighbours, as a procession of carriages had deposited them outside Walton House. It had seemed to take an age, but finally Eliza informed him that the last of the guests had now arrived, and so they made their way through to the ballroom.

Out of the corner of his eye he spotted Daisy, who

was taking Mrs Allen's velvet cloak. *If only I could dance with her tonight!* A pang went through him as he added this to the list of frustrations. But now he must forget his own heart, for it was time to move around the room, speaking briefly to as many guests as he could, while Eliza checked all was well with the staff, then gave the nod to the musicians to begin the dancing.

Knowing his duty, Hart led Lady Caroline out for the first dance. Miss Chester would no doubt be displeased, but could hardly complain, since Lady Caroline outranked her. As they moved through the figures of the dance, Hart considered Lady Caroline assessingly. She danced well—no doubt trained by the best caper-merchant in London. She looked well turned-out, too. And her company manners were good. She was also daughter to an earl, and offered an attractive dowry.

Since Miss Chester offered no greater attraction that could outweigh Lady Caroline's lineage, he supposed he should offer for her. And if he was going to offer for her, he should do so tonight. This, after all, was why Eliza had invited both young ladies. And why she had suggested a ball.

Yet all he could think about was how hurt Daisy would feel. He shook his head slightly. Daisy knew he had to wed.

As he turned in the dance, he saw his sisters. They were standing together, watching him and Lady Caroline, and wore almost identical expressions. He only had a brief moment to take it in, but he saw approval, perhaps mixed with relief. They, better than George Banfield, understood why he must marry soon. Why, even Daisy knew it, for he had spoken to her at length about his financial burdens—though not the reasons behind them. Even with Daisy he could not bear to speak ill of his father.

And he knew his duty. With that in mind he set out to be charming, and Lady Caroline bloomed under his compliments. She genuinely looked well tonight, her fair hair expertly dressed, her gown—

Wait. Who had dressed Lady Caroline's hair? Thinking back, he recalled Daisy telling him it was one of her skills. Now all he could think about was Daisy's hands, teasing the strands of Lady Caroline's hair into the curls and small plaits he could see. The thing was a masterpiece, now that he studied it closely.

Daisy's hands. Daisy's body. Daisy's—

He had to stop. Thankfully, the dance was at an end. He took Lady Caroline to the back of the room where the punch was being served, then handed her to her next dance partner with a sense of relief. As he made his way to Miss Chester to secure her hand for the second dance, he felt an overwhelming sense of injustice. Why must he be the sacrifice?

In this moment, he wished he had been born to be a servant.

Chapter Twenty-One

Sophia felt torn. While she had genuinely enjoyed working as a housemaid, tonight the role really chafed. It should have been her, dancing with the Earl in a glittering gown. Instead she was stuck in the ladies' retiring room, mending hems and fixing coiffures. Each time the door opened she could hear the music, along with a hubbub of conversation, and each time she had to stifle a sigh.

Tonight, she thought, *I am the other Cinderella.* The one with no fairy godmother, no beautiful ballgown, and no glass slippers.

And there was precisely nothing she could do about it.

'…the Earl is expected to make one of them an offer tonight!'

Sophia was suddenly all attention.

'But which one, my dear? Which one?'

The first lady—a plump matron in a green satin

gown—shrugged. 'If he has any sense, he will opt for the Pashley girl. A title is a title, after all.'

'But I heard—' her companion leaned closer, although there was no one present but the three of them '—that the Chesters are fabulously wealthy!'

Not as wealthy as the Van Bergens, I'd wager! was Sophia's immediate thought, but inwardly she felt devastation.

As the ladies moved on to gossip about other matters, Sophia's initial shock gave way to a deep sorrow. She knew—had always known—that an earl could not marry a maid, and that Hart had to marry well, given the perilous state of his finances. She just had not anticipated him *actually* making one of the ladies an offer while she was here to see them.

I should have told him the truth. Perhaps she did not need a fairy godmother. Perhaps the truth would have sufficed.

Abruptly, she was glad to have been assigned to the retiring room. He was no doubt out there charming whichever lady he had chosen, and Daisy did not want to see it.

The door opened again, to admit the Earl's sister, Mrs Dawson.

'Some oaf has trod on my hem!' she declared. 'See what you may do to mend it. Supper will soon be called, so there is little time.'

'Yes, Mrs Dawson.' Bending, Sophia inspected the

damage to the silk gown. The entire bottom flounce had come away at the back and on the right side. She tutted.

'Indeed!' Mrs Dawson concurred. 'I imagine this may take some time?'

'I shall be as quick as I can, Mrs Dawson. I shall aim for speed, even if it means I must sacrifice my usual neatness, if that is acceptable to you?'

'I am glad to see that you have the intelligence to see so quickly what must be done.' As Sophia found the best colour match she could in the candlelight, and began threading a fine needle, Mrs Dawson inquired casually, 'What is your name?'

'Sophia—that is to say, *Daisy*.' Sophia froze in horror. Her real name had slipped out in this unguarded moment, and she knew exactly why. Her immediate mind had been focused on threading the tiny needle, while her deeper attention was constantly wondering if Hart was now betrothed. Between the two, she had let down her usual guard.

Mrs Dawson chuckled. 'Well? Which is it? Sophia or Daisy?'

Sophia swallowed. 'It is Daisy, Mrs Dawson. I used to be called Sophia, but Daisy is a more appropriate name for a servant, is it not?'

Hart's sister nodded slowly. 'I suppose. I know many servants take on simple names in case someone in the family they serve might have the same name as them.' She sent Sophia a keen glance. 'So what were you before you were a servant, then? When you were called Sophia, I mean?'

Tears blurred Sophia's eyes as, abruptly, she wished she were safely at home in New York with her parents and sisters, and a heart that was intact.

'I was simply my parents' daughter, Mrs Dawson.'

A look of sympathy crossed Mrs Dawson's face, and she patted Sophia's hand. 'You are a good girl, Sophia, for I understand from Mrs Stone that both you and the other temporary housemaid are hardworking, skilled, and diligent.'

'Thank you, Mrs Dawson.' Kneeling, she picked up the bottom of Mrs Dawson's gown, moving her fingers to find the first torn part. How heartwarming it was to be addressed as Sophia once more! Yet, somehow, it made the armour around her crack further.

The door opened again, admitting Mrs Smyth, Hart's other sister.

'Oh, there you are, Eliza! I have news!'

Mrs Dawson straightened. 'Well, spit it out, Louisa!'

'He has taken Lady Caroline out on the terrace!'

Mrs Dawson clapped her hands. 'I *knew* he would prefer her over Miss Chester. I just *knew* it!'

'You said so from the start, Eliza.' She sank into an armchair. 'What a relief!'

'Indeed! He has been so distracted these past weeks, I despaired of him ever coming up to scratch!'

Keeping her head bent to her task, Sophia swallowed hard, resolving not to give way to sorrow. Dimly, she knew there would be copious tears in her future, if it was true that Hart was now betrothed. His sisters seemed certain of it. For now, she had to survive long enough to leave Walton House with her pride intact, even if her heart was in pieces. Tomorrow was Thursday, and the temporary servants were to leave on Sunday. Four more days. Surely she could make it through four more days?

Finally the ball was over. As Hart watched the last carriage depart up the drive, his gaze lifted to the gibbous moon and he shook his head slowly. A sense of failure shuddered through him, a feeling that he had let everyone down—himself, his family, and his name.

Oh, he had tried. He had danced with both ladies twice, had led Lady Caroline in to supper, had even asked her if she would like to take some air on the terrace. And then, he had baulked. Like a horse deceiving its rider with a strong run-up to a fence, he had turned abruptly at the last second, conversed with Lady Caroline about the cool night air and the music, then taken her back inside again.

She had been severely disappointed, he could tell. And why should she not be? If she had thought she was about to receive an offer, she had been exactly right. But when the moment had come, thoughts of Daisy had prevented him from saying the words.

Lord, he had been a fool, all these weeks, thinking he

could have both! That he could give his heart to Daisy and his hand to someone else.

Clearly, there was no possibility of marrying Daisy. To do so would mean a slow fall into bankruptcy and shame. He must not even think of it.

And so many people depended on him for their livelihoods, their homes—for food, shelter, a future. His thoughts flicked to Bess, his old nurse. What would happen to her if she lost her pension from the estate? Or John, once he gave way to old age and finally retired? His tenant farmers and their families? Mr and Mrs Stone, his butler, valet, steward, menservants, maids, and grooms. All his responsibility. And he had failed every last one of them.

His guests were gone—the locals in their carriages, the house guests—including his sisters—to their beds upstairs. The servants were busy tidying up, and he was standing at the front of Walton House, knowing himself to be unworthy of any of them.

Sally was collecting glasses, and had asked Sophia to gather together the cutlery. Much of it had already been placed in wooden boxes to be taken for washing and polishing, but various pieces were randomly scattered about the ballroom and supper-room. As she went about her task, her thoughts were elsewhere. None of the servants had mentioned their master's betrothal, which meant only that there had not yet been an official announcement. She would no doubt hear soon enough.

Her heart was broken. *Hart is my heart.* Why had she not told him the truth sooner? She was an heiress, and cared not what he might do with her dowry. She wanted only him. She loved him with every part of herself—mind, heart and soul. These past weeks, she had known happiness so strong that she knew she could never again in a hundred lifetimes experience anything like it.

'Any more cutlery?' she kept asking passing servants, and they would direct her to where they had seen wandering pieces.

'Yes—two spoons on the terrace, along with empty punch glasses,' said Reuben, hurrying past carrying a chair. All of the cutlery, china, and glassware had been counted out and would be counted back in. There had been at least one breakage—a drunk man had dropped a precious crystal brandy glass.

'Thank you!'

Making her way to the terrace, she braced herself. Here, just a few short hours ago, Hart had done something that would change his life forever. And hers, too.

Lord, her own stupidity knew no bounds. Why had she not told him the truth? Yes, he might have turned from her in disgusted by her deceit. But maybe, just maybe, he would have forgiven her, and then...

'Good evening, fair maid.' The deep voice behind her made Sophia whirl around. There, leaning against the doorway, his eyes bleary and his speech slightly slurred, was Mr Forsyth.

Instantly her heart stilled, then raced as she recalled Sally's words of warning. Neither Mr Banfield nor Mr Forsyth had had the opportunity during their stay of being alone with any of the younger housemaids. Until now.

'Mr Forsyth! I did not see you there.' Bending, she picked up the two spoons, leaving the glasses for others to collect. She must not show fear. She must plan how to get past him and into the house, where she would be safe.

'Hard at work, I see. Such a sad life for such a pretty girl.' He ambled towards her.

Feeling decidedly wary, Sophia stepped to the side and tried to pass him, but with surprising speed he grabbed her arm, pulling her towards him. And then his wet mouth was on hers and his hand was painfully squeezing her breast. For an instant she froze in shock, then bringing up her knee, she connected with his nether regions as forcefully as she could, dimly recalling Hart telling her how any injury to the ballocks was agony for a man. Forsyth staggered back, but as she tried to run past him he grabbed her hair, making her squeal in pain.

'How dare you, you little trollop!'

He was so much taller and stronger than her. Sophia knew she was in trouble. She could not fend him off by herself. There was only one thing for it.

'Help!' she cried. 'Help me!'

Chapter Twenty-Two

Moving her face left and right to evade Forsyth's seeking mouth, Sophia bent her knees so that he briefly held her entire weight. As he stumbled, she hooked her right leg behind his, at the same time pushing at his chest. His balance further impaired, he swayed—but tightened his grasp on her and they fell together, him landing half on top of her.

'Aha!' he muttered. 'Now I have you where I want you. You shall not escape me now!' He shuffled fully onto her, one hand lowering in an attempt to find the bottom of her skirts.

'No! You shall not!' Abruptly, Daisy gave way to Miss Van Bergen. This disgusting man must not be allowed to prevail. 'Help!' she bellowed, as loudly as she could—the sound fuelled by anger much stronger than her previous cry of fear.

This time she had been heard, and now distant steps were running towards them. Reuben, perhaps?

'Help me!' she called again—just as Forsyth finally

managed to find her hem. Then he was gone—hauled off her by two strong hands.

It all happened in an instant. One minute she was being pressed and assaulted, the next his weight was off her. A thump rang out as someone's fist connected with Forsyth's chin, and he fell beside her like a sack of potatoes.

'Daisy! Daisy!' Hart bent to help her up. 'How do you?'

Trembling from head to toe, Daisy could barely stand. If not for his reassuring—and safe—arms around her, she surely would have fallen again. Fear, anger, and relief coursed through her in equal measure.

'I was round at the front of the house,' he said, 'when I heard you. I came instantly.' He leaned back to look at her, his face deathly pale in the light of the flambeaux. 'Tell me honestly. Did he…?' He swallowed. 'Was he successful in his evil endeavour?'

Mutely, Daisy shook her head and he exhaled in relief.

'Thank the Lord for that! Now, I think you should be seated.' He guided her to the stone bench at the edge of the terrace, then left her to go to Forsyth, who was groggily rising.

'Did you hit me?' he asked the Earl, his expression filled with outrage. 'I believe you hit me!'

'I did. You are a guest under my roof, sir, and you have abused your position to dishonour Daisy—an innocent maid!'

'Innocent, pah! We are men of the world, you and I, my lord. These light-skirts are all the same.' He shrank back as Hart raised his fist once more. 'No, no, but I am only jesting, my lord!' He looked to where Daisy sat, shaking from head to toe. 'It was all a little misunderstanding, my dear. Was it not?'

Slowly, she shook her head.

'You will leave here early tomorrow morning and not return.' Hart's voice was like iron—cold, strong, implacable. 'You may be grateful to escape with only a single punch. Now,' he added, his voice dripping with disgust, 'get out of my sight!'

Forsyth went, reminding Sophia of a rat as he scurried off into the house.

Hart watched him go, then returned to her side, opening his arms. Gratefully she went into them, closing her eyes and telling herself that she was now safe.

'Daisy, my Daisy,' he murmured into her hair. 'All is well. You will never have to see him again.'

She cried then, telling him between sobs exactly what had occurred, and his arms tightened about her.

'That such a man is a guest at Walton House!' He stroked her hair. 'Thank the Lord I heard you!'

'Yes, for no one is around. The servants are between the ballroom and the kitchens, and the guests are all abed—or so I thought.'

'I saw him earlier, sleeping in a chair in the hall. Foxed. He must have come round and wandered back to see if the ball had finished. To think what might have happened!'

He looked down at her, his eyes dark and mysterious in the moonlight, then slowly bent his head.

For an instant revulsion rose within her, fuelled by fear. Then her mind and body caught up with one another, and she knew he was Hart. So she lifted her chin and accepted his kiss—the sweetest, softest kiss, and one which showed her that Forsyth would hopefully leave no permanent wound on her mind. *I am safe.*

Daisy did not sleep well, her rest punctuated by nightmares. Waking in the dark, her breathing ragged and her body frozen with fear, she reminded herself of Hart's intervention, and gradually convinced her terrified body to relax. This was an aspect of being a servant that she did not like one bit. Would a creature like Forsyth have importuned a Miss Van Bergen?

Recalling his words—*light-skirt. They are all the same*—she thought not. Such men chose prey they assumed had no protectors—women who seemed vulnerable. Why? *Because they could.*

Thank the Lord there were also good men in the world. Men like Hart. She lay there, willing herself to breathe slowly and evenly, and grateful that her distress had not awakened Mary or Sally. Sleep was elusive though, and as the dawn chorus began, she reminded herself with relief that it was Thursday, and that after meeting Hart she could return to her bed for a nap.

Breakfast for the family and guests was to be later this morning, given the late night everyone had had, and so all of the servants had also been permitted to sleep a little later. But it was Thursday, and both Sophia and one of the footmen were to have their day off as usual.

Pretending to sleep while Sally and Mary rose, dressed, and left, she got up, feeling as though she were moving slowly, as though she were a hundred years old. In a daze brought on by lack of sleep, she made her way through the house and outside, through the gardens and into the woods. Reaching the redwoods she looked around, her heart sinking. *He is not here.*

Hart had not slept well. His failure to make an offer to Lady Caroline and the associated feelings of guilt, shame, and negligence were screaming through him with every heartbeat. And his anger at Forsyth had not been relieved by that single punch.

How dared the man pester one of the Walton House maids? His assault on Daisy had been wicked, dishonourable, and essentially cowardly. Such men were a stain on society, their vice and degeneracy a blemish on the principles and ideals of the *ton*.

The fact that Forsyth's victim had been none other than Daisy added a potent dimension to Hart's anger, and Hart could hardly bear the pain he felt each time he tried to understand how she must have felt.

Worse yet, Daisy's time at Walton House was nearly

up, for his house guests would be leaving today and tomorrow, and the temporary staff would be let go on Sunday. His time was running out, and he still had no notion what to do about Daisy. Marriage was impossible, so his only choices were to let her go and live with a heart broken and bleeding, or to risk insulting her by offering to take her as his mistress.

His mind and heart were in turmoil, and worse, he had overslept—having struggled to sleep for hours. So he made his way to the redwoods with a head that was blurry and a heart that was sore. Still, seeing her there immediately lightened his mood.

'I was afraid you would not come.' It was almost a ritual by this point. Whichever of them arrived first would say it. Her expression was serious, and his heart melted.

He replied as expected, though meaning every word. 'Nothing could keep me away.' He took her in his arms. 'May I kiss you?'

For answer she kissed him, and he allowed her to lead—from gentle to passionate and back again. His hands remained chastely on her back, or in her hair, for he was concerned about the effect of Forsyth's actions.

'Let us walk,' he suggested, 'for we have much to talk about.'

She was quiet then, just when he wanted her to speak. They walked in silence through the woodland, her hand warm and small in his, and it killed him to know he would soon lose her.

'Daisy, I am here to listen, if there are things you wish to say to me.' Most of all, he wanted to know how much harm Forsyth had done to her spirit.

'Oh! I thought *you* wished to tell *me* something.'

This was a reminder that they needed to speak of the future, and his betrothal.

'First, I wish to know how you are, after last night's ordeal.'

'I confess I had nightmares, but I reminded myself that you were there, and that you kept me safe.' She swallowed. 'I do not deny how horrible it was, but I believe I am equal to it.'

'Of course you are! You are the strongest woman I know!'

She flushed a little at this, which he found adorable. They walked on a little further and finally, he knew he had to speak.

'I must speak to you of the future—of what will happen when your employment here ends.'

She was all attention. It actually looked as though she was holding her breath.

'I have learned that we cannot always have what we wish for. I do not wish to lose you, Daisy, but I cannot see a way forward for us.'

'Wh-what exactly are you saying?'

He exhaled. 'I have been honest with you about the state of my finances. It is imperative that I marry well. And I am sorry to say that marrying a housemaid would also not be the right thing to do.'

'So, did you make an offer to a lady last night?'

'I...did not.'

Her shoulders dropped, signalling relief.

'I tried to. Lord knows, I have tried for weeks to imagine myself leg-shackled to either of them. But—' he shook his head '—I cannot do it—not when you are the woman who fills my mind.' *And my heart.* The last he left unspoken, fearing it would make things harder for both of them. Still, it was the nearest he had come to telling her of his feelings—feelings that even now were threatening to overwhelm him. *Let us run away together—to America perhaps*, he wanted to say. With his skills and education, he could probably make a decent living there, in happiness with Daisy by his side.

But what of Bess? his conscience whispered. What of John, and the Stones, and all of them? Could he really leave them to the mercies of George Banfield?

No. I cannot. He had been raised to this responsibility, and could not abdicate. *I must do better than poor Papa managed.*

She was frowning, thinking deeply. She looked up at him.

'So, are you saying that we can never see one another again, Hart?'

Lord! Her words gave him a glimpse of a lonely future. *Never see one another again.*

He swallowed, drawing on every ounce of courage he had. Now was the time for honesty—no matter how brutal the truth might be. 'I cannot marry you, Daisy.

You must understand I am forced to marry someone else. But I want to keep you.' He took a breath. 'This is probably going to sound outrageous, and insulting, and I do not mean to offer you insult—'

She put a hand on his arm. 'Just tell me.'

'I should like to keep you—to pay all your bills, to rent a cottage for you, anywhere you choose. And I would ask you to wait for me.'

'For how long?'

He grimaced. 'Long enough to woo and marry an heiress, and get her with child. And I cannot do any of those things while you are near.' He ran a hand through his hair, as self-loathing shuddered through him. 'Lord, and I dare to criticise Forsyth? He is at least open with his wickedness, while here am I, cold-bloodedly planning to betray you, and to betray my future wife… No. It could never work.' Taking both her hands, he pressed them to his lips. 'Forgive me for even suggesting such a thing.'

Inwardly, he could almost hear his heart break. There was no solution but one. He had to let her go.

Tears were streaming down her cheeks. 'Oh, Hart, my Hart,' she was saying.

They clung to one another then, but she could not settle in his embrace.

'Hart! I, too, have something I need to tell you. And you will likely hate me for it.'

He kissed her. 'Never could I hate you, Daisy!'

She flinched, as if hating the sound of her name on

his lips. Now he was confused—and a little worried. What on earth was she about to say?

'You need to marry an heiress. I understand that.' She took a breath. 'If I were an heiress, would you marry me?'

'Of course! In a heartbeat!'

She nodded. 'Then, there is something I should tell you. I am indeed an heiress.'

He froze, bewilderment racing through him. That would indeed be the perfect solution, if it were true. But he could not simply go along with this delightful pretence and marry her. His sad situation meant the money itself was needed. It was as simple—and as cruel—as that.

He chuckled, trying to let her down lightly. 'I like that notion, and I absolutely would marry you, my heiress-housemaid, in the fairyland of our dreams.' Sobering, he added, 'Sadly, my responsibilities do not allow me to forget the real world—no matter how much I would wish it.'

She looked distressed. 'No really. *Truly.* Oh, Lord—I did not anticipate that you would not believe me. Well, naturally you do not. It is entirely unlikely, I suppose.' Her expression was earnest. 'I assure you, I am fabulously wealthy, and the people of Walton House are welcome to every last penny of it, so long as I can be your wife!'

He frowned. *Lord, she is lost, to have made up such a tale!* And it was he who had done this. He with his selfish extravagance. Oh, not the extravagance of gifts and money. No, he had bestowed on Daisy his time, his attention, and his demands. He had changed her from an innocent maid into—When he recalled some of the skills in which she had developed expertise these past weeks in the woods, he felt nothing but shame. He had ruined her, for his own selfish pleasure. *I have created a unique creature—an experienced virgin.*

Guilt rippled through him. He had been heedless of her future, her heart, her body... How would she explain her lack of innocence to a potential future husband? Oh, there would be a man who wanted her. But would he *love* her, knowing what she had done with another? Wrong as it was, virgins were expected to be...virginal. His head was whirling with confusion and regret, his stomach twisting with sick, sick guilt.

I have harmed her. Her heart had been engaged; he knew it as well as he knew her name. And worse, her fantastical story of being an heiress was surely a sign that her mind was temporarily disordered? This was no jest—she had been in earnest, just as though her fantasy tale could magically change his need for cash.

I must free her. But how? How could he undo weeks of courtship, the meeting of minds between them, the things they had said and done?

Foolishly, he had done the thing he had been determined never to do. He had fallen in love, and had behaved with the same degree of reckless abandon that had affected his father. Oh, it had played out differently, but the recklessness behind it was the same. And Daisy was paying for it. Would continue to pay for it, so long as she believed him to be some sort of hero from a Greek play.

Then I must fall from grace. Must show myself to be no hero, but rather, a villain. It would hurt her dreadfully, but in the end, it would sever the connection between them, something that must happen if she was to have any hope of a future.

'The truth is, Daisy...' he spoke slowly, his mind sluggish, 'I should never have dallied with you this summer.'

'D-dally?' Her eyes were wide, the colour draining from her face. 'Is that what this was? A dalliance?'

He managed a shrug. 'We both knew from the beginning it was all it could be, did we not?'

'I—I suppose so.' Her eyes searched his face. 'But I thought it had become something more.'

Now. Say it. Hurt her. 'Well, yes. The best dalliances tend to do that. But afterwards, one forgets.' He smiled, feeling as though it did not reach his eyes. 'I shall remember you with fondness, though. We had a good summer, did we not?'

Her throat was working, but no sound came out. Finally, she managed, 'I had thought so. I must now... I must now change my views, I think.' Her face was white as paper, and her shoulders shook. *Shock. Lord, what have I done?*

'I am sorry if I led you to believe we might have a

future together, Daisy,' he said softly. 'I cannot marry a servant, and you are too good to be my mistress. Somewhere out there is a good man who will wish to marry you some day.'

'Is there?' Her mouth twisted. 'I suspect I should prefer to remain unmarried, given the lessons I have learned this day.' Her eyes narrowed. 'I had not seen the truth before, but I see it now.' She laughed lightly. 'Lord, I have been a fool, dreaming of Cinderella, when all the time this entire episode has been exactly as sordid as others would view it.' She fixed him with a steely gaze. 'I hope you are proud of yourself, being the sort of man who seduces innocent housemaids. At least Mr Forsyth did it with violence, whereas you...' Her gaze showed contempt, and almost he wavered. But what would be the point? He had come this far. At least this way she would be freed from her *tendre* for him. 'You are the worst sort of man, I think, my lord.' Deliberately, she had chosen not to use his name.

'But I did not seduce you.' He could not help but remind her, stung by her disdain.

She sneered. 'Very clever, my lord. Yes, technically you did not *entirely* have your wicked way with me. But you have ruined me nevertheless.' She squared her shoulders. 'I expect we shall not speak again, my lord. I shall bid you farewell.'

Turning, she walked away, her head high and her shoulders rigid with control. As he watched her leave, it was all he could do to not call out to her, to fall on his knees before her and tell her the truth of his heart, begging for her forgiveness.

He watched until she was out of sight, then began making his own way slowly to the house. Hs guests would be descending for breakfast, and he must be there.

Duty called and, as always, he must be sacrificed to its demands.

Chapter Twenty-Three

Slowly, Sophia climbed the attic stairs, her mind and heart frozen with the shock of what had just happened. How many times had she climbed these stairs, these past weeks? And soon it would all end. *Thank the Lord.* Vaguely she remembered a fleeting notion at the start of the summer—that practiced rakes would be plausible, would seduce with flattering words and rehearsed kindnesses. She had thought it, then allowed herself to be taken by him anyway. Worse, he had not denied allowing his heart to become involved. *The best dalliances do that. And afterwards one forgets.*

She would never forget. Never. Neither the love, nor the betrayal he had just visited upon her. Oh, she had heard it said among women that men loved differently, but she had not believed it until now. He had shown her a sliver of his heart, all the while intending to break with her when he was done with her. She had been used for his dalliance, and was now discarded.

It was hard to comprehend or even fully remember

her relief this morning on hearing that he had *not*, after all, proposed to Lady Caroline—or Miss Chester for that matter. And that he had failed to do so because, according to him, his mind was filled with thoughts of her. And his heart? Perhaps a little, but not in a lasting way. She allowed herself to recall more of his words. He would marry her *in a heartbeat* if he could. Cynicism roiled within her, a hint of rage now boiling beneath her bewilderment. He had given her those words flippantly, yet they had come not from the heart, but from his cruelty. He would marry her in a heartbeat if she were an heiress, since he was physically attracted to her in a way that had not occurred with Lady Caroline or Miss Chester. Had either of those wealthy young ladies been a little cleverer with him, Sophia had no doubt the betrothal would already have been announced.

Anger and hurt warred within her in a cacophony of confusion, conducted by a deep cynicism. Whatever reaction she had anticipated to her finally telling Hart the truth, disbelief had not been part of it. Yet perhaps it did make sense, for why should he have believed her? Thank goodness he had not, for she might have ended up married to him—with his eyes on her money and his hands on his next 'dalliance', no doubt.

She had reached the top of the stairs—five flights, and never had they been harder to climb. Mary was coming along the narrow attic hallway. 'Ah, there you are, Daisy. All female servants are summoned to the servants' hall after the family and guests have breakfasted—even maidservants on their days off!'

Sighing, Sophia turned to follow Mary downstairs. There was no point going to her chamber, to give way to the pain within. Her rest would have to wait a little longer, it seemed. As would her ruminations. In truth her brain was too sluggish from lack of sleep, her heart too wounded by his cruelty, to fully figure anything out.

Hart watched the carriage depart with Cedric Forsyth inside, glad to see the back of him. He had not wished him well, nor engaged in any pleasantries with him. The man had decided to forego breakfast—presumably so that he would not have to face the surprised enquiries of his fellow guests as to why he was dressed for travel so early in the day, or why he was sporting a fine black eye. While many planned to leave today, such an early departure—and without the customary farewells—might draw comment. *George may explain Forsyth's sudden departure, if he can.*

Breakfast was something of an ordeal. A number of guests were clearly suffering from headaches and other consequences of freely imbibing the night before, and for most people, speech was at a minimum. George kept sending him angry glances—presumably on behalf of his friend—and Hart foresaw that he would be forced to speak with his cousin about Daisy's ordeal. Her *first* ordeal, that was. The second, she had been subjected to by Hart himself.

The Pashleys had clearly expected him to make Lady Caroline an offer last night. While Lord Pashley was his usual urbane self, Lady Caroline was stiffly correct, and her mother determinedly cheerful. The Chesters, all sharp eyes and interested expressions, kept looking from the Pashleys to Hart and back again, keenly interested, it seemed, in the fact that no betrothal was to be announced this morning. Between them and the garrulous Mrs Edgar, they maintained the bulk of the conversation, but their false liveliness was decidedly wearing.

Despite the guilty feelings within him with regard to his proposal, Hart was becoming increasingly certain he had made the right decision. Well, how was he supposed to credibly court other young ladies when he was head over ears in love with Daisy? The thought of facing Lady Caroline's coldness or Miss Chester's ebullience over the breakfast table for a lifetime filled him with horror. Surely there were other options?

As for his sisters, he dared not look at them. On the surface, both were behaving impeccably—as they had been raised to do. Yet he knew, with the instinct of a lifetime, that he would be held to account for his actions—or, in this case, his lack of action.

Once breakfast had finished and the guests dispersed to stroll around the grounds or gather in the drawing room, he made his way to his private study, there to pace, and worry, and wonder at all his choices—all the things he had done and not done. He was certain he would not remain undisturbed for long.

The servants' hall was a hubbub of conversation. Mary and Sophia slipped in at the back, wondering what it was all about. No one seemed to know.

A few moments later Mrs Stone appeared, Sally by her side. The room went quiet.

'I have called you together today primarily to thank you,' the housekeeper began. 'Last night's ball was, as you know, the first such event at Walton House in twenty-five years. Every one of you worked hard—far above your normal duties—and I wish you to know that I noticed and appreciated it. I thank you all.'

This earned a clap, and wide grins all around. Sophia could not help feeling a little proud at her part in it all. She had worked hard, too. Still, the events in the woods earlier had left her feeling as though she were back on the transatlantic packet. The world beneath her feet was uncertain and her new insight into Lord Hartington and being the subject of his 'dalliance' had left her reeling.

Mrs Stone was still speaking. 'As you know, we have had some additional temporary maidservants join us during the house party, and I am delighted to announce that we will be offering two of them a permanent position, should they accept it.' She paused. 'Jane Burrows, scullery maid!'

The girl gasped, then stepped forward. 'You may have some time to think about it if you wi—'

'I don't need no time, Mrs Stone,' the girl declared. 'I should love to stay!'

This earned a cheer, and a warm hug from one of the other scullery maids.

'We are also in need of a permanent upper housemaid,' the housekeeper began. She paused then, and Sophia was conscious that a number of eyes were now on her and Mary. *Lord, I hope Mary gets it!* Sophia was thinking.

'Mary Thorpe, step forward!'

'Well done!' Sophia touched her arm, needing to reassure Mary she was happy for her. Frowning, Mary stepped forward.

'I should like to keep you on as permanent staff, Mary,' said Mrs Stone.

'I am delighted to accept,' said Mary quietly, and again a round of cheers broke out.

Conversations then broke out all around the room, for one of the footmen had come in and was even now speaking quietly to Mrs Stone.

'I am so sorry, Daisy!' Mary was saying, having returned to Sophia's side. 'I wish they had kept you as well!'

'Honestly, Mary, all is well. I was hoping she would call your name. Now, when are you going to tell Reuben?' Strangely, Sophia's voice sounded reasonably normal. *Perhaps no one will even realise that my heart is breaking.*

Mary flushed, and Sophia was about to add another teasing comment, when Mrs Stone called for everyone's attention once more.

'I have just been informed,' she declared soberly, 'that two silver spoons are missing. This is a very serious matter, as they are worth a significant amount of money.' She named an amount that was more than a month's wage for an upper servant. 'A search must be mounted immediately. Those spoons must be found.'

Sophia, feeling decidedly guilty, immediately volunteered to help. What had she done with the two spoons on the terrace last night? She could not recall. But two spoons were missing, and it seemed likely that it was those two. So after Mrs Stone had dismissed them, Sophia went straight up to her and Sally, telling them that she had seen two spoons on the terrace last night, and offering to go and check instantly.

'Very well.' Mrs Stone inclined her head, and Sophia left, reflecting that both Sally and the housekeeper had seemed particularly cold, their visages wearing near-identical expressions that might have been carved from granite. No, surely she was imagining it? Or perhaps the spoons were a bigger concern than she thought.

Surprisingly, no one had come to his study yet, so Hart had decided to review the latest set of documents his steward had shared with him. The tidings were not good. Farm yields were no better than average, and repair work was needed on three of his tenants' houses. Since he could not very well deny people an intact roof, Hart knew he would have to approve the additional expenditure—which would reduce his reserves even further. Having already agreed to hiring a couple of extra female servants on a permanent basis—Mrs Stone had made a compelling case based on the amount of work required to maintain the house to a high standard—Hart knew his time to act was running short. Realistically, without an influx of funds by Christmas, he would have to make significant cuts in estate spending—letting servants go and completing only vital repairs. *Perhaps Daisy will be kept on.* Would that be a good thing, or no?

Sighing, he put away his papers and went to the window, staring out into the distance as if some solution might be found there.

Having searched the terrace and surrounding areas from end to end and back again, Sophia had found only one of the spoons. Having passed it to Cook, and knowing that others were still searching, she tried going over it all in her mind again. Nothing. The two spoons had been in her hand when Forsyth had grabbed her. The one she had found was close to that spot, so surely the other should have been nearby?

A little later, another meeting was called. This time all the manservants were there, too. One spoon was still missing, so the butler and housekeeper announced they had no option but to instigate a search of the servants' living quarters. At this, there were gasps all around. Surely they did not think that someone might have deliberately taken the spoon?

In answer to that exact question from one of the footmen, Mrs Stone replied grimly, 'We simply do not know. But we must find out. None of you are to go to your sleeping quarters until called. Everyone is to remain in this room.'

The butler then announced they would begin with a search of the footmen's chambers in the basement, and called a group of names, including Reuben. Sophia saw Reuben send Mary a reassuring glance, as if to tell her that he knew nothing of the missing cutlery and all would be well. Beside her, Mary's shoulders relaxed a little.

Once they had gone, a babble of conversation broke out all over the room. Mary turned to Sophia. 'Is it true you found one of the spoons? Where was it?'

'On the terrace. There should have been two, though. Last night there were two, but I searched the entire terrace just now and only found one of them. It makes no sense!'

'Have you told Mrs Stone?'

'Yes.' She paused. 'Do you think Mrs Stone is being particularly *stony* this morning?'

Mary smiled at her choice of words. 'She is very

concerned about the missing spoon—as she is right to be. It is worth a lot of money!'

'You are probably right.' But there was something more. Sophia could not exactly say what it was, but part of her yet-sluggish mind was worrying over it. 'Was Reuben pleased that you will be staying?'

Mary flushed. 'He was. Oh, Daisy, he has asked me to properly walk out with him!'

'Well of course he has!' Sophia hugged her friend. 'He is lucky to have you as his girl!'

'Well I do not know about that. I only know that I am the happiest girl in the world today.' *How odd!* This was probably one of the best days of Mary's life. Yet for Sophia…

'And I am delighted for you.' And she was. But Mary's evident happiness served only to underline Sophia's own concerns. How simple, in a way, it was for Mary and Reuben. They liked one another, they would walk out together, and unless something unusual or unexpected occurred, they would marry. She herself had chosen a different path. Reckless adventure. Nothing quiet, or simple, or usual about it. She had behaved with abandon and was now receiving her just rewards. And in two days she would leave here, never to see any of them again.

Chapter Twenty-Four

Finally, there was a knock on the door. With something suspiciously akin to relief, Hart turned from the window and invited whomever it was to enter. Best to get the difficult conversations done and over with.

'Cousin!' George was frowning, and Hart braced himself for unpleasantness. 'Why has Cedric left so suddenly?' he asked baldly, stepping inside and closing the door.

'What did he tell you?'

'Very little, save that you had insisted he leave. Why would you do such a thing?' George was purple with outrage.

Hart sat in one of the armchairs near the fireplace, inviting his cousin to be seated in the other. Huffily, George chose the sofa instead.

'How well do you know Mr Forsyth?'

George shrugged. 'Well enough. He is always about my set, and is invited everywhere.'

'I'll wager he does not get many repeat invitations, though.'

George's eyes widened. 'What has occurred?'

'He assaulted an innocent housemaid last night.'

George's jaw dropped. 'No! He would never— Why, he is as sound as any gentleman!'

'On what evidence do you base your assertion?'

'Well, he is my friend—and is friends with all my friends. We would know if he were a wrong 'un… Are you certain the maid did not lead him on, then pretend to be reluctant once seen?'

Revulsion turned Hart's stomach. 'Yes. I am a hundred per cent certain. She screamed for help, so I ran round from the front of the house to intervene.'

Unsurprisingly, George had nothing to say to this, so Hart pressed home his advantage. 'I cannot advise you, George, but if I could, I would tell you to be more discerning in your choice of friends.'

'Well, frankly, I do not believe your version of events.' He stood, straightening his waistcoat. 'And furthermore—' he glared at Hart, 'I would like to hear Cedric's story before I judge.'

Hart shrugged. 'You may do as you wish. But in future, you are not to bring any guest to this house without my express permission.'

With a curt nod, George was gone.

'Sally, Mary, and Daisy next please!'

Sophia followed the others upstairs and along to their little attic room.

'Stand by your beds, please!' Mrs Stone declared

crisply. 'Please place your belongings on your own beds.'

Bending, they all pulled out their bags and put them on the beds, as directed, then added anything else they owned from the little cupboard. Panic was now running through Sophia. *She will find my money, and ask how I acquired it!*

With minimal fuss, Mrs Stone searched through Sally's possessions, then all around and under her bed, checking under the mattress and pillow. She then moved on to Mary, and all the while Sophia was trying to work out how to explain her wealth.

I shall say it is the money left to me by my papa, plus savings I have made since. It is my old-age pension.

Mrs Stone had now reached Sophia, and frowned. 'Is something the matter, Daisy?'

'No, no, Mrs Stone. Nothing at all.' *Damnation!* Sophia could feel that she was sweating profusely—just as though she was indeed guilty of something. And there had been a decided tremble in her voice just now.

Yet I have nothing to fear. She had done nothing wrong.

But she did not wish for any drama associated with her—anything that might make things worse. These people—all of them—had become important to her. It was bad enough losing Hart—losing the man she had believed him to be. She did not wish to lose the respect she had here. Respect she had earned through honest toil, for the first time in her life.

Mrs Stone was rummaging through her bag. Sophia held her breath. An instant later she set the bag down and bent to check the space under the bed.

She did not find my coins! Whatever miracle had just occurred, Sophia was grateful for it. Perhaps it was simply that Mrs Stone was specifically seeking a spoon-shaped object…

Having checked under Sophia's pillow, and moving Sophia's tiny coin purse to the table, she then lifted the mattress—and froze. There, at the foot of Sophia's bed, was a silver spoon.

Sophia could not understand it. How did the spoon come to be under her mattress? Her mind was slow, befuddled, overcome by confusion.

'Daisy.' Mrs Stone's voice cracked. 'I am shocked, I must admit. I never took you for a thief.'

Thief! 'No! I am no thief! And I do not understand how it came to be there. I—'

Mrs Stone picked up the spoon, her expression like granite. 'You may have five minutes to pack up your things. Ensure you leave every part of your uniform on the bed. I shall ask one of the grooms to drive you to Derby—an act of kindness you do not, I think, deserve.'

Sophia just stood there silently, unable to think or speak. *What on earth is happening?*

'Come, Mary.' Mrs Stone made for the door. 'Sally, stay here and check the uniform.' Sally nodded grimly. Mary, Daisy saw, was crying, silent tears running down her face.

Hart must not think I did this! 'Mrs Stone!' the cry erupted from Sophia. 'May I speak to the master? He—'

'You may not!' Mrs Stone turned back, her expression full of anger. 'The very fact you would ask for such a thing gives credence to certain rumours I have been hearing.' She glanced briefly towards Sally, whose expression was equally grim. 'I shall have you know that I do not employ that sort of girl here.' She shook her head sadly. 'I thought I knew you, Daisy, but I did not know you at all.'

Daisy felt colour suffuse her face and neck. *That sort of girl.* Was that who she was now? Her parents would certainly think so, if they knew what she and Hart had been doing every Thursday. Hart had thought so too, and had set out to ruin her, for his own entertainment.

Then Mrs Stone was gone, and Mary too, and now there was only Sally, who was avoiding her eyes. Slowly, she removed her uniform, donning again Daisy's simple dress and shawl. As she folded her apron and dress, setting her little cap on top of them, Sophia felt something akin to grief run through her.

Her adventure was over, and it had ended in the most ignominious manner. Daisy would forever be remembered as a thief and a—what was the word Forsyth had used? *A light-skirt.* That was it. Someone who lifted her skirts for a man—as Sophia had done for Hart, many times.

Shame lanced through her—not simply because she

regretted her intimacies with Hart, but because of how others would judge her for it. They mattered to her, these people. Mrs Stone. Her husband, the head gardener. John, the head groom. All the maids. Mary. And now every one of them would think of her as a thief and a woman of easy virtue.

As she made her way down the back stairs and out through the servants' door, Sally at her heels, she felt numb, unable to plan or think. Grief and shame overwhelmed her, compounded by loss. There was no way to contact Hart, and she had no idea what to do about that. He had not cared for her anyway. *Perhaps it is better this way.*

A groom was waiting with the cart, his face rigid with disapproval. She climbed up beside him, avoiding his eyes, then sat stiffly as they began the journey to Derby, leaving Walton House behind forever.

Chapter Twenty-Five

'Come in!'

Hart stifled a sigh as the door opened, admitting both his sisters. While entirely expected, still he found himself having to brace himself to face their disapproval.

'Good morning again, Hart.'

'Good morning.' Rising from his desk, he seated himself in his preferred armchair, noting that Eliza and Louisa chose to sit together on the same sofa recently vacated by George Banfield. 'This is an unexpected pleasure,' he lied.

Eliza sniffed. 'It can hardly be unexpected, brother.'

'Oh?' He feigned confusion. 'How so?'

'You must know that everyone expected you to offer for the young lady of your choice at last night's ball. It was the perfect opportunity.' Louisa went straight to the point, her expression signalling frustration, disappointment, and anger. 'And yet, you have failed to do so, Hart. Why?'

Her use of words was interesting. 'The young lady

of my choice...' Daisy was his choice—or would be, if he were not constrained by circumstances. 'Tell me, how much choice did you have in the selection of a husband? As I recall, Mr Smyth was suggested for you by Mama, Louisa, but you seemed perfectly content with the suggestion.'

Louisa shrugged. 'He is a good man, and I am content.' She eyed him fiercely. 'I knew my duty.'

'And what of you, Eliza? Mr Dawson was *not*, as I recall, Mama's first choice for you. Indeed I seem to recollect some conflict between you on the matter.'

'It is true,' Eliza conceded. 'Our parents felt I could do better. But I loved him, you see.' She frowned. 'What is it you are trying to say, Hart? That you love someone else?'

'That is not what I am saying.' *That secret must rest within me.* 'I am saying I should have a choice.'

'But you had a choice!' Eliza countered. 'Both Lady Caroline and Miss Chester are perfectly eligible!'

'Then you should take them into your home. I promise you, you shall soon grow tired of them at your breakfast table or dinner table day after day.'

They exchanged a glance, then Eliza said, 'He has a point, sister. I found both young ladies intensely irritating, and I am not sure that either of them deserves to be mistress of Walton House.'

'But the finances! The dowry!' Louisa's brow was deeply furrowed.

Hart bit his lip, before continuing in a more measured

tone. 'I do not wish to insult either young lady. I am sure they will make perfectly good wives for someone.'

'But not you.' Louisa was yet to be convinced.

'Not me, no.'

Louisa sighed. 'But you must marry, Hart. The estate...'

'I know it.' He squared his shoulders. 'When do you make for London?'

'Not until later in the month.'

Eliza spoke up. 'I shall go in just a few days. I am still your hostess, you will recall, and so I need to ensure the townhouse is ready for us.'

'Then I shall follow you, Eliza. I shall attend all the balls and soirées you wish. I shall even go to Almack's. And I swear to choose a bride by Christmastide.' He sighed. 'Possibly even Lady Caroline or Miss Chester, if there is no one more suitable.' He shrugged. 'Despite what you may think, I do know my duty. I just—perhaps in London I might find a lady who has a good dowry and whom I can also tolerate!' He grimaced. 'Lord, it is a bad business, to be thinking of choosing a bride in such a way.'

Somewhat mollified, they agreed to this, departing with wry looks and a determination to be cheerful during this, the last day of the party. Many of the guests were supervising their packing at present, and he foresaw that the next few hours would be a flurry of farewells. He wandered to the window again, but thankfully no carriages had yet been brought round, meaning he could remain in the sanctuary of his study a little while longer.

In the distance, a cart rumbled down the drive, two figures atop it, though it was too far away for him to see which servants were in it. No matter. Whoever they were, they relied on him for their future livelihood—for food and shelter and security. And he would not—could not fail them.

At least I will see Daisy again for the next couple of days. See her, but only to feel the disdain she now felt for him, the hurt he had inflicted on her. Losing Daisy would be, he knew, the hardest thing he had ever faced. Never again would he ridicule love poems that spoke of heartbreak. Despite the arrogant assumptions of his former self, he now knew it was all too real.

Finally they were in Derby. Sophia had sat stiff and silent beside the disapproving groom all the way there. How different it had been to her original journey to Walton House, conversing easily with John atop the high carriage. She had been filled with hope then, and vivacity, and that sense of adventure had thrummed through her veins.

And now? As she jumped down from the cart and hefted her bag, politely thanking the groom, her spirits were low.

Without so much as a word the groom drove off, and this, the slightest of insults—for she barely knew the man—cut Sophia to the quick. As a child she had been chastised on occasion by those with a right to do so—her parents and teachers—but once she had become Miss Van Bergen she had been fawned over and feted everywhere she went.

The experience of being Daisy had been good in that sense. Until today's disaster—and she would dearly love to know who had schemed to discredit her by placing the missing spoon under her mattress—she had worked hard, and had earned respect through her own merits and efforts.

While being delighted for Mary, she could not help but feel a pang of disappointment that she, too, had not been offered a permanent position. Not that she wanted or needed it. But it would have been good to know that Mrs Stone had valued her.

And she *had*. Sophia was almost certain of it. At least until it emerged that Daisy was a thief and a light-skirt. *That sort of girl.* Mrs Stone had mentioned rumours of her involvement with the Earl. Had that influenced her selection of Mary for the permanent role? But then again, Mary was an excellent maid.

Belatedly realising she was standing by the side of the street staring into space, Sophia came back to the present. There was now no point in making for London, for she needed to go directly to New York, and never again return to England. And if Mama arrived in Liverpool after her departure, it mattered not. She could leave a letter with the Black Ball shipping company, explaining to Mama that she had changed her mind and was returning to New York. She could also write to Daisy to instruct her to tell the Earl she was returning to New York, then disappear. Lord Linford would be none the wiser.

Her decision made, she walked slowly to the coaching inn where she had arrived, innocent and hopeful, and with a heart that was fully intact, all those weeks ago. A coach was waiting outside, but the driver told her he was making for Newcastle, not Liverpool. No, he had no idea when the next coach to Liverpool would leave, but the company man inside would know.

The ruddy-haired man inside did know, and informed Sophia that the Liverpool coach would leave in an hour. That was timely, for she really should eat something before setting off. Not that she felt like eating. But last night's supper had been a long time ago, and she had a long day ahead.

The ticket prices were on the sign by the door, and she stepped aside to check her coin purse. Today she would have to pay for food, and the coach ticket, and her ticket to New York, as well as needing a room to stay in tonight.

Soon she would be on her way back to New York, there to recover, and forget, and hopefully never again open her heart to the devastation she was currently feeling. *But no.* She dared not think of him now. There were things to be done.

Finding a quiet corner, she decided to carefully take out some of her precious sovereigns and add them to her coin purse. Her passage to New York would be expensive, and it was probably safer to do it here than at the Liverpool docks. Rummaging through her bag, she could not initially find her coin bundle. Telling herself not to panic, she lifted the bag on to the bench beside her so she could search it thoroughly and methodically. One by one she removed her meagre belongings, hoping each time that the bundle would be mixed among them.

It was not there. Her money was gone.

The feeling that shuddered through her was like nothing she had ever experienced. Shock, Fear. Trepidation. On top of the heartbreak, shame, and disgrace she already carried.

Now she was truly exposed, without even her reserve fund to cover her. What on earth was she going to do?

Chapter Twenty-Six

By mid-afternoon the house was remarkably quiet. The Pashleys and Chesters had gone, as had George and his garrulous mother, thank goodness. Many of the remaining guests had retired to their chambers to rest, given the effect of last night's exertions. Hart therefore found himself unexpectedly free. And so, after nuncheon—when, disappointingly, Daisy had not made an appearance—he decided to ride out alone.

Making his way to the stables, he wandered about to talk to a few of the grooms, thanking them for the extra work they had done in looking after the horses and carriages of the guests during the ball.

John was relaxed about it all, which did not surprise Hart in the slightest.

'Ah, I knew all would be well,' he declared. 'It usually turns out so in the end.'

As the stable boy led Hart's horse towards them, he wondered aloud if he had omitted anyone in his thanks.

'Aye, you won't have seen Sam, for he's off in the cart to bring that serving maid to Derby.'

About to nod and ignore this, some instinct made Hart ask, 'Which serving maid? And for what reason is she in Derby?'

'Young Daisy has been let go—and without a reference as I understand. No one seems to know why, though apparently there was a silver spoon gone missing, I heard.'

Hart felt the ground beneath his feet sway alarmingly, blood draining from his head and limbs and leaving him feeling strangely weak.

'What? Daisy?'

John was looking concerned. 'Aye. A pity, for I liked her. I should never have taken her for a thief.' He eyed Hart closely. 'My lord! Are you unwell?' Reaching out, he made as if to touch Hart's arm.

Daisy is gone?

Pain arced through him, heart-deep and potent, followed by a surge of anger. Abruptly, he could move again. Turning on his heel, he ordered, in a tone he had never before used with any servant—never mind John, 'Prepare my carriage and bring it round. My valet must pack for me, but I shall travel alone. And send Mrs Stone to my study, instantly!'

'Yes, my lord.'

Daisy's mind had frozen for what seemed like an age, but now, slowly, she was able to think again. There was no point in going to Liverpool to wait for Mama, for what if she could not find her? She had not the money to pay for her passage home. And she could not return to Walton House. She was disgraced, and Hart had no regard for her.

So she had only one option. She had to try and reach London, to get money from the real Daisy, and from Aunt Agatha's man of business. Then she could return to Liverpool and buy her ticket. There was time, for Mama would not arrive for another few days.

Repacking her bag, she returned to the door. The ruddy-haired man had gone, and a balding fellow with a mustard-coloured waistcoat stood in his place.

'How much for London?'

'London coach doesn't stop here, lass. You need the King's Head. Or the Lion. Or even the Old Bell.'

'Thank you. Er—which is closest?'

Luckily the King's Head was in the next street, but when she was told the cost of a ticket to London, her heart sank. She did not have enough money.

She swallowed hard. 'Is there a cheaper option?'

'There is. You could take the slow coach, but I warn you, it will not arrive until Monday afternoon.'

'How much for that one?'

Thankfully, the price was just about within reach, and she nodded, relief coursing through her. 'Very well. I should like to buy a ticket please.'

The stagecoach man glanced at the clock. 'You're in luck, for that particular coach only comes through here on Thursdays and Sundays. They only have three of 'em, see?'

She didn't see, not at all, but nodded anyway.

'It should pass through here in about twenty minutes, lass.'

'Thank you.' A notion struck her. She needed Daisy to leave Kent and meet her in London. 'If I wished to send a letter to Kent, when would it get there?'

'Just two days, lass. The mail coach is the fastest thing in England.'

And so she bought from him some paper, borrowed his pen, and scribbled a short note to Daisy, letting her know she expected to be in London on Monday afternoon, as per the schedule of the slow coach. 'That'll be one penny, please, miss,' he declared. 'For the post.'

'Of course.' Never had she minded so much giving away a penny. Never had she so keenly understood the value of one. But she had a ticket, and her letter was written, and she had to hope that all would be well once she reached London.

Twenty minutes later she was in the coach, squeezed between a burly farmer's wife holding a caged chicken on her lap, and a man who smelled of onions. Having paid her fare—which included a simple dinner each evening and a few hours' rest at various inns each night, she had only two shillings left. *Two shillings!* There were street beggars with more money than her. Passengers on this route were expected to buy their own breakfasts—something that would be beyond her means.

Panic rose within her and ruthlessly, she pushed it down. If she could only reach Daisy, all would be well.

Hart paced up and down his study, filled with rage. How dared they dismiss Daisy? How dared they?

Telling himself to be calm, he stood by the window, recalling that he had actually seen the cart disappear down the drive around two hours ago. He had a few minutes to spare while his carriage and bags were prepared, and each second ticking by felt like an eternity.

There was a scratching at the door. 'You wished to see me, my lord?'

'I did.' He turned to face Mrs Stone. 'Why was Daisy dismissed?'

Her expression hardened. 'For theft. The missing silver spoon was found under her mattress.'

'And what makes you think she put it there?'

Her jaw dropped. 'Well, it was *her* bed. Yes, and there was something in her demeanour, too. She looked guilty, my lord.'

'She looked guilty? *Looked guilty?* This is what you have to say to me?' His rage was white-hot. 'I must hope, Mrs Stone,' he added, through gritted teeth, 'that should I ever face a judge, it will be someone with a little more discernment, insight and intelligence than you have just displayed.'

Her face was pale, yet she stood her ground. 'So what

would you have had me do, my lord? And before you reply, I should tell you that there have been rumours about Daisy.'

'Rumours? What rumours?'

Mrs Stone drew herself up, an expression of disdain crossing her face. 'I do not employ women of that nature here.'

There was a silence, as Hart tried to take in what the housekeeper was saying. Daisy was being judged for her trysting with him?

'And did you tell her this, Mrs Stone?' His tone was deceptively mild.

She lifted her chin. 'I did. And I stand by it!'

'Then perhaps you shall stand by it in some other household!'

She gasped. 'What? I—what?'

'I am considering dismissing you, Mrs Stone. I find myself unsure if I can continue to employ a woman of your *nature*.'

She swayed, reaching out to grasp the back of a chair. 'M-my nature?'

'Judgemental. Lacking in discernment. Daring to comment on *my* activities and choices.'

She put a hand to her mouth. 'You are right! I am sorry, my lord. I allowed my emotions to colour my judgement. It is just… I pride myself on everything being perfect, and—'

'Allow me to inform you, Mrs Stone, that I am not perfect, and I do not expect perfection in my servants.

What I do expect, though, is for people to be treated fairly while under my care. Irrespective of any connection I may have with Daisy, I believe you acted unjustly towards her. Now tell me, was she given her full pay?'

'I—no.' She hung her head. 'I did not pay her anything.'

'So you sent a young girl out with barely a penny in her pocket, because you had judged her and found her wanting? Despite the fact she has worked hard here for nigh on two months? Is that it?'

'I did, my lord. I—I thought…' Her voice trailed away.

'But you did not think, did you, Mrs Stone? Daisy was and is under our care, and if anything should befall her, I shall hold you personally responsible. Now get out of my sight.'

He turned away before he would say more. While he wanted to punish her, he knew that to dismiss his housekeeper for this one—albeit monumental—error of judgement would be disproportionate.

'Thank God!' Arthur, one of his grooms, had appeared outside, driving his best carriage, and as he watched his valet handed a travelling bag up, Arthur securing it atop the coach. Taking a sizeable amount of cash from his strongbox, he hurried outside, telling his valet to follow him to London in the coming days, then climbing into the carriage with a single, terse word to Arthur.

'Derby.'

'Yes, my lord.'

Seconds later the carriage was thundering down the drive.

The coach rumbled along. Derby was now gone, and Sophia knew she would never see it again. Never see Derby, nor Walton House, nor Mary, nor the other servants.

Nor Hart. *Hart, my heart.* The Hart of her imagination. She closed her eyes tight to stop tears from falling, conscious of onion-man snoring beside her, and chicken-woman looking out of the window to her left.

What would they tell him? Would he be told that she was a thief, and if so, would he believe it? *No. Surely not.* He knew her better than that.

As to how the missing spoon came to be under her mattress, she still had no idea. It was a clear, deliberate act of malice, and she was unused to the sensation that someone felt so angry with her that they had done such a dreadful thing. Methodically, she reviewed her interactions with every one of the servants—for it had to have been a servant, and most likely a female, since men were not permitted to venture to the attics, where the maidservants slept.

Sally? But no. Sally had seemed just as shocked as everyone else when the spoon had been discovered. And, although she was a little stiff and standoffish, Sophia had had no unpleasantness with her.

Though it may well have been Sally who had suspected her liaison with the Earl, she reflected, recalling the look that had passed between Sally and the housekeeper, the times when Sally may have seen or heard things that hinted at Sophia's activities in the woods.

What will Mary think of me? A pang went through her. Although Sophia's attention had been elsewhere for much of her time at Walton House, she had spent hours and hours in Mary's company, and had thought of her as a true friend. And now they would never see one another again, and Mary's memory of her would be forever stained. *At least she has her Reuben.*

In the midst of what felt suspiciously like grief, Sophia could only be glad for her friend. *Love, live well, and be happy*, she thought, sending good wishes in Mary's direction. At least someone had a happy ending. As Cinderella, she herself had missed the ball, and no one was coming to find her to try the glass slipper.

Hart had never before realised how many public coaches departed from Derby—and to all parts of the country. Having assumed Daisy would either be looking for work, or travelling, he had decided to seek news of her in all of the hostelries in the town, striking lucky at the fourth inn, where a ruddy-haired man vaguely remembered a brown-haired maid asking about coaches to Liverpool.

Liverpool! It made sense, for she had come from there, and she had clearly loved New York. They had not spoken of her future plans, and Hart cursed himself for not being more curious about whether she had another post lined up. Perhaps, despite being deprived of her Walton House wages, she had a ticket to America for another post? Or perhaps she was simply planning to seek work upon reaching the port town? Either way, he knew he must go there instantly, despite the fact he had sent his valet to London.

A bald man in a mustard-coloured waistcoat was standing nearby, and stepped forwards to disagree with his colleague. 'If it's the lass I'm thinking of, she wanted the London stage, not Liverpool, my lord.'

London! That made sense too, particularly if Daisy urgently needed work. While the two men debated, Hart stood silent, desperately unsure. *Daisy, where are you?*

The men had come to a conclusion, figuring that the London conversation had taken place *after* the Liverpool one. 'And where will the stage rest overnight?'

They scratched their heads at this, suggesting Birmingham, Coventry, Rugby, or Northampton, depending on which stage she had taken. Sadly, the man in the waistcoat could not recall which London coach she had opted for. He had sold many tickets for many coaches today, he stated regretfully, to Hart's frustration. *Well, that is not particularly helpful!* Still, at least he knew her ultimate destination—or hoped he did.

Belatedly he thought of his sisters, who would have to make his excuses with the remaining guests. Scribbling a quick note to them, which he passed to the stage-men for delivery, he explained that he had been called away on urgent business, and that he was sure they would say all that was correct to the guests. They would be displeased, he knew, but at this moment he cared not.

They may all go to the devil! In this he included not just his family and guests, but the servants who had treated Daisy so appallingly.

Thanking both men, he pressed a coin into each of their hands then returned to his carriage.

'London,' he said.

'Yes, my lord.' Arthur looked as though he wished to say something else.

'Well?'

'It is fairly late in the day, my lord. We can perhaps stop in Leicester tonight? And change horses in Northampton and Luton tomorrow?'

'Whatever you think best. Can we be in London tomorrow?'

'Yes, my lord. By evening, leastways.'

As to how he might find one particular serving maid on the road or in the capital, he had no idea. His mind was entirely focused on the challenges in simply following her. The stage coaches were long gone—she was more than three hours ahead, so even the fastest horses might not catch her. And besides, he could not guess her route.

Ten minutes later they had left Derby behind and he was on his way to London.

Chapter Twenty-Seven

It was after around eight o'clock on Thursday evening when Hart's well-sprung carriage pulled into the Blue Boar in Leicester. His groom checked with the landlord, returning to say that my lord could have a bedchamber for the night, although the landlord was sorry to say he would have to share the private parlour with two other travellers. Waving this away, Hart confirmed they would stop for the night, and exited the carriage.

During this first part of the journey he had encountered two public coaches, and stopped both to investigate. Sadly, Daisy had not been in either of them, and to his dying day he believed he would remember the bewildered faces of the passengers, who had clearly suspected him of having run mad.

And perhaps I have. There was something of madness in love, he conceded. Thoughts and memories of Daisy consumed him. Nothing else mattered but that he should find her and ensure her safety. Somewhere in the back of his mind he vaguely knew there could be no future for them, but that was less important than undoing the wrong done to her by Mrs Stone, and Forsyth, and all of them. While he could not marry her, and had even deliberately hurt her to try and help her let him go, never had he wished her any harm. Indeed, it was his highest priority that no one should harm her. *Ever.*

Forsyth! Having wracked his brain trying to work out who would have held animosity towards such a sunny character as Daisy, he had theorised that perhaps another serving maid was jealous of her—particularly if rumours had indeed been circulating that she and Hart were trysting—but it had not sat easily with him. Now there was a new possibility—that Forsyth had done it to punish her. But how? When? The man had been foxed… Vaguely, Hart now recalled something metallic protruding from the man's waistcoat. Or was his mind playing tricks on him?

But no. Forsyth had been to the attics before, for had Hart not seen him with his own eyes? *An interest in architecture? I think not.* He would not put it past Forsyth to be exploring the attics with more nefarious purposes in mind—wandering amid the maids' sleeping quarters, working out who slept where, getting some sick pleasure from creeping among their possessions… He shuddered.

As the inn staff fussed about him—the unanticipated arrival of an earl sending them into quite a fluster—he reflected that, wherever Daisy was tonight, she would not be meeting the same level of attention. He only hoped she was safe.

Sophia had managed to sleep for quite some time, flushing when she realised her head had been resting on chicken-woman's shoulder.

'Ah, never worry, lass!' she said, chuckling at Sophia's stuttered apologies. 'I'm glad to see you got some rest.'

The coach had stopped, and chicken-woman told her they were in Wolverhampton, and would soon have dinner. Relieved to be able to step out and stretch her aching body, Sophia accompanied chicken-woman into the inn, where she ate every morsel of the simple meal, before climbing back into what surely must be the slowest coach in England. Around midnight they stopped again somewhere—Sophia had no idea where—and she was shown to an attic where she fell into an exhausted sleep on a thin pallet on the floor amid female travellers and the inn's maids.

Hart's evening had improved, a little. What he needed most was distraction, and he found it in the shape of a middle-aged lady in the parlour reserved for members of the gentry and the aristocracy. On arriving he had been fully distracted by his own thoughts, but when his fellow guests had introduced themselves he had instantly honed in on the lady, his attention caught when she had said her name.

'A pleasure to meet you, Mrs Van Bergen,' he declared. 'My apologies for disturbing your peaceful dinner. I am Hartington.'

'Hartington, eh?' she asked. 'I knew the fourth Earl.'

'I am his son,' Hart confirmed. 'My father died six years ago.'

'I am sorry to hear it, Lord Hartington,' she offered. 'It is a long time since I came to England. I must be ready for similar tidings about others of my acquaintance, I suppose.' She indicated the seat opposite her own. 'Please join me, my lord.' Beyond perfunctory greetings both ignored the other guest—a Mr Speers, who had already finished his meal and was even now departing for his chamber.

So Hart sat with Mrs Van Bergen, and they spent two full hours in animated conversation, facilitated by good food and wine. Mrs Van Bergen, as he had surmised, was lately arrived from New York, and while there was no mention of his friend Linford, she indicated she was on her way to London to meet with her daughter, who had preceded her across the ocean.

'Sadly,' she informed him, 'my sister died during the crossing, and so my daughter is currently alone in England—apart from her servants. As soon as I received her letter I knew I had to come here directly, and thankfully the ship made excellent time as it crossed the Atlantic—indeed, the captain informed me that we arrived a full six days earlier than expected. Something to do with westerlies.'

'I am sorry to hear that. Your sister is—was—Lady Agatha Palmer? Am I correct in saying so? If so, she and my own sister are—were—well-acquainted.'

She gave him a warm smile. 'And this is why it is always a joy to visit England. In America, no one knows my background, or my family—though my husband is well-known.'

This provided him with the opening he had been waiting for. 'Will you tell me something of your life there? I have always wished to visit America.'

She obliged, and for the next hour he felt closer to Daisy—simply because Mrs Van Bergen was speaking of New York, where his beloved had lately spent some time. While Daisy had carefully never mentioned the name of her employer, he amused himself by imagining her working in the Van Bergen household. And it was a perfectly plausible notion, given how few ladies made a habit of crossing the Atlantic.

Mrs Van Bergen was likeable, sensible, and clever, and before long she had invited him to refer to her as Lady Harriet. 'Mrs Van Bergen is my American self. Here in England I find myself to be Lady Harriet again.'

Glancing at his pocket watch, he realised how late was the hour, and that he wished to be back on the road to London early in the morning. His groom was no doubt already snoring somewhere.

'Do you travel on tomorrow, Lady Harriet?'

She made a face. 'Sadly not, for my hired carriage has a broken axle, and it will apparently take two days to repair it.'

The solution was obvious. 'Then you must allow me to take you there. And your maid, of course.'

'That is very generous of you. Thank you, my lord.'

'We shall be in London by nightfall tomorrow, Lady Harriet.'

Waking with a stiff neck and a mark on her leg that she strongly suspected was a flea bite, Sophia rose groggily and made her way downstairs with the other female passengers. While they went to the taproom to order breakfast, Sophia went outside and drank her fill of water from the well in the inn yard, knowing it would only temporarily stave off hunger pangs. Then they all piled back into the carriage again, and Sophia braced herself for another day of tedium in a rumbling coach, supplemented by heartbreak, exhaustion, and with the added sauce of gnawing hunger. It would be a long, long time until dinner.

Friday morning passed easily, Hart and Lady Harriet continuing to deepen their acquaintance, while her abigail looked out of the window. At one point they passed another stage coach, Hart swiftly running his eyes over the passengers inside as they passed. While he could not today stop the coach for a detailed inspection as he had done yesterday, still he was fairly certain his Daisy had not been in this coach either.

'…a good thing she had my sister's maid with her. Young Daisy was a sensible girl.'

His head whipped round. 'Did you say Daisy?'

'I did. She was my sister's personal maid for her trip to New York.'

I knew it! His heart leapt, for here was an opportunity to speak of the woman he loved. 'How curious!'

'Why so, my lord?'

'One of the temporary maids at Walton House for my summer party was called Daisy—and she had lately travelled to New York.'

She shrugged. 'It is undoubtedly the same girl, my lord. There are not many temporary English maids who get such an opportunity. My sister only hired Daisy because her own abigail suffers dreadfully from seasickness.'

He shook his head in wonder at the coincidence, even as Lady Harriet's conversation moved on to her own daughter, and wishing again that she knew her Sophia was safe. But it was not truly a coincidence, was it? The only reason he had singled Lady Harriet out initially was because of her connection to Linford, and to New York. And as she rightly pointed out, very few temporary servants would ever be offered such an opportunity.

Had Lady Agatha's housekeeper hired her, he wondered? Or her steward? Did she even have a steward?

He frowned, recalling Lady Harriet's unaccompanied, vulnerable daughter.

'Will your daughter have been able to access funds in your absence, Lady Harriet?'

'Oh, yes,' she declared blithely. 'My husband gave her a bag of English sovereigns to take with her, and Agatha has a man of business…now, what is his name? Lynch! Yes, Mr Lynch will surely have the common sense to keep the household solvent until I get there. But the sooner I can get there, the better.'

As she spoke, there was a shout from the driver. 'Slow down, idiot!' he roared, at the same time pulling up his own horses. Instinctively bracing himself, Hart stretched a hand out across Mrs Van Bergen, as the carriage shuddered and reeled—first right, then left, and the sound of another carriage thundered towards them from the opposite direction.

Whatever evasive action Arthur had been attempting was only partly successful, for a moment later a team of four horses swept into view, their ears back and nostrils flaring in fear. *They are bolting*, Hart realised, before the other carriage crashed into the side of his own, sending them overturning into the ditch.

Chapter Twenty-Eight

Hours went by, and towns, and villages. Sophia had no idea where she was at present, and only vaguely recalled that it was now Friday. Which meant it had been just yesterday morning when she and Hart had walked in the woods, and he had not believed her when she had told him she was an heiress. When he had broken her heart. It felt as though a week had passed since then. Or a month, maybe.

'Whoa!' The stagecoach driver pulled up, and the passengers began clamouring to see why. There were currently six people in the interior of the coach, including onion-man and chicken-woman, and by the time Sophia's groggy mind began to react, the others had all half-risen and were looking out the window on the left-hand side, clamouring about a carriage accident of some kind.

'Empty!' declared the driver. 'Nothing to see! Right-o!' He clicked his tongue. 'Walk on!'

As her fellow passengers retook their seats and the

coach moved on, Sophia managed to see a glimpse of the wheels and underside of a carriage, which was lying on its side at the side of the road. *Lord! I hope no one was badly injured!* One thing was for certain—her troubles, bad as they were, could be worse. Much worse. She was intact, well and healthy, and headed for wealth and luxury. If hunger pains were gnawing at her at present, they would soon end. But for the poor unfortunates in the crashed carriage, who knew what injuries had befallen them?

The coach rumbled on, and eventually the other passengers stopped exclaiming, settling instead into the same hopeless silence that had preceded the accident.

That became the pattern for Sophia's days—a slow trundling of the coach along England's roads, a single meal each day, and sleeping in flea-ridden cots or pallets at night. *I deserve every punishment I am receiving*, was a half-coherent thought that flitted through her mind on the Sunday night. It was clearly justice for the way in which she had deceived everyone around her these past two months. The abandoned way in which she had behaved with Ha—with the rake for whom she had lifted her skirts.

Still, tomorrow she would be in London—although the notion did not seem quite real to her. Surely she would be stuck in this life forever, like Sisyphus or Tantalus, destined to repeat the same actions for all eternity, with never any satisfaction or resolution?

The Barley Mow in Watford was their final stop,

though it was now fully dark and Sophia could barely see the shape of the building. After dinner, she and chicken-woman—whose name was actually Mrs Coates—were allocated a small room under the eaves with two narrow beds. Not a pallet! Gratefully, Sophia half-undressed and sank down upon it, asleep almost before her head had hit the thin pillow.

In no time, it seemed, it was three o'clock, and time to leave. The inn servant who woke them had brought drinking water for each of them, and Sophia—despite feeling decidedly sluggish—drank every drop by the light of a tallow candle, knowing it would be the last sustenance she would get until she reached Daisy. And it already seemed a long time since dinner last night.

According to the coachman they would be in London by early afternoon, which was helpful. The last thing Sophia needed was for Daisy to be out when she arrived, but if that happened in the afternoon, then at least it would still be daylight when she called back a few hours later. As she settled into the seat beside Mrs Coates—onion-man having left them the day before—Sophia felt the beginnings of anxiety sprout within her. She had gambled away the bulk of her money on the ticket to London. Would she have been better seeking work in Derby and building up some cash, in case something should go awry in London?

Too late. It was done now. She and her two shillings were committed to their path.

* * *

After only six hours sleep, Hart was awake again, the result of a nightmare disturbing his sleep. In his fevered dream, Daisy had been sailing away to New York while he was standing on the quay, unable to reach her. Why, there might be a ship leaving for America this very morning! What if she had been bound for Liverpool all along, and his wild run to London had been entirely misconceived? No, there was nothing he could do about it, save continue on his way to London with Lady Harriet, and perhaps discover more about Daisy from those who had hired her—Lady Agatha's man of business. Mrs Stone, his own housekeeper. Vaguely he recalled mention of an agency.

Less than an hour later, having partaken of a decent breakfast, Hart was inspecting his new hired carriage. Thankfully it seemed sound, and comfortable enough to house Lady Harriet and her personal maid.

While none of his party had suffered serious injury—Arthur having been flung clean into a patch of brambles, and Hart having somehow protected Lady Harriet from harm—they had all been bruised and shaken, and the serving maid, Ellen, had suffered a sprained wrist. They had thought it broken at first, and Hart had spent the past two days in an inadequate inn in the middle of nowhere, dealing with doctors and carriage-makers.

Mr Rowntree, who had been called from Dunstable, described himself as the best wheelwright and carriage-maker in Bedfordshire. He vowed to haul Hart's carriage from the ditch today, and would begin the repairs with all haste. In the meantime he was honoured to offer my lord and his travelling companions the use of Mr Rowntree's own travelling coach.

An hour later they were on their way, Mr Rowntree's man atop with Arthur, Ellen nursing her right arm in a sling, and Lady Harriet leading the conversation with cheerful determination. Here, if his sister Eliza was to be believed, was his friend Linford's future mother-in-law. *Yes, Linford was able to sacrifice himself to the extent of becoming betrothed to an heiress he has never laid eyes on, yet I...* His mind shied away from completing the thought: guilt and shame were never far away.

Blossom's Inn in Lawrence Lane was in the heart of the city. Stepping down from the stagecoach, Sophia breathed in the scent of London. Smoke, horse dung, a hint of noxious odours from the river…it was entirely familiar to her as a New Yorker, and she felt something within her ease a little. Cities were known, familiar, safe. Here she could find work if needed, or shelter. But she would not need it, for Daisy was here. Or at least, so she hoped.

Bidding Mrs Coates farewell, she asked an inn servant how she might reach Mayfair, and was directed to walk through Cannon Street, Watling Street, and thence through Holborn, Oxford Street, and Great Swallow Street. It took only an hour, and Sophia was interested in everything she saw—the great cathedral of St Paul, the bustling streets, and the elegant architecture. Hope had returned—in the anticipation of food, and comfort, and *oh!* A warm bath. But for now she was focused on walking through London on a mild, dry day, and ignoring the cries of her empty belly.

Daisy had hopefully returned to Aunt Agatha's house, and Sophia knew the address by heart. Number 60, Grosvenor Street was an elegant four-storey townhouse in a quiet, fairly clean street. *Only the best for a marquess*, Sophia thought, recalling that the property had originally belonged to her grandfather, and had not been caught up in the entail.

Deliberately, she walked straight past the house, making for the nearby Grosvenor Square, which had a pretty garden. After removing her shawl, she folded it, placing it into the bag, at the same time retrieving the note she had written earlier—as the Barley Mow had had pens, ink, and cheap paper available for the use of its paying guests. The note was addressed to Miss Van Bergen. She then made her way back to the house, her heart pounding as the door opened to reveal a footman with a decidedly closed expression.

'I have a message for Miss Van Bergen,' she said, in as calm a manner as she could muster, holding out the folded note. 'I was told to await a reply.'

Thank goodness for Lady Harriet! Hart was far better in her company than sitting brooding and pining for Daisy over the endless hours of the journey to London.

The more time he spent with the lady, the more he liked her. She was a sensible matron with a lively mind and a ready wit. Occasionally, when she rolled her eyes or tilted her head a certain way, she even reminded him of Daisy, and pain would knife though him.

Was this to be his life now? Tortured by reminders, half-memories, and guilt? Daisy had only been in New York for a short time, but might she have picked up on some of Lady Harriet's mannerisms? Or was his imagination playing tricks on him?

Finally, they were now on the outskirts of London, and he would leave Lady Harriet at her sister's house before continuing to his own home.

'Grosvenor Street, Arthur!' he reminded his groom, shouting out the window of the carriage.

'Very good, my lord,' came back the reply. *Not long to go now.*

'Miss Van Bergen wishes to speak with you.' The footman was sadly failing to completely hide his consternation at events of which he clearly did not approve. 'Follow me.'

Almost, Sophia could imagine the man adding, 'And do not touch anything with your dirty hands!'

Her hands were, to be fair, a little grimy, but she could not help it. The dust from the road meant everyone and everything in the Slowest Coach in the World was grimy. Including herself.

A moment's panic assailed her as the footman led

her upstairs to what she supposed must be the drawing room. What if Daisy had developed a fondness for playing Miss Van Bergen, and did not wish to switch back? But no. Mama's arrival in the next week or so would put an end to that—even if Daisy would do such an awful thing, which Sophia was fairly certain she would not. Taking a breath, and conscious that her heart was thumping wildly, she stepped forward.

Chapter Twenty-Nine

'Your caller, Miss Van Bergen.'

Sophia entered, carefully closing the door behind her, but Daisy was already rising to embrace her. Overcome, Sophia threw her arms around the girl, saying,

'Oh, Daisy, Daisy! I am so pleased to see you!' It was true. The feeling was a mix of relief, and sorrow, and gratitude. She could not have had this adventure, not have fallen in love, not had her heart shattered into pieces, had it not been for Daisy's willingness to play her part in her charade.

'But you look so tired!' Daisy's expression showed genuine concern.

'I travelled by stagecoach, and had not enough money for breakfast,' she admitted, and Daisy promptly rang the bell for a maid.

'Bring tea,' she said with great authority. 'And bread, cheese, and fruit. Also some warm water and towels.'

'Yes, miss.'

Sophia eyed her with respect. Daisy had come into

herself in some way. All traces of the demure serving maid were gone, and in her place stood a confident young lady who was clearly comfortable with the role.

They talked then, of everything that had befallen them since leaving Liverpool—although Sophia was careful to leave out all references to Hart, and mentioned her dismissal only indirectly, describing it as an 'unfortunate incident'. The warm water arrived, and she washed her face and hands with great relief, declaring she would have a bath later. Daisy asked her how she had enjoyed being a maid, and she said with honesty that she had truly thrived on it. She spoke of needlework, and cleaning, of dressing young ladies' hair, and of making perfume.

'It sounds as though you excelled, Miss Van Bergen,' Daisy declared, genuine admiration in her eye.

'Remember, you are to call me Sophia,' she reminded her, 'for we are friends. And I am not sure that I excelled exactly. But I managed. Most of the time.'

'May I enquire,' Daisy asked, 'as to your plans regarding your betrothal—if that is not too impertinent a question?'

The food had arrived, and Sophia was enjoying every morsel. At this reminder of the inconvenient existence of Lord Linford, she frowned, then shrugged. 'I am determined to return to New York as soon as possible,' she declared, and Daisy caught her breath.

'Then, you do not wish to marry Lord Linford?'

Lord, certainly not! The thought of marrying anyone made her shudder inwardly. Once, Hart had been her ideal. Now she wished never to have to so much as dance with a man ever again.

'No. I am certain of it. I may never marry.' She tossed her head as she said this, hoping that Daisy would not sense the sadness beneath her defiance. 'I shall write to Lord Linford to explain that we should not suit, and he will never know that he never actually met me.'

Daisy made no objection, and once again she was grateful to the girl for supporting her in her foolish, beautiful bid for freedom. Linford, she was informed, would remain in Kent for another week, so unless Mama arrived later than expected she could try to persuade her to leave London without ever seeing the man she was once promised to in marriage. Or she could rest for a few days here before going directly to Liverpool. At present, her mind was too sluggish, her heart too sore to figure anything out.

Daisy passed her a beautiful shawl to wear, and gave her Aunt Agatha's strong-box. Seeing the riches within, relief flooded through Sophia. *I have money again!* That was something she would *not* miss about her time as a servant.

Sophia paid Daisy then, before they spoke together to Aunt Agatha's housekeeper, telling her Sophia's true identity, and describing Daisy as 'a friend'. Mrs Pattinson, though disapproving, could only accept the truth.

'Should I make up another bedchamber for your friend, miss?' she asked Sophia, a little stiffly.

'Oh, no,' Daisy replied instantly, 'for I am departing today. I must return to my—to my own family.'

Sophia's heart sank. She had recently lost Hart—or at least the Hart she had believed in—and Mary, and now Daisy was going to leave her, too.

But she had no time to try and persuade her friend to stay, for almost as soon as the housekeeper had departed, the door opened again, the footman standing to one side to allow someone to enter.

'Lady Harriet, Mrs Van Bergen!' he announced.

Chapter Thirty

Quick as a flash Daisy was up and away, standing to attention by the wall near the window. Sophia rose too, bustling forward to ensure she caught her mother's eye immediately.

'Mother!' Her tone reflected genuine shock. 'You are here a full week earlier than I expected!'

'Well, kiss me then, my dear, and do not just stand there as if I were a ghost come to haunt you!'

Sophia rose to embrace her mother, who continued talking just as though it were the most natural thing in the world to arrive in England a week early, having crossed an ocean.

'The captain was rather pleased to have made the crossing in such a short time—his fastest ever crossing, he said. I told him it was because I was willing the ship to speed across the ocean. I have been dreadfully worried about you Sophia. Are you well?'

'I am! But how are you? I cannot believe you are here so quickly!' Sophia shuddered as it began to dawn on her just how close they had come to disaster. Just a few hours earlier and Daisy would have been discovered, alone.

'What on earth are you wearing, my dear?' asked Mama, looking askance at Sophia's grey linen dress. 'And your hair! So plain and dowdy!'

'Oh, this?' She glanced at her simple linen dress, patting her hair. 'I am in mourning, remember, and did not intend to go out today. I do have other mourning gowns in bombazine and silk, but I save those for when I must be out and about.'

They spoke then of Aunt Agatha, and Mama confessed how much she would miss her sister. Sophia then turned the conversation back to Mama's journey, asking if she had hired a carriage to bring her from Liverpool.

'It has in fact taken three carriages, and a great deal of luck and kindness for me to reach London!' Mama declared. Sophia was just about to question this, when a soft sound from Daisy drew her attention. The girl's face was paper-white.

'Daisy? What is amiss?'

'Lord Linford is arriving, miss.'

The two girls eyed one another in horror, then Sophia rose. 'I cannot see him, Mama!' Even she heard the panic in her own voice. *Lord! What am I to say to him? He will know instantly that I am not me, but Daisy is!*

'What? Lord Linford? Your betrothed?' A frown of puzzlement creased Lady Harriet's brow.

Sophia knew she had only seconds in which to act.

'I do not like him, and we should not suit. I have said nothing, waiting for your arrival, but now that he is here...please do not make me marry him!' Her distress was real, and Mama responded instantly.

'Of course! I should not dream of doing so. But tell me, has he...harmed you in some way?'

'Oh, no! He is just *persistent*.' Lord, would Mama think Lord Linford some sort of lecher, like Forsyth? The poor man had done nothing to deserve such aspersions. The web she had spun was becoming more tangled every moment.

'Is he, now?' Lady Harriet's jaw was set. 'He must desperately need your dowry, I suppose.' Guilt ran through Sophia. Lord Linford was probably a perfectly agreeable gentleman—a fact she could allow now that no one was to make her marry him.

'We can speak of this later, Mama. I promise. But now I must go to my bedchamber. Come, Daisy!'

She led the way out onto the landing, hearing the footman one floor below open the front door. Stifling a shriek of pure terror she ran up the stairs to the next floor, and Daisy showed her where her chamber was situated. Once the door was safely closed, she paced about the room in distress, barely noticing how pretty it was. She could not fathom it. Why was Linford here, in London? It did not match what Daisy had told her earlier, when she had first arrived.

'I thought you said he was to remain in Kent for another week! I had hoped to persuade Mama to leave

London immediately. Now what am I to do?' It would have been so much easier if Mama had never met Linford.

Daisy reported that Linford had said he would not travel until next Wednesday at the earliest; she seemed genuinely confused by his early arrival.

Walking to the window, Sophia peered down at the street below. 'We must stay here until the carriage is gone.'

Daisy followed her. 'And then I must leave this house and never return.'

They spoke of Linford then. Interestingly, despite the misgivings she had hinted at on the ship, Daisy now seemed to hold him in high regard. 'He is, I think, a good man,' Daisy concluded, her gaze wistful.

'Then I am sorry to have deceived him.' It was true. Linford was yet another casualty of Sophia's actions.

'Was it worth it?' Daisy clapped a hand to her mouth. 'Forgive my impertinence, miss!'

Sophia was unperturbed. 'A good question, Daisy.' She thought for a moment, memories flashing through her mind. Sitting atop the carriage with John. Learning how to scrub spots from brass. Dressing Miss Chester's hair... Walking in the woods and lying there with Hart...

'Yes,' she mused. 'Despite everything, it was worth it. I shall never regret my adventure in Derbyshire.' It was true. The pain of that last conversation with Hart was still a searing, open wound, but she had been changed forever by her summer in Derbyshire. She had known the challenge of hard work, the experience of being a different class, the pleasures of passion and now, the agony of heartbreak. *I shall never see him again.* For a moment grief threatened to overcome her, but no! She must not give into such emotions now. 'But it is all over now, and we both must return to our real lives.'

'Yes. Yes, we must.'

'What will you do, Daisy?' She eyed her friend curiously.

'I intend to use your generous payment to buy a one-way ticket to New York. I shall find work there, and never risk seeing anyone who met me these past two months.' Her expression was bleak, and Sophia felt a pang of guilt. Her adventure had affected many, many people.

'Would you stay here as my maid, Daisy, and return to New York with me?'

The girl shook her head. 'I cannot remain in London, and risk being seen by the people who believe me to be Miss Van Bergen. I must leave today.'

Sophia nodded slowly. She herself was in no state to travel today. She needed more food, and a bath, and at least a week's worth of sleep. 'A sensible plan. Please send me a note when you are settled there. Perhaps you can work for me, for I hope to live independently if I can persuade my papa to allow it.' It was the best option, given that she would now never marry. 'But—forgive me—I know what it is to consider leaving one's home forever. It is a wrench—although—' her eyes grew distant '—in the right circumstances I believe I could be happy here forever.' *If he had loved me. If we could have married.* But the man she had believed him to be did not truly exist. He was a phantom, created by his practiced charm and her willing foolishness.

Again her mind returned to her own masquerade—a different form of deceit. She had cheated everyone, and was now entirely entangled in a net of her own making. *I am a terrible person, and I deserve every ounce of agony.*

Finally Linford left, glancing up at the window where they stood and tipping his hat to them. Daisy left immediately afterwards, Sophia accompanying her down to the first floor landing, where they made their farewells. Daisy had given her a letter to be passed to Lord Linford, should the truth come out, and Sophia promised to ensure he received it.

With one last look filled with shared understanding and secrets they parted, Sophia making for the drawing room, and Daisy continuing downstairs to the ground floor, from whence she would leave the house, and leave London forever.

Bracing herself, Sophia re-entered the drawing room. Mama was there, looking severe.

'Sit down, Sophia.'

Lord, does she know? Sophia sat, her knees quaking.

'Tell me again why you do not wish to marry Lord Linford.'

'I—we would not suit.'

'Lord Linford disagrees. In fact, he has expressed a strong desire to marry you.'

Her jaw dropped. 'But why? Is he really so desperate for my dowry?'

She shrugged. 'Apparently not. He wants a new settlement, where your dowry is held in trust for any children you may have.'

Sophia could hardly believe it. This was an entirely unexpected complication, and at this moment she had no notion how to counter it. 'I do not understand.' She shook her head, genuine confusion racing through her.

'Foolish girl! Have you not thought of the obvious explanation?'

Sophia eyed her blankly.

'I had the strong impression that he loves you.'

Her jaw dropped. Linford did not love her, for he had never even met her. *He loves you.*

No. *He loves Daisy!* It was obvious to Sophia now. Daisy had seemed sad earlier—because she was leaving the man she loved. A man she had deceived at Sophia's behest. Lord, was there no end to the harm Sophia had caused with her masquerade?

It was all too much. Burying her head in her hands, she muttered, 'What a muddle!'

'A muddle?' Mama's voice was sharp. 'What manner of muddle?'

'He does not love me!' The words erupted from Sophia. 'He loves another girl, and I love anoth—' She broke off, before she inadvertently revealed everything.

Mama's eyebrows were raised. 'To be fair,' she replied wryly, 'that does sound like a muddle. I can see you have been missing wise counsel, for you have had neither me nor Agatha to advise you. But never fear, all will be well.'

'But how? Linford is insisting on marrying the wrong woman—*me*, and if I marry him we shall both be miserable! My h-heart belongs to another, and I strongly suspect that, despite his kind words, he is in love with someone else.' It was true. Despite his treatment of her, Sophia's heart still belonged to Hart. *Hart, my heart.* How foolish could one girl be? He had told her, had *shown* her what he truly was, yet her idiotic heart clung to its adoration of him.

Mama shrugged. 'Then do not marry him. You have no need to do so. I should like…' she mused, 'to see the two of you together. That will tell me everything I need to know.'

'Can we not leave this place, Mama? I wish to go home to New York. England has not been what I expected. Not at all.'

'Do not be so idiotish, Sophia. I have only just arrived, and am looking forward to reacquainting myself with all my old friends. Or at least, those who yet live.'

'Well, I do not intend to go out in society! I shall stay in this house until it is time for us to go home.'

Mama gave her *that* look—the one that told Sophia she was being unreasonable. *And I am. I know it.* 'You may do as you wish, Sophia. And when you are ready to quit this childish tantrum, I shall permit you to accompany me to the teas and soirées that I fully intend to enjoy for the next month and more.' A thoughtful look came across her face. 'If I recall correctly, the *ton* will gradually return to London this month, and it is likely to be October before the balls and soirées begin. By that time, I trust you will have returned to good sense! Now, please ask the housekeeper to show me to my chamber, for I need to rest. It has been a long few days.'

Chapter Thirty-One

Once Mama had gone, Sophia paced about the drawing room in agitation. What a day! Still, at least Daisy was safely away, and Mama would not force her to marry Linford. She foresaw that she would have to meet him and formally put an end to the betrothal, but if he truly loved Daisy…what should she tell him?

Ringing the bell for a maid, she asked for a bath, and spent the next hour in various stages of mindless bliss. Removing her servant's dress for the last time, she patted it fondly before turning away. That part of her life was done. It was time to be Sophia Van Bergen again.

After her bath one of the maids helped her dress in her own finery—a delicate chemise and petticoat, then an expensive day gown of figured muslin. The maid dressed her hair in a suitably elaborate style, and as she sat before the mirror watching her own transformation from serving maid back to lady of quality, her mind drifted to Mary who had proved to be a quick learner in dressing hair. Was Mary even now helping Lady Caroline or Miss Chester to dress for dinner?

But no, for the party was ended, the guests gone. Had Hart proposed to one of the young ladies following Sophia's departure? It was possible, for he had clearly indicated that Sophia's presence was his barrier. *He did not truly love me—he made that clear.* But she had taken his attention, his focus, meaning that he had found it impossible to court another. So a *tendre* then, intense while it happened, yet afterwards forgotten. For men like Hart, an *affaire* was simply something to be indulged and enjoyed at the time, without ever lasting. She had heard of such things of course, having seen on multiple occasions New York ladies rolling their eyes at some husband's current peccadillo while never challenging the assumptions that lay behind it.

Descending to the drawing room, Sophia felt completely unsettled. Mama was still resting, and there was nothing to turn her mind from her own heartache. For the first time since Mrs Stone had found the spoon beneath her mattress she had time and vitality enough to think, and her thoughts at this moment were of one person only: Hart.

What was he doing now? Perhaps he was in his study, working. Or in the drawing room with his sisters and nieces. Perhaps he was even walking in the woods— their woods. Was he thinking of her, as she was thinking of him? No, he had probably already put her from his mind.

Focused on her own thoughts, she was entirely oblivious to the sound of the door knocker, nor male voices in the hall below. And so, as with Mama's arrival earlier, she was entirely unprepared when the drawing-room door opened.

'The Right Honourable the Earl of Linford,' the footman announced.

Hart was glad to finally have reached his elegant townhouse in Mayfair. A journey that should have taken less than two days had taken four. Thankfully, his valet had arrived and was now assisting him to dress for a light dinner. The staff had not known when to expect him but his cook, he was certain, would produce a creditable repast.

'How are things at Walton House?' he asked, and his valet, seemingly surprised by the question, assured him all was well.

'When I left your guests had all departed, my lord, and it is my understanding that Mrs Smyth plans to return to her home on the morrow, while Mrs Dawson was to set out for London.'

'And what of the servants?' Hart persisted.

'I believe...' replied the valet with an air of great care, 'there is a certain consternation among some of the upper servants although, naturally, I did not enquire as to the cause.'

Consternation, eh? Good. Hart had still not forgiven Mrs Stone, although to be fair she would have no reason to suspect that one of the guests might have deliberately sought to pretend Daisy was a thief. His jaw tightened as he thought of Forsyth. Yes, he had unfinished business there.

And then there was Daisy. *Where are you, my love?* He had already written to Mrs Stone, requesting any details which might help him locate her. Her previous post had been with Lady Agatha Palmer, whose man of business was, according to Lady Harriet, a Mr Lynch. Had he hired Daisy for the trip to New York? Hart intended to call on this Mr Lynch just as soon as his London servants were able to identify the man's place of business. There was still hope, and he intended to cling to it. Although he could never marry a servant, and knew he urgently needed to remove Daisy from his heart as best he could, the burning injustice of what had been done to her was driving him mad. He could not rest until he had undone the wrongs that had been done to her—especially since the wrongs he himself had committed were greater than any.

Sophia whirled around when she heard the announcement, but it was too late. Her betrothed was already there.

'Good aft—' He froze, his jaw dropping and his words unfinished. They eyed one another for one long, horrified moment, before his brow cleared. 'Ah!' he remarked. 'Are you one of Miss Van Bergen's sisters, perhaps?'

A lifeline! 'Yes!' she declared. 'Yes, I am! I—'

Shame overcame her. She was tired of telling lies, and she had already wronged this man. She had half-risen, but now she sank back into her seat, hiding her face in her hands. 'No! No, I am not. Oh, it is all such a muddle! I should never have—' Bringing her hands to her side, she eyed him directly, lifting her chin. 'Please, be seated, my lord.'

He sat, his expression grim. 'You had better tell me the truth, Miss—whoever you are. Something decidedly havey-cavey is going on, and I do not appreciate being taken for a fool.'

'Very well, but you will not like it.' She took a breath, then told him. All of it—including the fact she had worked as a servant all summer.

'Why on earth would you do such a thing?' His expression indicated sheer bewilderment.

She tried to explain. 'It was the most wonderful experience of my life. You, a man, cannot know what it is to be hemmed in and managed, every moment of your life since the day you were born.'

'So you did not want this marriage? Is that what this charade was about? Well, I would never have wished to marry an unwilling maiden. All you had to do was say.'

'I believe my parents would say the same. No.' She shook her head. 'I was reconciled to the marriage. I simply wanted freedom first.'

He frowned. 'Then you will insist on proceeding with the wedding? Even after—'

'No, no, of course not! It is clear that we should not suit.'

'On that, at least, we agree.' He was clearly relieved not to be forced to marry her. Well, what man could ever forgive such duplicity?

She bit her lip. 'I know you are angry with me, and rightly so. I am sincerely sorry for deceiving you. And please do not blame Daisy! It took an age to persuade her to be part of my scheme.'

He had more questions, but his conclusion when it came was damning. He spoke harshly of Daisy, and Sophia was moved to try and defend her. 'But no! Daisy would never—'

'Permit me to say that I suspect I know her now, and better than you ever did! She is a liar, a deceiver, and a cheat!' He rose. 'I believe it is time for me to leave now. I hope our paths do not cross in future.'

'Wait!' She bit her lip. 'I must give you something, and I must ask a boon of you.'

He rolled his eyes. 'Your self-regard knows no bounds, Miss Van Bergen. Well?'

'One moment.'

Quickly, she ran to her room, retrieving Daisy's letter from her reticule. She went to hand it to him, but he looked at it, then shook his head. 'I do not wish to read whatever lies she is telling to try and excuse herself.'

Sophia stood firm. 'You are angry now, and I understand that. But some day you will wish to know what is in that letter, and so I urge you to keep it.'

With a bitten-off expletive he stowed the letter inside his coat. 'And the boon? Though I must inform you I am not in a mood for beneficence.'

Despite quaking inwardly, she managed to eye him steadily. After the hardships she had experienced, she was not going to allow an angry man to oppose her—even if his anger was fully justified. 'My mother knows nothing of this, and so—'

'You wish me to keep your sordid scheme a secret? Very well, for no one can come out of this looking good. But I intend to tell my sister and my aunt the truth, for this—this *servant* deceived them, too.' His tone dripped with disdain, and she winced inwardly.

'Thank you.'

There was a pause, as they eyed one another. 'What are your intentions now, Miss Van Bergen?'

'To return to New York as soon as possible.'

'Good. I trust we shall not be forced to meet again. I shall wish you a good day—and a better one than I am experiencing.'

His bow was slight, his tone curt, and as he departed she sank down into the chair, as hopelessness coursed through her. She deserved every ounce of disdain he had just shown her.

As for Hart, given Lord Linford's reaction she had been right not to tell him the truth. The deception she had served on her former betrothed had been distant, yet he had been hurt and angry beyond measure. What she had done to Hart was worse, for it had been intimate, and had involved emotions, and confidences, and quiet closeness. She knew Hart's hopes, and dreams, and frustrations—and he had shared them in good faith with a serving maid called Daisy, with whom he had had a light dalliance to while away the summer. How could she criticise him for his deception when all the time Daisy was a woman who did not really exist?

Chapter Thirty-Two

Kent, Friday 18, September

Hart felt tears welling up inside. *Actual tears!* He was standing in the little chapel in the grounds of Linford House, watching his friend take his wedding vows, and happiness was radiating out of Linford.

That happiness contrasted sharply with the pain he was currently hiding. It filled him as though it were a living thing, twisting and biting at every turn. Two weeks since Daisy had been dismissed from Walton House. His attempts to find her had come to nothing. Both Mrs Stone and Mr Lynch had cited the same agency, but the owner—an interesting woman called Mrs Gray—had claimed not to have seen Daisy since appointing her to the two posts he knew about.

Which suggested she had not, after all, returned to London to seek work. *New York, then?* Perhaps he should ask Mrs Van Bergen for advice. He had seen her a number of times while out on house calls, as the *ton* gradually made its way back to London, and was continuing to develop a strong liking for her. He had not yet met her daughter who was apparently unwell, but the cynical part of his mind had identified that an heiress whose mother was now a firm friend could be a definite prospect for him—particularly as the rumours she was to marry Linford had plainly been false.

Indeed, Linford had eyes only for his bride—a Miss Marguerite Boyd-Parker, the daughter of his former business associate. She had been staying in Linford House all summer as a guest of Linford's aunt, and it was plain to everyone present that this was a love match.

The 'I dos' were done, and Hart dutifully signed the register alongside Lady Arabella Linford, the bride's witness. Afterwards there was a wedding breakfast which included most of Linford's tenants and servants—a nice gesture. Hart himself was much more conscious of the needs and wants of servants these days—a direct consequence of his love for a certain housemaid.

The evident happiness all around him was delightful. He was genuinely pleased for Linford and his bride, but could only contrast their joy with the pain he carried—an invisible burden, yet one that made every conversation, every smile more difficult.

The newly wedded couple eventually departed for their honeymoon, and Hart called for his carriage, relieved to know he could be back in London by nightfall.

Each day was a trial, every moment a reminder that she was missing from his side, that she had been hurt beyond measure, and that he would never see her again.

Mama was not pleased. 'Enough, Sophia!'

Sophia had once more declined an invitation to accompany her mother on her rounds of house calls. Mama was delighting in picking up old threads, and reacquainting herself with friends she had not seen in many years. Freed from the burdens of four daughters and a prestigious home to manage, she seemed happier than Sophia could recall her being in a long time. Her chances of agreeing to return to New York soon were decidedly slim.

And now she had clearly had enough of Sophia's refusal to engage, and was metaphorically stamping an elegant little foot.

'You may have one more day of moping, then you are done! You did not want Linford? So be it. It was you, remember, who agreed to marry him in the first place.' Her expression softened. 'When I first arrived, you mentioned someone else—another man who had taken your fancy.'

Sophia stiffened. *How can I speak of him?*

'Is he a gentleman of good character? A single gentleman?' Sophia could only nod, but Mama seemed satisfied. 'Then I do not see why it is such a problem. Unless…' She frowned. 'Not every man will return your affections, you know. And every girl should have her heart broken at least once.'

This sparked Sophia's curiosity. 'Did you, Mama?'

'I thought so at the time. A most unsuitable gentleman. I had a lucky escape, I think. But we are speaking of you, not me. Now, I command you to leave this house tomorrow. Go for a walk, perhaps. Today is your last day to be confined to this house, and hiding from visitors.'

The truth was that Sophia was terrified even of her own drawing-room. She had been taken unawares twice there—first by Mama, then by Linford. In her imagination the trio would be completed when Hart appeared.

He was in London, she knew, for Mama had mentioned calling on him and his sister Mrs Dawson in the Hartington townhouse. Thankfully Mama had not seemed to notice how Sophia froze when his name was mentioned. She could not even ask Mama how she knew the family, for she had shown no interest in any of Mama's other acquaintances.

The next day, accompanied by a maid, she left the house, walking as far as Grosvenor Square Park and back again. It terrified her to do it—an astonishing development considering the courage she had found within herself since arriving in England. But her sense that Hart would inevitably find her was strong, and horrifying. *A liar, a deceiver, and a cheat!* Those had been Linford's words, and why should Hart react any differently? Particularly since they were true. *Amoral—*

another word Linford had used, and it made Sophia die a little inside each time she recalled it. Because it was true. She had had no thought for anyone but herself when she had embarked on her masquerade—not Daisy, nor Linford, nor any of the people she had deceived at Walton House. Mrs Stone. John. Mary. Reuben. Sally.

Hart.

By the time she had returned to the house, her feelings of relief were not as overwhelming as she had anticipated, and she told Mama she would try to walk a little further each day. The courage she needed now was of a different nature to her headstrong impulsivity at the beginning of the summer. She needed to accept what she had done and to take the consequences. Yes, she might see him in the street, or he might call to see Mama. And if that were to happen, she would simply have to be sorry, and take his rage and disappointment.

But she missed him. She missed him quietly in every moment. She missed him when the rain fell, and when the sun shone. She missed him when she noticed flowers, or trees or birds. She missed him when she saw couples together, and when she saw other lonely people.

Despite his betrayal, she loved him yet—fool that she was. Loving him had become a habit with her. For many weeks he had been her obsession—her last thought before sleeping and her first thought on those cool early mornings. And it was a habit that was proving hard to shake off.

Still, she persisted. Well, what else was there to do? And gradually, each day, she felt a little calmer inside. On Friday she even joined Mama in the drawing room, making reasonable efforts to converse with Mama's callers, who all declared her to be a 'delightful young lady' and that they were glad to have been the first to meet her. Afterwards, Mama pointed out, a little wryly, that they would now surely expect to find would-be suitors calling, for she had been keeping them away with the news that her daughter was unwell.

This was an unanticipated problem. 'Oh, no, Mama! But I do not wish to marry!'

'Nonsense! I am certain there will be a man among them who catches your eye. Now I am going to see my mantua-maker. I have a notion to ask her for a new gown in that Clarence blue silk twill that seems to be all the rage.' She sent Sophia a piercing glance. 'You may safely stay here, for the at-home hour is done.'

But Mama was wrong, and once more Sophia was to be shocked by an unanticipated visitor. The footman scratched at the door—a new rule introduced by Sophia herself, so that she might have at least a few seconds of warning.

'Enter!'

'The Right Honourable the Countess of Linford to see you, miss.'

Chapter Thirty-Three

Well!

Sophia sank into her chair as her unexpected guest departed. Who would have thought it? Daisy had married Linford—a love-match, just as Sophia had suspected—and was marvellously happy. What was more, her true name was not even Daisy, but Marguerite Boyd-Parker, and she was the daughter of a gentleman. So she had been keeping her own secrets, even while masquerading as Miss Van Bergen all summer. Lord, stepping into deception had led to all manner of complications—and not just for Sophia herself!

While Sophia was, naturally, delighted for her friend's good fortune, she could not help but contrast Daisy's—*Marguerite's*—good fortune with her own sorry lot. Marguerite had married the man she loved, and happiness radiated from her like a glow of sunshine.

What was more, Sophia had now allowed Marguerite to persuade her to attend an upcoming ball in the

Linford townhouse—a ball which Hart would be attending! Marguerite had pointed out that knowing the *exact* time and place when she would see him again had to be better than her current uncertainty. Which made sense, but now that she had agreed to it, Sophia felt rather sick.

Yet, why should she avoid him? Yes, she had deceived him, pretending to be a servant rather than an heiress. But what he had done was, to her mind, a thousand times worse. He had pretended to love—or at least, had led her to believe…

Come to think of it, he had never spoken of love, had he? The thought was lowering. While she had been busy deceiving everyone around her, Sophia had also been lying to herself. With time and distance now between them, her recollections of looks and touches were fading, and only the more concrete memories remained—the words he had actually spoken, the things they had done together. She pressed both hands to her cheeks, feeling the flush of shame-ridden desire. Even now, if he took her by the hand and laid her on a soft bed of grass beneath a sunlit forest, she would willingly…

All of it was on her. She had deceived herself.

'Miss Van Bergen has recovered, and is now receiving visitors.' Louisa's tone held a hint of slyness, and Hart shuddered inwardly. He was already tired of hearing about the American heiress, and wished to God Linford had married her, for his sisters had both decided she was a better prospect even than Lady Caroline and Miss Chester. The young lady—despite her reclusiveness up until now—was apparently being courted by every bachelor in London. Or at least, those who could be bothered to seek an introduction.

'And?' He cut at his beef with rather more vehemence than was required.

'And you have not even called upon her! Come now, you do not wish to fall at the first hurdle, do you? Her dowry is said to be simply enormous!'

He snorted. 'Which suggests only that she is either ugly, or half-witted, or unpleasant.' To be fair, he liked her mother.

'Brother! How can you be so disagreeable about a lady you have never met?'

Because I am filled with rage, and loss, and fears about what might be happening to Daisy. It eats at me, every minute of every day. He shrugged. 'No doubt I shall meet her eventually.'

'She plans to attend the Linford ball, apparently.' His friend and his new wife were launching the autumn gathering of the *ton* with a full ball—a good way for his friend's new wife to make her mark, for the former Miss Boyd-Parker was unknown to the *ton*.

'Then I shall see Miss Van Bergen there.' Oh, he knew his terse answers were frustrating his sister, but he could do no better. Despite committing himself to choosing a bride by Christmas, his heart knew only Daisy.

Having tried to find her using every method he could think of, he now realised the futility of finding one woman among the multitudes. He did not even know her plans. *She is gone, and I may never see her again.*

Abruptly, all vitality left him, as it often did these days. He felt flat, empty, listless. The thought of returning to Walton House to feel her absence every moment, was untenable. Perhaps here in London, he would learn to forget her—at least enough to permit him to find an heiress by Christmas.

I am a fool! Daisy had never been suitable as a possible wife—her low birth and lack of fortune meant that it had never been possible. Sometimes he wondered what might have happened if he had found her that day when she had been forced to leave Walton House. *Likely I would have secured a special licence and married her within the week!* Yes, and then his slow descent into bankruptcy would have continued, with all its implications for those who depended on him.

No, perhaps it was better this way. He could live without a heart, and marry some other lady in whom he had no real interest. Anything else was beyond his control.

The day of the ball dawned, and the flutters in Sophia's stomach, which had been steadily growing since her agreement with Dais—with *Marguerite*—now felt enormous. Knowing that Marguerite and her servants would be busy all day, she knew not to call—which was a pity, since Marguerite's optimism and common sense generally calmed her when her fears and regrets threatened to overcome her.

Mama approved of her new friend, and had accepted her marriage to Lord Linford without so much as a blink. When Sophia had asked about it once, she had shrugged, saying, 'They clearly adore one another. I assume this is the lady you mentioned to me?'

'She is. I knew he loved her, and not me.'

'And you were right, my child.' Which she was, but not for the reasons Mama assumed. And Mama had not connected the new Lady Linford with Daisy, the serving maid who had accompanied Aunt Agatha to New York all those months ago. Sophia sighed inwardly. The ripples from her deception would haunt her, she knew.

Lord Linford had been friendly and warm towards her—a warmth she did not deserve, she knew. The first time she had met him since his marriage, and since the day he had coldly told her he hoped they would not be forced to meet again, she had been filled with trepidation. But he had been welcoming, and forgiving, and had ruefully confessed to being excessively delighted by how the situation had resolved itself. He also understood from his wife that she and Miss Van Bergen were firm friends, and so, he said, that was good enough for him.

At least that was one thing she did not need to worry about tonight. Not that she had any space in her mind to worry about Linford, for she was consumed by the knowledge that tonight, she would see Hart. She fully expected him to turn from her in disdain as Linford had, and using similar epithets to those used by his friend. Or perhaps he would think it all a great lark, and try to court her for her dowry, which in a way would be even worse. Thankfully she had not known in Derbyshire how close the two men were, but had been informed of it on multiple occasions recently—not least by Marguerite herself.

There was a queue of carriages outside the Linford townhouse, for Mama had decided to arrive a little late—no doubt wishing to make an entrance. Sophia could feel her nervousness increase the longer they waited. Mama must have sensed it, for she said, in a rallying tone, 'Hold your head high, Sophia. We are Van Bergens, and you are granddaughter to a marquess.'

It helped, a little. This time, she was no fraud. So why did it feel as though she had been more truly herself when she had been masquerading as Daisy? *Because I was with Hart.* All else may have been false, including his courtship of her, but her own heart had been true.

Finally, it was their turn. Carefully holding up her skirts a little so the delicate hem would clear the mud, Sophia made her way towards the house on the wooden pallets that had been placed there, noticing there were only two more carriages after theirs. Blinking in the sudden light of the entrance hall, she saw Marguerite with her husband, ready to greet their guests as Lord and Lady Linford.

'Mrs Van Bergen! And Miss Van Bergen!' My lord greeted them, even as his wife was pulling Sophia into a spontaneous embrace.

'How do you, my friend?'

'I am here. I am ready.'

'Good. I am glad to hear it. And in that gown you will outshine them all!'

'Your own gown is stunning, Marguerite.' She meant it. As a married lady, Marguerite was now permitted to wear a much wider range of colours than she had previously enjoyed. Lady Linford's ball gown was of blue silk, with delicate embroidery and no fewer than three ruffles at the hem.

Lady Linford smiled happily in response, but the next guests behind them were waiting, and so she had to turn away. 'The ballroom is actually on this floor but has a balcony entrance up this way. That is where everyone is being announced—the servants will show you the way.' Mischief danced in her eyes as she referred to 'the servants', and Sophia shared a moment of shared understanding with her before proceeding towards the staircase, suddenly nervous about her gown.

It was of white satin, studded with a thousand tiny beads and crystals that caught the light as she moved. The bodice and sleeves were simply cut, and Sophia's neck was bare of jewels, Mama having decided that tonight was a night to avoid wearing any of the priceless necklaces they owned. Sophia's hair had been expertly dressed, and at the last Mama had permitted a few silver pins, each with a precious diamond.

'Perfect!' she had declared, and in truth Sophia had seen how the occasional sparkles in her dark hair tied with the extravagance of her gown—the whole thing kept in check by the clean plainness of her bare neck and long gloves of white satin.

'Yes, let us go this way,' Mama murmured, 'for if I recall correctly…' Her voice tailed off as they began to climb the stairs, and Sophia was struck by the beautiful scenes painted on either side of the staircase. They reached the top, where a major-domo confirmed their names. He nodded to a pair of footmen, who opened the double doors beside them.

'Mrs Van Bergen, Miss Van Bergen,' he announced, his voice seeming to bellow into the space.

Chapter Thirty-Four

Sophia barely had time to take it all in. She took one step forwards, realising they were on an elegant balcony, a wide staircase descending before them to the ballroom proper. There were people everywhere—it felt a little overwhelming, but then, it had been quite a while since Sophia had attended such a large event. Hart's ball did not count, for she had seen little of it, being assigned to look after cloaks and mend torn hems.

As the major-domo's call rang out, every eye turned to look at the Van Bergen ladies as they slowly descended the staircase. There seemed to be a brief dip in the hum of conversation before it resumed, a little louder than before.

They had barely reached the foot of the staircase before the first people reached them. 'Mrs Van Bergen! Such a delight to see you again And Miss Van Bergen!'

Sophia smiled and agreed to dance with various young men, but all the while she was subtly, anxiously searching for one particular man. And she could not see him anywhere. She accepted a drink from someone and sipped nervously, trying her best to make polite conversation. No doubt they would think her dull-witted, but she had not the wherewithal to even care. She had met some of them before, for their little drawing room had been besieged by the *ton* since the word went about that Sophia had recovered from her 'illness'.

'Let me see your card, my dear!' Lady Linford had issued dance cards to all the ladies, and Sophia's was rapidly filling up. Mama had been speaking to one of the ladies—something about the dances—and now turned, seeking Sophia's card. Taking the tiny pencil tucked into the card, Mama wrote something, then handed it to the young gentleman who was waiting his chance to add his name.

'And that is the last, I am sorry to say. A pity,' he declared, 'for I should have liked to dance with you twice!'

'Oh, no,' she replied firmly. 'I have told everyone the same. I shall dance only once with each gentleman tonight.'

He bowed. 'Then I am honoured to have secured the only spot left.'

'Mrs Van Bergen!' Mama's smile was genuine as she saw the lady who was even now approaching. Sophia's heart sank. It was Mrs Dawson, Hart's sister. The woman for whom she had mended a torn flounce at the ball in Derbyshire. *Will she recognise me?* And if she did, what would she say? Bracing herself, and trying to contain the dread within her, she prepared to meet her doom.

Hart was at the back of the ballroom, trapped in conversations about pineapples with Lord Pashley, when he heard a commotion at the far end of the room. 'The Van Bergens!' someone said, so he turned to look—as did everyone else, it seemed. The ballroom was large, and all he could see at first were two slim female figures, descending elegantly. As they got closer he recognised Mrs Van Bergen—reflecting that he ought to speak to her tonight, for her intelligence, wit, and common sense might help him survive the ordeal of his first social appearance since his own ball—not counting Linford's wedding, which had been a quiet affair from a *ton* perspective.

The girl behind her sparkled and glittered as she moved, her neck and arms bare of jewellery. He approved, and wondered if those who had come tonight dripping in precious stones might now be regretting their choices.

A pang went through him as the way Miss Van Bergen moved reminded him of his Daisy—but then, he was becoming accustomed to seeing traces of Daisy everywhere he went. Even Linford's new wife had the same colouring, and he had found himself forced to not dwell overmuch on Lady Linford's glossy brown curls and blue eyes, while wondering if he would ever see Daisy again.

A swarm surrounded the Van Bergen ladies just as soon as they reached the ground, and he decided now would be a good time to replenish his glass of fine punch. Taking it onto the terrace he stood for a moment, trying to take some peace from solitude and the cool night air, till a call from behind him made him stiffen.

'Cousin!'

'Mrs Van Bergen! It is so lovely to see you.'

'Mrs Dawson. The notion is entirely mutual, my friend. Let me introduce my daughter.' She did so, and as she rose from her curtsy Sophia saw Mrs Dawson's jaw loosen in shock. *She knows me!* 'But—I do not understand. You are Miss Van Bergen?'

'I am. It is a pleasure to make your acquaintance, Mrs Dawson.'

Mrs Dawson shook her head quickly, as if ridding herself of impossible thoughts. Her eyes narrowed, and Sophia felt nausea swirling within. 'I trust you have recovered from your ailment, Miss Van Bergen? I am sure your mama was most concerned about you.'

'I am, thank you.'

'And I was…but she is well recovered now, are you not, Sophia?'

Sophia! Mrs Dawson's eyes widened again, and then her face hardened. *She knows. She suspected, and now she knows.* Recalling that she had given Mrs Dawson her correct name in a slip of the tongue, the night she had knelt on the floor mending her gown, Sophia shuddered. *Oh, Lord. She knows.*

Turning slightly, Mrs Dawson beckoned Lady Arabella, Linford's sister, to come and join them. Lady Arabella already knew the truth, since Daisy—Marguerite—had had to explain their charade to Linford's family. Thankfully, Lady Arabella's gaze showed only polite enquiry, not suspicion or disapproval, as they all conversed politely. If she and Mrs Dawson had shared what they each knew, there was no sign of it in Lady Arabella's demeanour. Not that it made much difference. Staying in London, going out in society...all of it had increased the chances of Sophia's masquerade coming to light.

The next few minutes were agony, but when Mama was safely distracted by Lady Arabella, Hart's sister saw her chance.

'Miss Van Bergen? Your given name is Sophia, is that correct?'

'Yes.'

'A pretty name.' Her eyes narrowed. 'Daisy is also a pretty name, do you not think?'

Sophia swallowed, her stomach sick. 'I suppose so.'

'We must speak some time, you and I.'

'Yes.' Sophia squared her shoulders. 'Yes, I shall speak to you, Mrs Dawson—of names and choices and regrets. And hopes,' she added softly.

'Hopes?' Her eyes widened. 'Hopes,' she repeated, her expression thoughtful.

Hopes! Why had she said that? When she knew that to hope Hart might court her would only result in having her heart broken all over again, for this time he would have marriage on his mind, not a simple dalliance. And yet, she did hope. Somewhere deep within she hoped for some sort of miracle—that the man she had imagined would somehow spring back into existence. Stifling a cynical laugh, she turned her face away from hope, instead focusing on the fact she would need every ounce of courage just to survive the upcoming reunion.

Every girl should have her heart broken at least once. Mama was wise, and Sophia was strong. Strong enough to survive this night, and whatever it might bring.

Behind Mrs Dawson, Lord and Lady Linford were taking to the dance floor, the musicians striking up for the first dance. A nervous-looking young man arrived to claim his promised dance and Sophia graciously curtsied, making her excuses to Mrs Dawson and allowing the young man to lead her out. *I am Miss Van Bergen*, she reminded herself, *daughter of Mr Oscar Van Bergen and Lady Harriet Palmer. I am granddaughter of a marquess and fabulously wealthy. I need no approval from any man here tonight.* She needed no husband, and never again would she allow any man close enough to hurt her.

* * *

'Cousin!'

Hart winced, knowing exactly who was behind him. *Damnation! What fool let him in?* He turned slowly, taking a long draught of punch before facing his heir.

George was all smiling affability. 'You remember Cedric, do you not?'

They remain friends, despite what I told George? His jaw hardened, as surprise gave way to cynical acknowledgement. *George can see no wrong in his friends.*

Cedric looked decidedly uncomfortable, as well he might. 'Good evening, my lord. I trust you are well.'

'Cousin.' He ignored the other man. Were they really intending to act as if nothing had occurred?

'I—er—pleasant ball, is it not?' George now looked decidedly uneasy—Hart's coldness clearly landing exactly as intended. Perhaps he had genuinely put Forsyth's perfidy from his mind. Unfortunately for Forsyth's sake, Hart had not.

Hart shrugged, replying to his cousin. 'I hope so. Lord and Lady Linford are good friends of mine.'

There was a silence. 'About that other thing...'

'Yes?' He was not going to make things easy for George. For either of them. But the longer he stood there, the more rage rose within him, recalling what Forsyth had done—and attempted to do—to Daisy.

'It was all a misunderstanding, Hart. Cedric explained it to me. That serving maid made advances

towards him, then clearly changed her mind. She...'
His voice tailed off, as he looked from one to the other.

Hart stiffened then, carefully, he set down his glass. Adjusting one cuff, then the other, he then moved like lightning, grabbing Forsyth by the throat and pushing him up against the wall.

Chapter Thirty-Five

'I say, cousin, what—do you not think you should not be doing that? We are at a ball, man.'

Hart barely heard George. Rage was pulsing through him, knowing he finally had his hands on the man who had importuned Daisy, then had caused her to be dismissed. The lies Forsyth had told to George had been for Hart the final feather that broke the horse's back.

'Tell him the truth.' His voice was low, rough, and implacable. Forsyth simply stared at him, eyeballs bulging in shock and fear.

'Speak the truth,' he repeated, 'or I shall strangle you with my bare hands, right here.'

Hart had never been a man of violence, but the thought of what this vile reprobate had done was too much for him. Plus, Cedric Forsyth was a coward. He would not actually need to murder him. Or at least, he did not think so.

'Cousin! Should this not be settled on the duelling field, between gentlemen?'

'Absolutely not,' Hart retorted, never for an instant taking his eyes off Forsyth. 'For this creature is no gentleman, and does not deserve such consideration. In fact I believe him to be the sort of man who dishonours innocent housemaids. Now, will you admit it, or must I—?' He tightened his grip a further notch.

'Yes, yes,' Forsyth spluttered. 'Very well, I shall admit it was *I* who tried, not she.' Hart heard George gasp. 'Well, and how is a man to know who is game,' Forsyth continued, 'if he does not try?'

Hart tightened his grip again at this, very slightly. 'Tell him the rest.'

'The rest? What rest? There is no rest! You came and pulled me off her. Punched me, too.'

'The silver spoon. The attic. Tell us both what you did.'

If it were possible, Forsyth's eyes widened further. 'How did you know about that? No one saw me!'

'If no one saw you, then how do I know *exactly* what you did?' Hopefully Forsyth was too frightened to see through his bluff. 'Speak!' he commanded.

'I did not intend to take her money. I did not even know it was there! I only wished to be certain which bed was hers!'

Money? What money?

Almost instantly Hart figured it out, with fleeting gratitude for his own velocity of thought. 'You searched in her bag for her letter of engagement, so you would know where to plant the silver spoon.'

'I—yes. But it was only a jest—a little punishment. It was her fault that you planted me a facer that night.'

'Her fault? Really?' He twisted his hands a little harder, until Forsyth's breath became raspy.

'No! My fault! All mine!'

'And the money?'

'I shall pay it back—every last sovereign! I swear!'

Pay it back? When no one knew where she was? Forsyth's words sank in. *Sovereigns?* So he had stolen a substantial amount. Probably Daisy's life savings. His contempt knew no bounds.

Before he did something he would later regret, he shoved Forsyth away, hard enough to send him sprawling.

'George.'

His cousin stalled in the act of moving to assist his friend. 'Y-yes, Hart?'

'If I see or hear of you in this creature's company one more time, I shall cut you off without a penny, and bar you entirely from Walton House. Do you understand me?'

'I—I do.'

'Good. Now get out of here, and take your former friend with you. No, not through the house. Go that way.' He indicated the garden. 'Once outside this house, you shall part ways, never to connect again.'

'But—Lord Linford!'

'I shall explain the situation to Linford. In great detail. Indeed I suspect Mr Forsyth here will soon find all doors closed against him. What he did to that innocent girl is enough to merit it, but to then deliberately place a valuable item under her mattress, and steal her money...' He shook his head. 'He does not deserve the title of gentleman.'

'No indeed.' George straightened, his expression sober. *Perhaps there is hope for him yet.*

'Now go.'

Hart stood alone for a little longer, ignoring the music and merriment in the ballroom behind him, as gradually his rage settled, leaving behind only hopelessness. In Walton House while under his protection, an innocent maid had been assaulted, accused of theft, and summarily dismissed. He now knew that this reprobate had also stolen her money. And Hart could do exactly nothing to aid her. Worse, he himself had harmed her, too. Had all but seduced her, while knowing they could have no future together.

His duties called. He had spent almost an hour skulking on the terrace at his friend's ball, and had done all he could to avenge Daisy tonight. He could not forget her, but also, had not succeeded in finding her. Now it was time to see if he could manage to smile politely at Miss Van Bergen. Squaring his shoulders, he returned inside.

Sophia's mind was awhirl. She had danced with multiple partners, and could not recall any of their names. Hart was not here, and his sister had recognised her. As the latest dance came to an end she curtsied, declining the gentleman's offer of refreshment. There was to be one more dance before supper, the musicians striking up the distinctive tempo of a waltz to alert the crowd, and there was a sudden surge as gentlemen made for the ladies of their choice.

Sophia stood by a gilded pillar, allowing it all to wash over her. No doubt someone would be along in a moment to claim her hand, but for now she wished only to escape. *I wish this ordeal was over.* She closed her eyes.

'Lord Hartington!' Hart turned, smiling as he saw Mrs Van Bergen approach.

His greeting was genuinely warm, for he continued to believe that Mrs Van Bergen was one of the few matrons of the *ton* who displayed common sense, wit, and warmth.

'Lady Harriet!' After they had enquired after one another's health, Hart forced himself to ask politely, 'Is your daughter with you tonight? I understand she is recovered.'

'Yes indeed—although I have barely seen her, for her hand has been claimed for every dance! But I must confess something to you, Lord Hartington.'

'Oh?' Hiding his relief that he would not, after all, be forced to dance with the heiress, he enquired, 'And what is that?'

Mischief danced in her eyes, making his heart turn

over. Daisy had used to wear exactly the same expression. *Ah, still I see her everywhere!*

'I saw that Sophia's card was almost full, so took the liberty of adding your name for the supper dance. This next dance, in fact.'

'You did?' Momentarily taken aback, he recovered quickly. 'I am grateful you have done so, for I should dearly like to meet your daughter.' It was true, in a way. He liked Mrs Van Bergen very well, and was curious about Sophia, whom he had heard much about on the long journey to London.

'And I should like Sophia to meet you—for you are quite my favourite you know!'

He grinned at this, and her shoulders sagged in relief. 'I am glad you have taken my meddling in good spirit.'

'You may be easy on that score. Now, where is your daughter?' He looked about him, but at present could not think of what her daughter looked like.

'I see her! Let me introduce you.' She led him through the crowd, and he glimpsed her briefly as the crowds shifted—a slim young lady in a well-fitting white dress that seemed to glitter and sparkle. Ah, yes, no diamonds. *How elegant!*

As they got ever closer, something odd seemed to be happening to him. *She looks like Daisy!* While he was becoming well accustomed to the sensation, this time it was not going away. The shape of her face, the turn of her jaw, the little, straight nose... Miss Sophia Van Bergen had her eyes closed—likely weary of all the attention, particularly as she had been unwell recently. Yes, once she opened her eyes he would see that it was not Daisy. Why, the very notion was preposterous!

'Lord Hartington, please allow me to introduce to you my daughter, Sophia.'

At this, her eyes snapped open, fixing almost instantly on his. He froze, as the impossible and the miraculous seemed to be happening right before him.

'Thank you, Mama. Lord Hartington and I have already met.' She dipped into a deep curtsy, honouring him. As she rose she kept her eyes locked with his, hers showing fear, regret, and determination. And he could no more resist Daisy than he could deny his own name.

'We have indeed!' he managed, his heart racing and his mind desperately trying to understand how Daisy was being introduced as Miss Van Bergen. He turned to Mrs Van Bergen who was eyeing them both, surprise and a gleam of speculation in her eye. 'Though I did not know at the time she was your daughter.' *Is she? Is she truly Mrs Van Bergen's daughter? But how—?*

The musicians began the dance proper, and there was a rush of couples to the floor. He held out his hand, and Daisy placed her small hand in his. Without even a glance towards Mrs Van Bergen, they took their places for the waltz.

Chapter Thirty-Six

Hart's head was spinning. *How is this possible?*

The dance began, and he took her in his arms for the Marche. The waltz was believed to be shocking by some of the older members of the *ton*, for it involved not only an increased physical connection between the dancers, but also required sustained eye gaze between them throughout. In fact, it was perfect.

In her eyes he saw the fear begin to fade. Had she really thought he would denounce her? Confusion still dominated, tempered by relief and wonder. *It is Daisy! I have found her!* Or, more accurately, she had found him.

For the next few moments they simply danced, moving in harmony, their eyes locked upon one another, and Hart's bewilderment gradually giving way to joy.

'Daisy?' he managed eventually, as they promenaded together in time to the music.

She nodded. 'Yes. I am Daisy.' She grimaced—a look of regret and sorrow. 'And I am also Sophia. Sophia Van Bergen.'

He shook his head, disbelief and bewilderment still strong within him. 'But how? And more importantly, why?'

'My Aunt Agatha died on the ship, leaving me without a chaperone. I asked my maid Daisy if I could take her place for a short time. It was to be an adventure, nothing more. No one knows what I did—not even my mother.'

The audacity of her! The wonderful, beautiful audacity! He could not help grinning, picturing her planning her adventure, then executing it with such ruthless courage.

She frowned. 'Actually, there are a couple of people who know, but I do not think they will tell anyone.'

Truthfully, he cared not! His Daisy was already wonderful, yet now here was another layer of admiration to be added. Happiness was building within him, as reality began to sink in. Daisy was Miss Van Bergen!

The Marche ended and they moved into the Pirouette part of the waltz. Facing one another, they each took a sidestep away, so that his right hip was aligned with hers. He then placed his right hand on her left hip, while she reciprocated. Their free hands they then joined in a lovers' arch above their heads, and they turned slowly to the music, eyes fixed upon one another. Not since they had lain together in the woods had they been this close.

Fleetingly he was reminded of Lord Byron's scathing verse condemning the waltz as little more than public fornication. 'Hands which may freely range in public sight', Byron had said, and in this moment, Hart knew the poet to have been not wrong.

Daisy was here, and his hands were upon her, and *Lord!* The hunger for her surged within him. Seeing his expression she gasped, and he knew she matched him. *Daisy!*

All the while, his mind was busy realigning itself with this new knowledge. As reason reasserted itself, another memory came to him. 'You told me, that last morning, that you were an heiress.'

'I did!' Her expression was guarded. 'But you did not believe me.' She shrugged. 'And why should you? By that time it seemed unlikely even to me myself!'

Vaguely he was aware that they were being watched. *We need to be alone!* When the music paused and couples began preparing for the lively Sauteuse part of the waltz, he saw his chance. Bending to speak directly in her ear, he murmured, 'The terrace?' and she paused, considering his request.

In his haste and happiness he had not considered events from her perspective, and now it all rushed in on him. His talk of a dalliance, soon to be forgotten. His need to marry an heiress. The ruthless way in which he had broken with her, having spent the summer encouraging her to all manner of acts of Eros. *Lord, this is bad. Very bad.*

She nodded then led the way, her boldness a welcome reminder of the way in which she had embraced their time together, before. It took on new significance now that he knew of her daring adventure—a well-reared young lady taking on the role of servant, simply for adventure? *She is formidable. And I am in deep, deep trouble.*

Once outside, he closed the door before following as she made for the edge of the terrace. Turning to face him, she said, 'Well?' Her expression was closed, her manner forbidding. She was every inch Miss Van Bergen, her lack of jewellery testament to her wealth and standing.

'I know how the spoon came to be found among your possessions.' It was all he could think of, to share something that would surely be of interest to her.

She shrugged. 'I could lose a thousand such spoons, and barely notice. But what I will never forget is injustice and deceit—from whatever quarter.'

She was intrigued, though. He could tell.

'It was Forsyth.'

At this she gaped, her eyes widening. 'I had not thought to suspect him. Are you certain?'

'He admitted it tonight. He also admitted to stealing money from you.'

She nodded thoughtfully. 'I had wondered about that. Still,' she straightened, once more an ice queen in glittering white, 'it is all in the past now. One forgets these things.'

She is quoting me! He winced, and she raised a cynical eyebrow.

'Have I said something to offend you, my lord?'

'You have quoted my own words back to me.'

She feigned puzzlement. 'I have?' She laughed lightly. 'You must forgive me, my lord. A summer adventure must soon be forgotten, I think.'

'Not by me.'

Vaguely he was aware that the waltz had ended, and that the supper bell was sounding. *Good. We shall not be disturbed.* He needed every second with her, for this would likely be his one chance to put things right. If such a thing were even possible.

Her gaze was filled with scorn. 'Indeed? I do not recall you asking for my direction, or offering me any protection from Mrs Stone. I was nothing to you, forgotten once discarded.' She sighed theatrically. 'Such is the way of the world, I understand. And now, if you will excuse me, my lord, I believe I must return to the ballroom.'

She went to move past him and he caught her arm. 'Daisy!'

'Unhand me, sir.' She was cold as ice, and entirely unreachable. Instantly he dropped his hand, the parallels between himself and Forsyth already too strong for his disordered heart. Still, his mind was functioning, for which he was grateful.

'Mrs Gray!' he called after her and she turned, her brow furrowed.

'Who is that?'

'She owns an employment agency here in London. It

was there that Daisy—the real Daisy—was appointed to her last two posts. The trip to new York with Lady Agatha Palmer, and a summer appointment at Walton House.'

'And what of it?' Her eyes glittered in the dim light, her expression wary.

'I met with her, two days ago, seeking information about Daisy Jennings.'

'Why would you do such a thing?'

Oh, he could see it in her expression, hope warring with hurt and cynicism.

'Because I had lied to the woman I love. I had lied to try and help her recover from the pain of breaking with her. I cared for her too well to make her my mistress, and so I wished to make her hate me, so that she would strike me from her heart. It was the least I could do.' She was listening—clearly uncertain, but listening. 'When I discovered that you had been dismissed by Mrs Stone I had strong words with her, then immediately followed you to Derby.' He described the men from the coaching companies he had spoken to, and her eyes widened at the mention of a certain mustard-coloured waistcoat. He told her of meeting Lady Harriet, of their coach overturning, and of having no way of knowing how to find her once he had reached London.

'We did pass an overturned coach,' she mused, clearly wavering, then something else occurred to her and her expression hardened once more. 'But tell me, my lord, is your current *devotion*,' her tone dripped with disdain, 'in direct proportion to my dowry?'

Chapter Thirty-Seven

The words hung in the air between them, time seeming to stand still for an instant. *Here it is.* The insurmountable problem. They both knew he needed to marry an heiress, and that he had broken with Daisy—with Miss Van Bergen—when he believed her to be penniless.

Protestations of love were not enough, he knew. Taking a breath, he understood this moment required him to bare his soul. Nothing less would do.

'I have told you before of my papa,' he offered quietly, 'of the expectations and the challenges I was left with. He was a good man, but his flaw was that he lost his good sense in his need to love and be loved. I believe he stood in my shadow, in my mind, that morning in the woods when I rejected you. They all rely on me, you see. John. Bess my old nurse. Even Mrs Stone.' He gave a short laugh. 'I wanted to run away with you, to begin a new life in the New World and work for my living.'

There was a pause. 'But you could not do it, could you?' Her voice was low, her expression inscrutable.

Slowly he shook his head. 'If I did, then eventually George would have inherited, and filled the place with friends like Forsyth.'

She considered this, her eyes filled with sadness. 'So I was the sacrifice.'

'No. We both were.'

He held himself completely still as she thought about his words, praying for eloquence. For the inspiration to say all of the right things, and none of the wrong things.

'Yes...' she said slowly. 'Yes, I can see how that might be the case. But why did you hurt me so...so *deliberately*?'

Now he could read pain in her—in the stiffness of her body, the pallor of her face, and in—oh, Lord, the expression in her eyes. Agony was emanating from her in waves, and he could hardly bear it. How he longed to take her into his arms! But he could not. Not when she still doubted him.

And so he spoke of their long summer together, of how he had come to love her, and why. 'This was never a dalliance,' he declared finally, 'and I should never have characterised it in that way, even in a misguided attempt to free you from me. The truth is, I was never much in the petticoat line, and am certainly no rake. And if I had intended a dalliance, I certainly would not have chosen an innocent maid in my employ. Besides, we were never master and servant. Not after the first time I saw you in the woods, hugging a redwood tree.'

'We shook hands.'

'We did.'

'And then you kissed me.'

'Ought I not to have done so? For everything flows from that moment.'

There was a long silence.

Finally, she spoke. 'I am glad you did.'

His heart leapt at her words. There was hope yet! Carefully he nodded, hoping he would not misstep. 'We built trust between us, slowly, all summer. And then I shredded it in one single conversation.'

'Yes.'

'I am sorry. Truly. I hurt you, and I should not have done it.' He let this land, then daringly, threw down a challenge. 'But have you really forgotten all the other days? The conversations between us? The way we kissed? I was not free to speak of my love for you, but I tried to show it in a hundred other ways.'

'I—I thought so, at the time.'

'And what do you think now?'

He held his breath. His entire future life depended on her reply.

Sophia could barely think. He was standing before her, and was waiting for her answer. In a flash, it all went through her mind. A hundred examples of his caring for her. Love in his eyes, his touch. Even his words, indirectly. Each time he had spoken of something he admired about her. Each time he had opened up a little more, trusting her with his deepest secrets and worries. But the wounds of that last conversation ran deep, for they provided an entirely contrary narrative to his motivations all summer.

And yet... Would a cold-hearted rake have been interested in where she had gone? In finding out who had incriminated her? In her mind's' eye she could see an overturned coach, a letter of engagement signed by Mrs Gray, a man in a mustard-coloured waistcoat...

She looked at him again. The flambeau on the edge of the terrace was now shining directly on his face, and she saw there only sincerity. *I know him.* She did. She knew him, knew everything about him. His honour, his weaknesses, his strengths and his flaws. And it would be exactly the sort of foolish thing he would do—to reject her in a misguided attempt to make it easier for her to recover from a broken heart.

Sometimes in life, one gets the opportunity to be brave, to take a chance. Her heart knew what it wanted, and her head was satisfied.

'Hart!' Her voice cracked, and she reached out a hand. 'I—'

She got no further, for his arms were about her, and now his lips brushed hers, retreated, then brushed again. Stretching, she claimed his mouth with her own and she feasted on him—his taste, his passion, his familiarity. *This is right.*

'Daisy! My Daisy!' he murmured against her mouth, and she thrilled in the memories awakened by her other name on his lips. 'I love you!'

He retreated to say it again, this time adding, 'And I have never said those words to any other woman. Only you. Forever, only you.'

'And I love you, Hart.'

Swooping, he claimed her mouth again, this time in a ferocious kiss, all the passion they shared in it.

Eventually they surfaced, to smile in wonder at each other and wonder aloud how anyone could be so lucky as they.

'I thought I had lost you, Daisy. I was such a fool!'

'I believe I was also a fool. I see now that I should have told you the truth. Should have trusted you.' She shook her head. 'If I had done so, these past weeks would have been very different for both of us.'

He gave a wry smile. 'You did try to tell me, as I recall. I thought you were so desperate for us not to part that you were making up tales for us.'

'Well I was desperate,' she declared frankly. 'But I had no idea how to overcome your disbelief. The truth was so unlikely, was it not?'

He waved this away. 'What matters is that we have found one another again. And this time, we will never be parted.'

'Never!'

A few moments later, when they were ready to speak again, she declared, 'I would have done it, you know.'

'Done what?'

'Become your mistress. Lived alone in some isolated cottage until you had done your duty by your wife. It would have been worth it, if we could have been together afterwards.'

'Lord, I am ashamed to have even suggested it!'

'But why? It was a perfectly logical suggestion, given the situation—or at least, the situation as you believed it to be.' She bit her lip, recalling Linford's anger. 'And what of my deception—pretending to be a servant all those weeks? Are you very angry about it? And Mrs Dawson knows me, I believe. I have created a muddle, and I should not wish for it to affect you.'

He grinned. 'I think that you are audacious, and brave, and quite, quite mad, my love, and I am not angry in the least!'

Warmth spread through her at his words. *He understands!* 'Well I am sorry for having deceived you, but I cannot be sorry for having done it, no matter how hard I try! It was my one chance to escape the burdens of family, and duty, and responsibility, and I am forever altered because of those two short months.'

'And in spending time with you instead of courting the young ladies at my house party, I too was taking time out of my own responsibilities.' He thought about this for a moment. 'Ever since I inherited the earldom I have done little that was spontaneous, so I can only admire the manner in which you seized the opportunity you were given. You are formidable, Daisy! Do you know that?'

She dimpled at him. 'You will have to learn to call me Miss Van Bergen, you know!'

He shook his head. 'No. I should much prefer to call you something infinitely more dear.'

She caught her breath as he dropped to one knee before her. This was it. The most important moment of her life.

'Daisy. Miss Van Bergen. Sophia.' He gazed up at her, his eyes filled with emotion. 'I love you. I love you so much I contemplated abandoning all of the duties and responsibilities I have been raised to uphold. Even when you were a servant, I knew you to be far above me in quality, and heart, and goodness.'

He squared his shoulders, and she wondered if he would acknowledge the fact she was an heiress, for it was that which had both complicated and smoothed their path. She was exactly right, for he continued, 'The fact that your father has provided you with a dowry means that together, we can look after Walton House and all of the people who depend upon it for their livelihoods. That is all. I do not want your dowry for myself. I never did. What I want is you by my side as we journey through life.' She nodded, smiling mistily at him. He swallowed, continuing. 'I should like to set up a legal agreement that means you shall not lose control of the money you bring with you to our marriage. I do not know if such a thing is even possible, but I should like to try.' He took a breath. 'Say you will marry me, and I shall never know sorrow again!'

'Of course I shall marry you, Hart! I should like nothing better!' He rose, taking her in his arms, and proceeded to plant light kisses all over her face. Bringing her hands up she held him, hands on his cheeks, her eyes on his. 'I love you.'

They kissed then—a kiss like no other. It held reverence, and commitment, and the promise of a lifetime of togetherness. Sophia had never known a person could feel so much happiness, so much love. Then, stepping back, they held both hands and gazed at each other—until the door to the ballroom opened.

'Ah, there you are, Sophia!' Mama moved briskly towards them, seemingly ignoring the fact they had hurriedly dropped hands. 'You have missed supper, you know.'

'Mrs Van Bergen,' Hart's voice was thick with emotion, 'might I call upon you tomorrow? There is something in particular I wish to ask you.'

'Is there, now? I did wonder about that.' She glanced at her daughter. 'Sophia, is this the man—the reason why you would not—?'

'Yes! It was always Hart, but there was a…misunderstanding between us.'

'A misunderstanding which has now been resolved,' Hart added firmly. 'And which included my confusing her with someone else, so I did not realise until tonight that she was your daughter. I apologise.'

Mrs Van Bergen waved this away. 'I am quite certain I do not need to hear the details. In my husband's absence I have full authority to make decisions regarding our daughter's marriage.' She made a face, a hint of wryness in her tone as she added, 'Although I think that I shall have to word my letter to him very carefully!'

Chapter Thirty-Eight

Lord Hartington called upon Mrs Van Bergen the very next day, and came away from the meeting entirely satisfied. His Daisy—or Sophia, as he must now learn to address her—had been relieved and delighted, and he had checked with her again, once her mama had tactfully left them alone after formally agreeing to their betrothal, that she was still content to pardon him for his wrong-headed coldness that last morning in Derbyshire. She had assured him in the warmest of terms that he was entirely forgiven, and they had enjoyed fevered kisses right there in the Grosvenor Street drawing-room.

As to the announcement of their betrothal, he had suggested to Lady Harriet and Sophia a ball at his own mansion, since his friend Linford had put the notion into his head. 'My sister Mrs Dawson is my hostess as you may be aware, and so I shall ask her if she does not mind organising another ball.' He grinned. 'The one she arranged for Walton House was excellent.'

Lady Harriet had clapped her hands together. 'How wonderful! Please assure your sister that my daughter and I stand ready to assist, for it is no little undertaking.'

An hour later, whistling, he sauntered into his townhouse, the butler there greeting him with the news that Mrs Dawson wished to speak with him urgently in the drawing room.

'Well that is convenient,' he declared, 'for I wish to speak to her, too!' Taking the stairs two at a time he bounded into the drawing room, planted a smacking kiss on his sister's cheek, and asked her how she did this fine day.

'I—Hart! What on earth ails you?'

'Ails me? Why nothing at all, dear sister. Indeed I have not felt better in a long, long time.'

She sniffed. 'If it were not so early in the day I might suspect you of being bosky, but you must be sober, for there is something I must inform you about. Something most concerning.'

The hairs stood up at the back of his neck. He and Sophia had been too busy last night kissing and being happy to complete their conversations, but he now recalled that she had mentioned Eliza at some point.

Mrs Dawson knows me, I believe, Sophia had said. Well, if that were the case, then Eliza was likely about to warn him—and would no doubt disapprove strongly. And since no one must ever criticise or disapprove of his beloved Dai—Sophia, his mind was already dancing around, seeking a solution.

'And I have news for you—news which I think is not concerning at all. Quite the contrary, in fact.'

Her eyes widened.

'Should you like to speak first, or shall I?'

She baulked, as he had hoped she might—his unusual behaviour probably unsettling her. 'You first.'

'Very well. As I recall, you were already aware that Mr Van Bergen was seeking a suitable husband for his daughter, and that Linford was a possible candidate.'

She nodded, an air of bewilderment about her.

'The truth is—I was also a candidate, but Miss Van Bergen and I were not certain if we should suit. And so—'

His sister, with the sharpness of mind he loved, immediately completed the story. 'She concealed herself as a servant in order to get to know you better!' Her brow cleared. 'Thank goodness there is an explanation! I confess once I realised who she was I could not account for it. She is truly Miss Van Bergen, for I say she is the double of her mother and aunt—even if others cannot see it. And besides, her mother stands with her.' She frowned. 'But it is extremely daring, to have done what she did. She is American, and so the same rules of behaviour may not govern young ladies on the other side of the Atlantic, but still, I am not certain the *ton* would approve.'

'Ah, but you are forgetting something, Eliza. The *ton*

does not know, and nor shall they ever know.' He lowered his voice. 'It was done even without Lady Harriet's knowledge, so please do not speak of it to anyone but Sophia herself.'

'Of course! My lips are forever sealed on the matter.' She sent him a keen glance. 'Sophia, eh?'

He nodded. *Of course she would notice that I used her intimate name.* 'You may wish me happy, Eliza. I am come directly from Grosvenor Street.'

She was overcome then, and hugged him, and cried happy tears. 'Oh!' she declared, dabbing at her face with a lace-edged handkerchief, 'to know that all your worries are at an end, and it is all safe! Bess, and John, and every one of them!' Another thought struck her. 'George Banfield is likely to be most put out—yes, and his mother, too! And when I think of how you snatched away the Van Bergen heiress, when every bachelor in the *ton* swarms around her as though she was honey... and she is the granddaughter of a marquess! I am so happy for you!'

Inwardly, Hart knew he would have married Sophia for herself alone, had he been able to safely shed the earldom—and that his beloved knew it. She had made it plain today that she cared little for dowries, and that she considered it *their* money, not hers. 'It is for the tenants, and the servants, and everyone who relies upon us!' she had said, passion in her eyes. 'And what is more, I should like to be your companion in matters of business, for Papa has taught me well.' This had warmed his heart, and knowing Sophia's lively mind he had no doubt they would make good decisions together.

'Lady Harriet and I discussed the announcement, and I suggested perhaps a ball, here. Would that be acceptable to you? I do not wish to impose upon you any further—'

'Impose? *Impose?*' She clapped her hands. 'This is no imposition. This is the rarest opportunity of my career as your hostess—yes, and the last, too. Such an announcement! The *ton* will be agog, I tell you!' She rose, bristling with purpose. 'We shall have a ball, and it shall be the finest ball this house has ever seen! Now, let me check my invitations.' She bustled across to the desk in the corner, rustling through various papers and cards. 'Yes! I knew it! There is nothing on Tuesday week—not so much as a musicale! We shall hold our ball then.'

'Ten days?' he asked dubiously. 'Can you really organise everything in just ten days?'

'Watch me!' she declared, then changed her mind immediately. 'Actually, do not, for I need to meet with the housekeeper, and the butler, and with Cook...'

'Lady Harriet has offered to assist. Sophia, too.'

Her face lit up in a wide smile. 'Perfect! I shall include them, and gladly! Now, go, and leave me to it!'

Epilogue

The Hartington ball glittered and sparkled—just as much as the Linford event a little less than two weeks earlier. Everyone knew that Lord Hartington and Lord Linford were firm friends and had been for years, and there was some speculation that there had been some sort of wager between them as to who could throw the most lavish ball—for how else could one explain Lord Hartington's unexpected event? Still the *ton* came, as they had for Lord and Lady Linford. They came, and they mingled. They danced, and drank, and ate a fine supper.

The Van Bergen ladies were there, the heiress looking resplendent in an understated silk gown laced with silver thread, the diamonds and sapphires at her throat tonight reminding everyone of that tremendous dowry—the one coveted by every bachelor in the *ton*.

Her wealth was not her only attribute, for many had been struck by her beauty, her wit, and her warm nature. She was friendly to almost everyone—save a couple of gentlemen she had seemingly taken an aversion to—but not one of the hopeful bachelors could honestly say she had shown him any particular attention.

And so it was with genuine shock that those members of the *ton* present reacted to Lord Hartington's announcement. Somehow, in only a matter of weeks, he had secured her hand! Many a pang went through the assembly at the realisation the greatest prize on the matrimonial market had already been won—and so swiftly!

But they clapped regardless, and they watched with great interest as Miss Van Bergen stepped forward to stand by Lord Hartington's side. The look that passed between them was clear to anyone with an ounce of wit.

'A love match!' someone declared, and there was a murmur of agreement around the ballroom. Mrs Van Bergen and Mrs Dawson stood together, wearing near-identical expressions signalling pride and happiness, while the more observant (and less bosky) among the guests noted that Lord and Lady Linford seemed unruffled by the announcement—and indeed were among the first to congratulate their friends.

Those who specialised in hindsight then worked their way through the crowd, declaring themselves to be unsurprised, for they had seen more than a week ago which way the wind was blowing. Some even referred to watching the couple waltz at the Linford ball, declaring they had known at the time a love match was brewing there.

The couple themselves, inured to all speculation,

took to the floor for the first dance after supper—and so in harmony were their steps, so loving their shared gaze, that no one could deny, or regret their betrothal (although Mr George Banfield was afterwards said to have been rather put out, as were Lord Pashley's daughter and a young lady called Miss Chester, whose bodice was shockingly low-cut).

By the time they were married a couple of weeks later, the *ton* gossip had moved on to newer, fresher topics, and Lord and Lady Hartington departed for their honeymoon in Derbyshire with little comment.

As the gates of Walton House came into view, Sophia suddenly experienced an attack of nerves. 'Lord, what will they all think of me?'

'They will think nothing, my love,' said Hart, kissing her cheek. Having spent more than a week since the wedding wending their way northwards in a leisurely fashion, they had had seven blissful nights in each other's arms—seven nights of a real bed, and uninterrupted privacy. They had made the most of it.

The Walton House servants had been informed by letter that my lord had been recently married in London, to a lady named Miss Van Bergen, and that he expected to bring his bride to Walton House in the coming days. They would have been experiencing significant nerves ever since that letter arrived, Sophia knew. She could only imagine the deepest of deep cleans that would have been completed these past days.

'Look.' As the carriage turned into the drive, the stable boy appeared, running ahead of them at full pelt. 'Slow down a little, Arthur,' Hart ordered, and the groom did so. Their other carriage—containing Hart's valet, one of Aunt Agatha's maids, and a tremendous amount of luggage—had been sent ahead this morning, so the Walton House servants would already be aware that today was the day they would finally meet their new lady.

The carriage pulled up outside the front door, and Sophia was reminded of the fact that the first time she had arrived, she had entered the house via the kitchens. Ignoring the nerves fluttering within her, she stepped down, and Hart tucked her hand into his arm.

Knox, the elderly butler, was the first to greet them, as was correct. Mrs Stone was next, and launched into what was clearly a rehearsed speech.

'Welcome, my lady. It is an honour to meet you.' Eyeing her closely for the first time, Mrs Stone paled. 'I—I—' Her mouth was opening and shutting, but no further words came out.

'Quite,' murmured Hart, moving on.

The house servants were lined up to meet their new mistress, and as she went down the line it was interesting for Sophia to note which of them recognised her. Most did not, but Reuben's eyes widened, Sally's jaw dropped, her expression one of utmost horror, and Mary—*dear Mary*—gasped in shock.

Once the inspection was done Hart ordered tea in

the drawing room, then called for the housekeeper to join them.

Mrs Stone's hands were trembling, Sophia saw, and her heart went out to the woman. While Hart was still angry for the way in which Daisy had been dismissed, Sophia saw that Mrs Stone could have come to no other reasonable conclusion at the time.

'Mrs Stone,' she began softly. 'When I arrived in England in July, I saw an opportunity to get to know one of my suitors in an unusual way, and I took it. Not many know of my masquerade, and it is something which will not be spoken of in this house after today, but I wish you to know that I came to respect and admire you during my last stay here.'

Tears started in Mrs Stone's eyes. 'Oh, my lady! I am so sorry! My lord—' She turned to Hart, 'What you said that day was correct. I was too harsh, too judgemental!'

'The true thief has since been discovered, you may be interested to know.' His tone was brusque, and Sophia wished he would let it go. 'Mr Forsyth had attempted to importune… Daisy, and when she rejected him, he saw an opportunity for revenge.'

Mrs Stone put a hand to her mouth. 'And I was his tool!' She shook her head. 'I shall never forgive myself!' she declared, clearly genuinely upset.

'Well, you must,' declared Sophia, in a practical tone, 'for I have forgiven you, and that has put an end to it.'

'Yes, my lady.' The housekeeper dabbed at her eyes with a linen handkerchief.

'I believe we shall deal very well together, you and I,' Sophia continued, 'but I must request something from you.'

'Anything, my lady!'

'I wish for Mary Thorpe to be my personal maid.'

Her brow cleared. 'Well, that is easily done, my lady. I shall send her to your chamber directly.'

'Er—no.' Hart intervened once more. 'I shall be accompanying my wife to the master and mistress suite shortly. You may have half an hour to make all ready, then please ensure there are no servants within.'

'Yes, my lord.'

Once she had gone, Hart swept Sophia into his arms. 'So, Lady Hartington, how does it feel to be mistress of a house where you once cleaned and scrubbed, fetched and carried?'

She considered this. 'It is less odd than I anticipated, Hart. You see, I *know* this house already. I know every inch of it, and every servant who tends to it. I am advantaged beyond anything any new lady has ever experienced.'

'And I am similarly advantaged, for I know you—every thought in your head, every kindness of your heart, every delectable inch of your body.' He made as if to kiss her, but she paused him with a finger on his lips.

'Speaking of kindness, you will be good to Mrs Stone, will you not?'

He grinned. 'I shall. I think she has suffered enough. Now, where were we, Lady Hartington?'

This time, she did not resist.

* * * * *

If you enjoyed this story, make sure to read the previous instalment in The Heiress Switch miniseries

The Maid's Masquerade

And why not check out Catherine Tinley's The Triplet Orphan miniseries

Miss Rose and the Vexing Viscount
Miss Isobel and the Prince
Miss Anna and the Earl

MILLS & BOON®

Coming next month

RESCUED BY THE RAKISH LORD
Sarah Mallory

'It is a rather delicate matter. It concerns Lord Graddon's guest, the one with the roguish epithet Devil Blackbourne.' Lady Kenton declared. 'You will recall we all thought he had quit Graddon Hall.'

'But he has returned?' Selina replied cautiously.

Lady Kenton nodded.

'And now, I suppose, it is all over the town and all the poor mamas are once again anxious for their chicks. But is this all, ma'am?' Selina asked, still anxious. 'I cannot think it warrants you driving here especially to tell me.'

'You are quite correct, if it was only the rake's return I would have left it until we met, or you heard it from one of your other friends. As it is, Sir Alfred came home today with the most alarming report and as soon as I heard it, I came to warn you.'

Selina was now thoroughly alarmed. Was news of her masquerading as a serving maid all over Torrisford now? She waited anxiously while Lady Kenton tapped her fan against her palm, clearly struggling to find the right words to express herself.

'Oh, my dear Selina,' she exclaimed at last, 'The rogue has made you the subject of the most outrageous wager!'

Continue reading

RESCUED BY THE RAKISH LORD
Sarah Mallory

Available next month
millsandboon.co.uk

Copyright © 2026 Sarah Mallory

COMING SOON!

We really hope you enjoyed reading this book. If you're looking for more romance be sure to head to the shops when new books are available on

Thursday 23rd April

To see which titles are coming soon, please visit
millsandboon.co.uk/nextmonth

MILLS & BOON

TWO BRAND NEW BOOKS FROM
Love Always

Be prepared to be swept away to incredible worldwide destinations along with our strong, relatable heroines and intensely desirable heroes.

OUT NOW

Four Love Always stories published every month, find them all at:

millsandboon.co.uk

FOUR BRAND NEW BOOKS FROM
MILLS & BOON MODERN

Indulge in desire, drama, and breathtaking romance – where passion knows no bounds!

OUT NOW

Eight Modern stories published every month, find them all at:

millsandboon.co.uk

OUT NOW!

Available at
millsandboon.co.uk

MILLS & BOON

LET'S TALK
Romance

For exclusive extracts, competitions and special offers, find us online:

- **f** MillsandBoon
- **X** @MillsandBoon
- **◉** @MillsandBoonUK
- **♪** @MillsandBoonUK

Get in touch on 01413 063 232

For all the latest titles coming soon, visit
millsandboon.co.uk/nextmonth